Principles of Textual Criticism

Principles
of Textual Criticism

by JAMES THORPE

THE HUNTINGTON LIBRARY
SAN MARINO, CALIFORNIA

Contents

Preface

This book is an effort to present, in a reasonably comprehensive way, a discussion of the basic principles which underlie the practice of textual criticism. All criticism involves judgment, and so does textual criticism. The principal judgments of textual criticism concern decisions about the words which should make up the text, and the goal of textual criticism is to determine the text of what we are to read as the work of literary art.

The establishment of the text is basic scholarship in the sense that most other forms of literary study depend upon the availability of a suitably reliable text. The need for textual criticism is not limited to a few works, nor to long ago and far away, nor to trivial details. The texts of most poems and plays and stories and essays of all periods become corrupted, often in features that are important to a thorough understanding of them; and we run serious risks when we use, for careful study, texts that have not been scrutinized in accordance with some principles of textual criticism.

Textual study—or, to use a more enveloping term, editorial work—has been booming in the recent past. I imagine that more and more editions large and small will be launched in the future. Under these circumstances, it seems timely to offer a statement of principles to those who may have (or may develop) an interest in textual studies, either as producers of texts or as consumers of them. In fact, I have the feeling that all literary scholars should be aware of the kinds of textual problems that exist, of their extent, and of the principles that may be used in trying to solve them. Indeed, if we bow out of editorial work in favor of those whose sole specialty is the text, I am afraid all scholarship will suffer. Nevertheless, I certainly do not wish to exaggerate the importance of editorial efforts; as Samuel Johnson observed with some counter-exaggeration in his *Preface to Shakespeare,* "it is not very grateful to consider how little the succession of editors has added to this author's power of pleasing. He was read, admired, studied, and imitated, while he was yet deformed with all the improprieties which ignorance and neglect could accumulate upon him." But removing the accumulation of improprieties ought to bring us a little closer to our true literary heritage.

This book is not a manual which is intended to teach editorial procedures to the reader. Neither does it unlock a secret box full of handy rules of thumb that can be guaranteed to solve hard problems. Instead, it deals with basic topics, even with attitudes and outlooks, that seem central to effective work as a literary scholar. Principles are developed through a discussion of relevant problems, either literary problems or scholarly problems. This is a literary book, I hope, in returning regularly and frequently to real examples involving literary works. The chronological scope is, mainly, from the Renaissance to the present and the focus is on English and American literature; I believe that the same textual principles are true for all periods and for all literatures, but it would be confusing (and beyond my powers) to apply them in one book to more remote examples which have other characteristic problems.

The chapters which make up this book were written to develop a set of ideas progressively, and each depends on what has preceded it. Since I am afraid that any later chapter will give a distorted impression if taken out of its context, I hope that readers will begin at the beginning of the book. Chapter One, "The Aesthetics of Textual Criticism," was first published in *PMLA* in December 1965 and several times reprinted; it was after writing that essay (which has now been revised) that I felt the wish to extend the ideas there set forth. The second chapter, "The Ideal of Textual Criticism," has also been revised since its appearance in the William Andrews Clark Library Seminar Pamphlet of 1969. An abbreviated form of Chapter Five, "The Treatment of Accidentals," appeared in 1971 in the Books and Bibliography Series of the University of Kansas Libraries, under the title "Watching the Ps and Qs."

"Among these candidates of inferiour fame," wrote Johnson in his *Preface to Shakespeare*, "I am now to stand the judgment of the publick; and wish that I could confidently produce my commentary as equal to the encouragement which I have had the honour of receiving." I have had the honor of holding a John Simon Guggenheim Memorial Fellowship, for which I am deeply grateful. I have enjoyed the encouragement of a multitude of friends (particularly A. Walton Litz and Hallett D. Smith), to all of whom I offer my affectionate thanks. And it was my good fortune to write this book at the most agreeable version of the Happy Valley I am likely to know—the Huntington Library and Art Gallery, to the staff of which I express my enduring appreciation.

JAMES THORPE

Principles of Textual Criticism

CHAPTER I

The Aesthetics of Textual Criticism

WILLIAM BLAKE's *Book of Thel* used to begin, in most editions, with these words:

> The daughters of the Seraphim led round their sunny flocks.
> All but the youngest, she in paleness sought the secret air.

Blake did not, however, write "the Seraphim"; he wrote—and engraved—"Mne Seraphim," which a succession of editors altered into sense. The *TLS* reviewer was exasperated beyond endurance when two editors chose to print "Mne," especially as they did so "without a word of protest, without pausing to say whether they think it sense or non-sense. It turns what was a beautiful and natural line into an ugly and a pompous one. That, apparently, does not matter." The reviewer reserved his particular scorn for the reason that the editors printed "Mne"; the reason was no more substantial than "that Blake's pen wrote the word."[1]

Many people on occasion prefer a textual error to an authentic reading. One mistake by a compositor of Melville's *White-Jacket*—setting "soiled fish of the sea" instead of "coiled fish of the sea"—achieved an adventitious fame some years ago. Various readers have since declared themselves in favor of the error, on the grounds that "soiled fish" makes a richer, more interesting

---

[1] Review of D. J. Sloss and J. P. R. Wallis, *William Blake's Prophetic Writings*, in *TLS*, July 22, 1926, p. 493. "Mne" is the reading now given in all "standard" editions, but "the" is still used in many current texts intended for general or student consumption. As one might expect, a considerable body of commentary has grown up around "Mne."

passage than the ordinary "coiled fish of the sea." In short, the error seems to them to create a better work.

The preference for one reading over another, the basic decision of textual criticism, is in this case being made on what are called aesthetic grounds. And the decision is made despite demonstrable proof that the preferred reading is in one case an editorial invention and in the other a compositorial mistake. Most bibliographers, editors, and textual critics would at this point join in a chorus of denunciation of the person so ill-advised as to make such a preposterous decision.

On what grounds shall we decide which party to join? Does the wretch who hugs the error deserve denunciation because he decided on aesthetic rather than textual grounds? Because he put out the palace fire in Lilliput by improper means? Because we mistrust his taste? Because we fear lest the taste of any individual become the norm? Or because he contumaciously refused to prefer what the author wrote?

On the other hand, suppose we side with the man who chose the error. What is our reason? As a vote for value in a topsy-turvy world in which the worse is so often preferred? As a protest against those vile mechanics, the textual bibliographers, who claim that their findings alone are logical, scientific, and irrefutable because they involve infinite pains? As a forthright preference for the best work of art?

Some choose one way and some the other. A recent writer has suggested a rearrangement of Ben Jonson's eulogy on Shakespeare by transferring lines 51-54 to a point ten lines before the place that Jonson chose to put them. The passage "would seem less awkward following the lines just quoted than where it actually occurs." The transposed passage "forms with the lines preceding and succeeding it, a perfectly coherent unit." In short, "I think," the writer says, "a good case can be made that the change is an improvement."[2] The case rests on the greater literary

2Wesley Trimpi, *Ben Jonson's Poems: A Study of the Plain Style* (Stanford, 1962), p. 151.

merit of the resulting passage. A Shelley scholar has argued that "Music, when soft voices die" was changed from a "good poem" to "a unique achievement" by an editorial reversal of the two stanzas; now "it does not represent its author's intentions in either aesthetic form or literal meaning. In large measure we must thank accident for the composition of this lovely poem, almost such a happy accident as the random selection of lines by some mechanical device might eventually produce."[3] Upon seeing the text of Emily Dickinson's "After great pain, a formal feeling comes" in the standard edition ("edited according to the superstitiously literal lights of modern scholarship by Thomas H. Johnson"), a scholarly reviewer said that "in despair, one begins to think of nice things to say about Victorian family editors."[4] The first flowering of William Empson's genius as an anatomist of language, his *Seven Types of Ambiguity,* included discussions of several passages in which he found the authorial readings inferior to revisions which he could make. In Rupert Brooke's line about "The keen/Unpassioned beauty of a great machine," he considered "unpassioned" as "prosaic and intellectually shoddy" in comparison with his own word, "impassioned," which provided a daring and successful image. Similarly, his high evaluation of the playful dignity and rhythm of the line "Queenlily June with a rose in her hair" depended on his misreading the first word as "Queen Lily" rather than as an adverb, which made the line (he thought) ebb away "into complacence and monotony."[5]

On the other hand, writers have suggested changes which resulted, they thought, in a text of less literary merit. In his edi-

[3]Irving Massey, "Shelley's 'Music, when soft voices die': Text and Meaning," *JEGP,* 59 (1960), 436–438. Massey maintains that the non-authorial "version has by now a tradition of its own, and cannot simply be dropped from the records of English poetry" (p. 438). He was answered, rather severely, by E. D. Hirsch, Jr., in "Further Comments on 'Music, When Soft Voices Die'," *JEGP,* 60 (1961), 296–298.

[4]Edwin Fussell, *AL,* 33 (1961–62), 234–235.

[5]London, 1930, pp. 260–261, 83; see also p. 34. These examples were retained in the revised edition (London, 1947).

tion of Shakespeare, Samuel Johnson replaced the passage in *Hamlet* which editors had been printing as "In private to inter him" with the original reading "In hugger mugger to inter him," which had apparently been considered inelegant. "That the words now replaced are better," Johnson observed, "I do not undertake to prove: it is sufficient that they are *Shakespeare's*." He went on to give his rationale for retaining the authorial reading in the face of a possible improvement. "If phraseology is to be changed as words grow uncouth by disuse, or gross by vulgarity, the history of every language will be lost; we shall no longer have the words of any authour; and, as these alterations will be often unskilfully made, we shall in time have very little of his meaning."[6] In wanting to conserve the past, his argument is basically historical.

Thus the choice in all of these cases seems to be between the better word and the words of the author. The choice is immaterial under any theory of literature by which the reality of the work of art is independent of its written or printed form. "To every man who struggles with his own soul in mystery," wrote D. H. Lawrence, "a book that is a book flowers once, and seeds, and is gone. First edition or forty-first are only the husks of it . . . . One submits to the process of publication as to a necessary evil: as souls are said to submit to the necessary evil of being born into flesh."[7] Nor is such a choice likely to arise under an earlier view of textual study which assumed that the authorial version was always the "best" reading. If the power of a divine afflatus enabled the poet to create, he could hardly be improved upon. Shelley, for example, maintained in "A Defence of Poetry" that "poetry is indeed something divine" and that verse is "the echo of the eternal music." Vasari reports, toward the end of his life of Fra Angelico, that that painter would not alter the initial version of one of his paintings on the grounds that

[6]Notes to *Hamlet* (IV.iv.84 in modern editions, IV.v in Johnson's edition).

[7]Introduction to *A Bibliography of the Writings of D. H. Lawrence,* compiled by Edward D. McDonald (Philadelphia, 1925), pp. 14, 13.

6

it was as it was because of the will of God. George Lyman Kittredge was horrified by the notion "that prompters and proofreaders can (or could) improve Shakespeare."[8] With a less romantic view of the act of artistic creation, one can face this possibility with equanimity: if you happen to believe that the compositor improved on Melville, the Great Chain of Being is not endangered.

Whether our preference lights on the better words or on the words of the author, and whatever reason we give for our decision, we have done more than make one elementary choice. For all textual decisions have an aesthetic basis or are built on an aesthetic assumption, and it is idle to try to dissociate textual grounds from aesthetic grounds as the reason for our choice. Consequently, to make one kind of textual decision is to commit oneself, in principle at least, to a whole series of related decisions. Before we realize what we have done, we may have decided who should be called the author of MacLeish's *J. B.*, whether the eighteenth-century emendations to *Comus* deserve to be incorporated into the text, and which one of the versions of Hardy's *The Return of the Native* is the "real" novel.

Before we make our choice, it might be useful to bring into the open at least the first aesthetic assumption which lies behind textual criticism, and to expose it to scrutiny. The basic questions are no different from those which one confronts in every form of literary study, and in the course of this essay I will discuss three assumptions about the work of art, assumptions which have a controlling effect on the practice of textual criticism. The most fundamental question is this: what is the phenomenon or aesthetic object with which textual criticism properly deals? The things which can be called aesthetic objects because they are capable of arousing an aesthetic response in us are (permit me to say) of three kinds: works of chance, works of nature, and works of art. Works of chance are any objects which are formed by random activity: a painting created when a can

[8]Ed., *The Tragedy of Hamlet* (Boston, 1939), p. viii.

of paint is tipped over by the vibration of an electric fan and spills onto a canvas; a poem formed by combining an entry (selected by a throw of dice) in each column of a dictionary; a musical composition made by recording the sounds of traffic at a busy intersection; a sculpture consisting of a wastepaper basket into which an office worker has tossed the envelopes which brought the day's mail. Works of nature are any objects or effects which are formed by natural phenomena: a changing pattern of cumulus clouds against a blue sky, the sound of the wind whistling through the boughs of a tree, the smell of the blossoms of *Viburnum carlesii*. Since language is a human invention and not a natural phenomenon, literary works cannot by definition be works of nature. Works of art are any objects created by human agency for the purpose of arousing an aesthetic response. These are the works which satisfy our conventional ideas of the painting, the sculpture, the symphony, the poem, the play, the novel. Since the work of art is an intended aesthetic object, the idea of either a random or a natural work of art is self-contradictory. Human intelligence was purposefully engaged in the creation of the work of art, but it may not have been successful; the term "work of art" is thus descriptive rather than evaluative, and it includes failures as well as successes. The language of the literary work, whether judged a success or a failure, is a fulfillment of the author's intentions.

Having pushed all aesthetic objects into these three rooms, we cannot, however, very properly slam the doors and go on our way rejoicing. For everything is an aesthetic object for somebody. The complex organization of some human beings will respond in aesthetic experience to the stimulus of any object, particularly if its usual scale is altered or its ordinary context is displaced. Moreover, memory stands ready, on the least hint, to supply the substance for aesthetic response. A classified ad describing a cottage for sale in Florida, with the beach on one side and an orange grove on the other, may create a response which is indistinguishable from that which derives

8

from Marlowe's "Passionate Shepherd to His Love"; for a melancholic reader, however, the ad may be the poor man's "Dover Beach." Likewise, a random pile of beer cans may arouse a response similar to a sculpture, and so forth. These facts make the situation complicated, but we cannot simplify it by saying that people do not or should not have aesthetic experiences from such objects, or that they are all mad if they do; they do in fact have such experiences, and the invocation of madness may in these cases be the last defence of a bewildered man. Moreover, these examples do not represent clear types; there are innumerable objects which may be responded to as sculpture between the pile of beer cans on the one hand and the Pietà of Michelangelo on the other, and there is no convenient line that can be drawn which marks the limit of where the "normal" person "should" make an aesthetic response. It took "the wise men of the society of Salomon's House," in Bacon's *New Atlantis,* to be able "to discern (as far as appertaineth to the generations of men) between divine miracles, works of nature, works of art, and impostures and illusions of all sorts."

The problems of criticism become immense, even intolerable, if every object must be taken seriously as a potential source of aesthetic experience, if criticism is invited to preside over all creation. So, in self-defence, we are always on the lookout for ways to cut the area of responsibility but never in search of less authority. In the last generation or two, one tendency in criticism has been to limit attention to the aesthetic object and to move away from the complex problems associated with the artist as unpredictable personality. We have been taught, by the French Symbolists and their followers at second and third hand, that the intentions of the artist are not to be trusted, that the intentions of the work of art are all-important, and that the task of the reader or critic is to understand the intentions of the work of art. Paul Valéry put the case sharply: *"There is no true meaning to a text*—no author's authority. Whatever he may have *wanted to say,* he has written what he has written. Once published, a text is like an apparatus that anyone may use as he will and according to his ability: it is not certain that the one who constructed it can use it better than another. Besides, if he knows well what he meant to do, this knowledge always disturbs his perception of what he has done."[9]

Though one may not like to think of art as gymnastic apparatus on which to exercise, the focus on the work of art seems manifestly sound as a way of trying to understand its intentions and its meaning. However, two secondary effects present themselves. First, we may be suspicious of anything that can be called authorial intention, for fear of committing the "intentional fallacy." Thus the authority of the author over the words which make up the text he wrote is subtly undermined by confusing it with the authority of the author over the meaning of his text. While the author cannot dictate the meaning of the text, he certainly has final authority over which words constitute the text of his literary work.

The other secondary effect is that of overturning the distinction between the aesthetic object (the genus) and the work of art (a species), of thinking that all automobiles are Fords. The fact that it generates an aesthetic response does not mean that it is a work of art. These two effects are interconnected, of course, at least under the definition I have given for the work of art, as an object created by human agency with the intention of arousing an aesthetic response. If the element of intention is minimized, the work of art tends to blend into, and be indistinguishable from, works of chance and works of nature. Indeed, these distinctions seem less important and less useful if commerce is restricted to the aesthetic object and to the general aesthetic response of the individual. The loss of these distinctions, however, leads to confusion and (ultimately) to abandoning conceptual thinking about works of art.

The difficulties which arise from these confusions are not

[9]"Concerning *Le Cimetière marin* (1933), in Paul Valéry, *The Art of Poetry* (New York, 1958), p. 152.

merely visions of theoretical possibilities or of the ineluctable deviations from ideal purity. In every art one can point to aesthetic objects which in fact blend art, chance, and nature to a significant degree. Indeterminate music, for example, combines art and chance. The composer supplies blocks of music for the performers, who are to play the sections in whatever order they fancy on a given occasion; thus the composer incorporates in the work itself a variable governed by random chance. Examples of aesthetic objects which are not primarily works of art can be multiplied: the paintings of Beauty, the chimpanzee at the Cincinnati Zoo, for whose works there has been a ready commercial market; "happenings," or unstructured episodes with characters; self-destroying machines, which are designed to follow an unpredetermined course in destroying themselves. Let me say again that each of these examples will be the occasion for aesthetic response on the part of some people, perhaps a few and perhaps a great many, and no amount of laughing at them, of saying that they are being duped by frauds, will alter the fact that they are responding to aesthetic objects.

In the literary line, there are various current examples of aesthetic objects which depend on chance. The "novel" by Marc Saporta entitled *Composition No. 1,* published by Simon and Schuster in 1963, consists of loose printed pages which are to be shuffled before reading. *The Story of O,* by Pauline Réage (published in an English translation by the Grove Press in 1966) has alternate beginnings and endings. Many poems have been written by computer. These examples may sound familiar in their resemblance to the language frame described in the Academy of Projectors in *Gulliver's Travels.* That engine was actually a device to insure a random arrangement of words. All of the words in the language had been written on pieces of paper which were pasted on all the sides of bits of wood, which were linked together by wires. This device, twenty feet square, had forty iron handles on the sides which could be used to shake the frame and thus change the words which showed. Any groups of words which made part of a sentence were written into a book, and a rearrangement of those broken sentences was to produce the body of all arts and sciences. Swift's machine was a satire on modern learning; we are taking similar experiments in wise passiveness, perhaps because we are not sure of our grounds for responding otherwise.

The question of importance that these distinctions about aesthetic objects raise is whether criticism can deal with works of chance and nature as well as with works of art. I think that it can, but in very much more limited ways. It can give an account of affective qualities, and these reports may range from crude impressionism to elaborate psychological inquiry. It cannot ordinarily deal with those features on which criticism is most useful, matters of genre, tradition, and convention, without giving vent to a large amount of foolishness. Since textual criticism cannot traffic in works of nature, we need only distinguish between the kinds of authority it can have in dealing with works of chance and works of art. It is of course possible to establish a set of principles by which textual criticism could be applied to works of chance. In view of the random element in all works of chance, however, it is evident that an irrational variable of indefinite importance would always have to be included in the textual principles. Thus the operation of those principles would in the long run be little better than guesswork, and the results of a textual criticism established for works of chance would be about like pinning the tail on the donkey without peeking.

Let us return for a moment to the question of choosing between "Mne" (Blake's word, reputedly nonsensical) and "the" (an editorial substitution that seems to make sense), or of choosing between the "soiled fish of the sea" (the compositorial error) and the "coiled fish of the sea" (the authorial reading). What should our decision now be? Obviously we should choose the one which better fulfills our purposes. If we want to maximize our aesthetic experience by getting the biggest return from our attention, we are free to choose whichever reading satisfies that condition—with the error just as valid a choice as the authorial reading. Those readers who prefer the compositor's error—which is a simple example of a work of chance—can thus find perfectly logical grounds for their choice. It is a choice which repudiates the value of differentiating among classes of aesthetic objects, however, and the consistent application of it will, consequently, aid self-gratification on non-intellectual grounds. On the other hand, critics whose prime aesthetic interest is at that moment in works of art must choose the authorial reading whether they think it better or worse. Their main concern is to understand the literary production as a work of art, as an order of words created by the author; they cannot permit their attention to be pre-empted by any auxiliary effects, and they cannot properly set up in business as connoisseurs of all human experience. I certainly do not mean to suggest, however, that people should in general limit their aesthetic experience to works of art. In "The Conundrum of the Workshops" Kipling cast the Devil in the role of rejecting sources of pleasure on the grounds that they are not Art:

> When the flush of a new-born sun first fell on Eden's
>   green and gold,
> Our father Adam sat under the Tree and scratched with
>   a stick in the mould;
> And the first rude sketch that the world had seen was
>   joy to his mighty heart,
> Till the Devil whispered behind the leaves, "It's pretty,
>   but is it Art?"

It would be a sadly reduced world if we went about avoiding sunsets and other innocent forms of beauty. Only this: although one person may from time to time enjoy aesthetic experience from a wide variety of sources, he is not in a position to deal with works of nature and works of chance in his role as a textual critic; he is left, then, with literary works of art as the sole practicable subject for textual criticism.

II

Emily Dickinson's poem "I taste a liquor never brewed" was first printed, in May 1861, in the Springfield *Daily Republican.* The first stanza there reads as follows:

> I taste a liquor never brewed,
> From tankards scooped in pearl;
> Not Frankfort berries yield the sense
> Such a delicious whirl.

That was not, however, precisely what she had written. Her stanza had been more forthright and less delicate:

> I taste a liquor never brewed—
> From Tankards scooped in Pearl—
> Not all the Frankfort Berries
> Yield such an Alcohol!

The editor of the *Daily Republican* apparently thought that the stanza deserved a rhyme; he may well, like any sensible man, have objected to the logic of the third line. The version which he printed was a new stanza, produced under that power reserved by the editor to correct rhymes and alter figures of speech; he thought it (I feel sure) a notable improvement over Emily's crude work. Emily Dickinson was not at the time averse to publication; but she was, in the words of her distinguished modern editor, Thomas H. Johnson, concerned "how one can publish and at the same time preserve the integrity of one's art."[10] This is a topic which can lead into the central question, even paradox, relating to the creation of the work of art: whose intentions are being fulfilled, who can be properly called the

[10] *The Poems of Emily Dickinson* (Cambridge, Mass., 1955), I, xxvi.

14

author? The obvious answer in the present case—Emily Dickinson—is true enough, and it will serve perfectly for the manuscripts of those poems which she did not communicate to anyone. But once works of art are performed—even in elementary bardic song, or on the stage, or by a reader from copies reproduced from the author's inscription—then complex questions begin in time to arise.

In examining the nature of authorship, I am trying to inquire into what constitutes the integrity of the work of art. Whatever it is, it is apparently something which various classes of persons either do not respect or else define with such latitude that it includes their own efforts. On many magazines, for example, the editorial practice has been to alter the author's text to suit the policy or need of the magazine while retaining the author's name. The author is a tradesman, his work is a commodity which can be made more or less vendible, and the magazine is in a more favored position in the commercial hierarchy than is the author. A multitude of examples of the results can be gleaned from the pages of Frank Luther Mott's study of American magazines. When A. J. H. Duganne refused to furnish further chapters for his serial story, *The Atheist*, the editor of *Holden's* simply wrote the final chapters himself; Emerson's peculiarities were edited out of his contributions to the *Dial*.[11] William Dean Howells acted the part of an "academic taskmaster freely blue-penciling the essays of his unhappy pupils," and he said that his proofreading "sometimes wellnigh took the character of original work, in that liberal *Atlantic* tradition of bettering the authors by editorial transposition and paraphrase, either in the form of suggestion or of absolute correction"; James Russell Lowell (the second president of the Modern Language Association) wrote to a contributor to the *North American Review* that "I shall take the liberty to make a verbal change here and there, such as I am sure you would agree to could we talk the matter over. I think, for example, you speak

[11]*A History of American Magazines 1741-1850* (New York, 1930), p. 504.

rather too well of young Lytton, whom I regard as both an imposter and as an antinomian heretic. Swinburne I must modify a little, as you will see, to make the *Review* consistent with itself. But you need not be afraid of not knowing your own child again."[12] Edward Bok, the editor of the *Ladies' Home Journal*, once deleted a substantial portion of a story by Mark Twain; and the editor of *Collier's* modified a story by Julian Hawthorne about a seduced maiden by inserting a secret marriage and legitimizing the child.[13] When extracts from *Huckleberry Finn* were printed in the *Century Magazine*, they were carefully altered by Richard Watson Gilder, the editor, with Twain's full consent, even though they had already been pruned both by Mrs. Clemens and by William Dean Howells; Gilder excised about a fifth of the extracts, including descriptive passages and those which (like "to be in a sweat") he thought too coarse or vulgar for his audience.[14] Examples could be multiplied indefinitely. Sometimes the editor is a famous man of letters and the author a hack, and sometimes it is the other way around; sometimes a change seems to later critics to have been improvement, and sometimes debasement.

The reflection on these facts might be simple were it not that when authors publish their periodical contributions in book form, they very frequently retain the changes which have been introduced by the editors. Thus, by inference, they validate the changes and give them some kind of authority. Nathaniel Hawthorne, for example, retained the changes, despite his objection to editorial meddling; at least, in the case of the four short stories for which the manuscript is extant, he seems not to have restored the original readings when the editors altered his text, in punctuation, spelling, capitalization, and diction.[15] Similarly,

[12]*A History of American Magazines 1865–1885* (Cambridge, Mass., 1938), p. 21.

[13]*A History of American Magazines 1885–1905* (Cambridge, Mass., 1957), p. 37.

[14]Arthur L. Scott, "The *Century Magazine* Edits *Huckleberry Finn*, 1884–1885," *AL*, 27 (1955), 356–363.

[15]Seymour L. Gross and Alfred J. Levy, "Some Remarks on the Extant Manuscripts of Hawthorne's Short Stories," *SB*, 14 (1961), 254–257.

when Thomas Nelson Page's stories were collected by Scribner's, he did not reintroduce the omitted passages (about drink, religion, and horror) nor the original Negro dialect; the changes made by the editors of the *Century Magazine* were largely allowed to stand.[16] Charles Reade objected strenuously to the editorial pressure from *Blackwood's* on *The Woman Hater*, but he then used the serial text as copy for the book, with only a few inconsequential changes in phrasing.[17]

On the other hand, occasionally authors have restored their original readings in book publication. When Thomas Hardy's novels were first published in periodicals, the texts were considerably changed at the urging of editors. Sometimes the alterations were verbal, as the change from "lewd" to "gross," "loose" to "wicked," and "bawdy" to "sinful" in *Far from the Madding Crowd*; sometimes they were more substantial, as the omission of the seduction scene from *Tess of the D'Urbervilles* and the substitution of a mock marriage. When Hardy got his manuscripts ready for book publication, however, he restored nearly everything that the magazine editors had made him change.[18] But not always, even with Hardy. Many editorial changes were made in his manuscript for the first serial appearance, in the *Atlantic Monthly*, of *Two on a Tower*. This edited text then served, with few changes, as copy-text for the first London edition, and the edited version has continued in all later editions of Hardy.[19]

In cases of these kinds, there is generally some uncertainty as to the interpretation to be put on the author's actions. Often

[16]John R. Roberson, "The Manuscripts of Page's 'Marse Chan'," *SB*, 9 (1957), 259–262.

[17]Royal A. Gettman, "Henry James's Revision of *The American*," *AL*, 16 (1945), 295.

[18]Oscar Maurer, " 'My Squeamish Public': Some Problems of Victorian Magazine Publishers and Editors," *SB*, 12 (1958), 21–40.

[19]Carl J. Weber, "The Manuscript of Hardy's *Two on a Tower*," *PBSA*, 40 (1946), 1–21.

we cannot be sure whether he makes suggested changes because of a compliant nature, whether he allows editorial alterations to stand in later editions out of laziness, whether he reverts to earlier readings out of pertinacity, or whether there is reasoned conviction in support of his actions. Once another hand helps to prepare a work of art for dissemination, it is usually difficult to distinguish with certainty which part is not by the author.

One of the most common kinds of intervention in the publication of books is made by the publisher's editor—the person whose job it is to read material before publication, to recommend acceptance or rejection, to "house style" the text, to query anything which seems inaccurate, ineffective, or offensive, and to make or suggest any changes which appeal to the editor as desirable. I suppose that almost every writer—even the lowly scholar—has found his deathless prose altered by a publisher's editor, who is sometimes an eminent man of letters and sometimes a mere slip of a girl barely out of college. Some authors blanch at the thought of any alteration, some accept any change gratefully as an improvement. There appears to be a perennial joke among editors of "educational" publishers that they completely rewrite the books of some authors, reducing the text to half of its original length, and the authors never realize that any changes have been made.

Probably the most celebrated editor of this century was Maxwell E. Perkins of Charles Scribner's Sons, editor for Fitzgerald, Wolfe, Hemingway, and a dozen other writers of consequence. Perkins was rather reluctant to offer any specific suggestions to authors except about legal or libelous matters. Frequently he sent long letters or memoranda of advice to "his" authors about their manuscripts; but his suggestions were general and undemanding. He was like a kindly parent, proud of his children, always encouraging them to fulfill their potentialities, ready to offer a guiding hand in time of need. It was only when an author called for help that he would be party to the making of important changes in a manuscript. The most significant revi-

18

sions he ever made, presumably, were his extensive cuts in Wolfe's first two manuscripts, trying to bring order out of chaos.[20] The cuts were apparently made by Perkins with Wolfe's acquiescence, and they reduced *Look Homeward, Angel* (for example) by thirty percent.[21] Wolfe gave his own view of the role of an editor by saying that his editor, after reading a certain number of portions of manuscript submitted to him, "called me to his home and calmly informed me that my book was finished. I could only look at him with stunned surprise, and finally I only could tell him out of the depth of my own hopelessness, that he was mistaken, that the book was not finished, that it could never be completed, that I could write no more. He answered with the same quiet finality that the book was finished whether I knew it or not. . . ." Wolfe soon came to agree, and thus were the scope and structure of the novel determined.[22]

Wives serve as editors, too. Mrs. Hawthorne made a thorough revision of her husband's notebooks while preparing them for publication. She was careful, for example, to root out his colloquialisms: in her hands, "boozy" becomes "intoxicated," "soft soap" turns to "praise," "squint" and "peep" are "look," and "speechifying" gains the dignity of "making speeches."[23] To mention only one more of an almost unlimited number of instances, Theodore Dreiser had the advantage—however un-

[20]*Editor to Author: The Letters of Maxwell E. Perkins,* ed. John Hall Wheelock (New York, 1950), pp. 171–174, 175–180, 286–294, 227–230, 98–102.

[21]Francis E. Skipp, "The Editing of *Look Homeward, Angel,*" *PBSA,* 57 (1963), 1–13. On the basis of analyzing the material cut, Skipp is of the opinion that the changes improved the work.

[22]Thomas Wolfe, *The Story of a Novel* (New York, 1936), p. 74. Also, as for Wolfe's last fiction, "to say the least, now that they are finally disclosed, the 'polishing' and alterations made by [Edward] Aswell [of Harper] after Wolfe's death are alarming, for he took liberties with the manuscript which went far beyond acceptable assistance." (Richard Walser, rev. of Richard S. Kennedy's *The Window of Memory: The Literary Career of Thomas Wolfe,* in *MP,* 61, 1963–64, 324.)

[23]*The English Notebooks of Nathaniel Hawthorne,* ed. Randall Stewart (New York, 1941), pp. ix-xxi.

likely it seems—of several editors, notably Louise Campbell. She acted as literary assistant, revised eight of his books while preparing them for publication, and even wrote character sketches for publication under his name in *Esquire*.[24] What is called ghost writing, however, goes a little beyond the usual requirements of editing.[25]

Then there are some books the final forms of which (it would be accurate to say) are not so much written as constructed. Mark Twain, for example, left *The Mysterious Stranger* unfinished; Albert Bigelow Paine put it together somewhat arbitrarily and added a last chapter found separately among the author's papers. Bernard de Fallois reconstructed Marcel Proust's *Jean Santeuil*, that first rough version of *Remembrance of Things Past*, by the use of seventy notebooks and several boxes of torn and detached pages made available to him after Proust's death by Madame Gérard Mante-Proust.[26] *More Stately Mansions* was made by Karl Ragner Gierow by shortening Eugene O'Neill's partly revised script.

Editors play an important role in the production of magazines and books, and they are often responsible for changes in the author's text. I am not trying to say whether these changes are or are not improvements, whether they are made willingly or reluctantly by the author, whether there should or should not be editors—only that textual changes for which an editor is responsible do in fact take place, frequently and regularly.

This editorial activity results in the embodiment of the editor's intentions in the work of art. In a complex way, the integrity of the work of art is thereby, in some measure, the effect of a juncture of intentions.[27] Another major entanglement, this one mainly accidental in nature, occurs in the trans-

[24]Robert H. Elias, rev. of *Letters to Louise: Theodore Dreiser's Letters to Louise Campbell* (Philadelphia, 1959), *AL*, 33 (1961), 90–91.

[25]For an interesting account by a noted editor (of O'Neill and Faulkner, for example) who had been a prolific ghost writer, see Saxe Commins, "Confessions of a Ghost," *PULC*, 22 (1960), 26–35.

[26]Marcel Proust, *Jean Santeuil* (London, 1955), pp. ix, xxi-xxii.

lation of the text from authorial to public form—the physical process of turning the author's dictated or typed or handwritten copy into print or (in earlier times) into scribal manuscript form. To speak only of printing, I suppose it is true to say that few if any books of any size have ever been printed without mistakes, even that "No book is completed until *Error* has crept in & affixed his sly Imprimatur." The usual assumption is that every printed book includes many errors, and it is easy to see why this must be: a page of type may contain from one to five thousand characters; there is only one way of getting each of them right, and many ways of getting each one wrong. No matter how experienced the compositor, he will make changes, the proofreader will fail to notice some of them, and every change is an error. The editors of the Centenary Hawthorne have sought to minimize this state of nature by having all proofs "read at least five times and by three or more editors."[28]

Proofreading by authors was not usual before the eighteenth century; indeed, early proofreading normally consisted of a reading (by the master printer or his assistant) of one of the first sheets printed off, without recourse to the copy, and marking any apparent errors for correction; in the meantime, of course, a certain number of uncorrected sheets would have already been printed. The fact that proof sheets were later run off, and given to the author for correction, is certainly no guarantee that all the mistakes were caught. Careless proofreading is not uncommon, and writers differ in their interest and skill in handling such details. It has been said that F. Scott Fitzgerald's *This Side of Paradise* is an "inexcusably sloppy job, and that the blame must be distributed between author and publisher"; the first edition contained a large number of

[27]An unusually detailed and explicit account of the modifications made in a novel as a result of suggestions by editors and others is set forth in Irving Wallace's *The Writing of One Novel* (New York, 1968), particularly pp. 110–136. The novel discussed is Wallace's *The Prize,* 1962.

[28]*The Scarlet Letter* (Columbus, Ohio, 1962), p. xlvii.

21

misspellings, inconsistencies, and other examples of carelessness which neither the author nor the publisher corrected—indeed, some of the errors noted by the reviewers in 1920 have not yet been corrected.[29] Even when the author and publisher both take care, there are still errors. Sinclair Lewis, for example, wrote as follows to his publisher after he had seen a list of errors and inconsistencies observed by Mr. Louis Feipel in the published version of *Babbitt*: "J. Henry! This man Feipel is a wonder—to catch all these after rather unusually careful proof-reading not only by myself and my wife but also by two or three professionals!"[30] Sometimes misprints become, in effect, a permanent part of the text.[31]

Sometimes an author prefers the mistakes to his own work. Richard Ellmann has described such a preference on the part of James Joyce. It occurred while Joyce was dictating *Finnegans Wake* to Samuel Beckett. "There was a knock on the door and Joyce said, 'Come in.' Beckett, who hadn't heard the knock, by mistake wrote down 'Come in' as part of the dictated text. Afterwards he read it back to Joyce who said, 'What's that "Come in"?' 'That's what you dictated,' Beckett replied. Joyce thought for a moment, realizing that Beckett hadn't heard the knock; then he said, 'Let it stand'."[32]

Perhaps the play is the form of literary art in which the principles associated with the integrity of the work and the

[29]Matthew J. Bruccoli, "A Collation of F. Scott Fitzgerald's *This Side of Paradise*," *SB*, 9 (1957), 263–265.

[30]Matthew J. Bruccoli, "Textual Variants in Sinclair Lewis's *Babbitt*," *SB*, 11 (1958), 263–268.

[31]M. R. Ridley, "The Perpetuated Misprint," *TLS*, August 28, 1959, p. 495.

[32]"The Backgrounds of *Ulysses*," *KR*, 16 (1954), 359–360. I have heard it said that Joyce retained some of the printer's errors in *Ulysses* because he preferred them to what he had written, but I have been unable to find any evidence of this claim. "Of course, any editor must be cautious when he goes beyond Joyce's own corrections and emends from the manuscripts; Joyce's 'love of accidentals' is well known, and some of the apparent errors may have received his silent sanction." (A. Walton Litz, "Uses of the *Finnegans Wake* Manuscripts," in *Twelve and a Tilly*, ed. Jack P. Dalton and Clive Hart, London, 1966, p. 100.)

identity of the author are most visible. If the playwright wants his play to find its way onto the stage, he must accommodate his text to the financial claims of the producer, the presentational claims of the director and actors, and the undefined claims of the theatre-going public. William Gibson has given a detailed account of his struggles in revising and rewriting *Two for the Seesaw*. From the time that the first draft was completed until it opened in New York, Gibson rewrote the entire play several times and recast some parts of it as many as five times. These changes were made in trying to meet objections and accommodate the text to the various claims made on it. For example, the male star did not like the character which he was to portray, and the changes made for his benefit covered a wide range: from the deletion of those speeches in which the character talked aloud to himself (since the actor "personally did not talk aloud to himself") all the way to the assurance that he would not "go onstage with one line unrewritten that he felt uncomfortable or untruthful with."

Gibson came to feel that the play as it was produced was not quite his: his collaborators had made a new play. It was a successful play, one which was (he thought) much better and more effective because of the revisions which had been forced on the writer. But not quite his. He told of visiting the studio of a painter and envying her because "she was working in a medium where she alone could ruin it. This seemed to me a definition of art." When Gibson turned over a text to his publisher, he could not bear to put his name to the final version: so he rewrote once more, using much of the stage version, restoring much of what had been surrendered, writing new bits, and ending with a composite of several versions.[33]

The rewriting of plays to meet the demands of performance has for some time been typical of theatrical practice. Oscar Wilde, for example, wrote *The Importance of Being Earnest*

---

[33]William Gibson, *The Seesaw Log: A Chronicle of the Stage Production, with the Text, of "Two for the Seesaw"* (New York, 1959), pp. 32, 37, 101, 43, 140.

as a four-act play, and he did not submit it until it had passed through three stages of composition; when Sir George Alexander (the manager of St. James's Theatre) told him to recast it into three acts and to reduce the length in order to allow time for a curtain raiser, Wilde complied. It is only a few writers of strong will, fierce independence, and eminence—such as G. B. Shaw and Eugene O'Neill—who have been able to see their work performed in accordance with their own intentions, and they have had to fight for their convictions.[34] For the most part, Moss Hart's description in *Act One* (New York, 1959) of the birth of *Once in a Lifetime* is more characteristic: throughout rehearsals and tryouts the author is busily engaged in rewriting the text, adjusting it to the realities of performance, trying to make it into a show which will be a public success.

This process is by no means limited to the work of commercial experts. The conversion of Archibald MacLeish's *J. B.* is an instructive—if rather sad—example. MacLeish spent four years writing the play, which was published by Houghton Mifflin in book form in March 1958 and produced in the Yale University Theatre the next month. Alfred de Liagre, Jr., bought the play, engaged Elia Kazan as director, and brought Kazan and MacLeish together. Kazan thought the play "needed important changes for professional production," gave detailed directions, and MacLeish enthusiastically agreed. The story of the revision of the play, from July through December 1958, is one filled with demands for changes by Kazan and agreement by MacLeish. "You are right to want something from Nickles at the end of Act I," says MacLeish. "Hell, you are always right. Why should I mention it? Here is what I propose." After the Washington opening, Kazan told MacLeish that the play needed a "recognition scene," and he outlined where and why it should

[34]"Often the rehearsals of an O'Neill play would degenerate into a series of running battles between the playwright and the producer, the director, and the actors. Invariably, O'Neill was able to stand his ground against them all." Croswell Bowen, "Rehearsing *The Iceman Cometh*," in *O'Neill and His Plays: Four Decades of Criticism*, ed. Oscar Cargill and others (New York, 1961), p. 460.

take place. MacLeish agreed, and in two days supplied the scene.[35]

It appears likely that the production of plays has always occasioned considerable modification of the text. Undoubtedly a few dramatists at any given time have been able to stand their ground in the running battle with actors, directors, producers, and public; but usually the writer seems to have thought of his words as variable in the process of converting a text to a finished performance.[36] Thus there are, in theory at least and often in practice, two or more versions of every produced play. In Elizabethan times, the author's foul papers represent a non-produced version and the prompt book a produced version.[37] For *J. B.*, the Houghton Mifflin edition (1958) is a non-produced version, while a produced version was printed in *Theatre Arts* (February 1960) and by Samuel French, Inc.; the versions are naturally different.

In dramatic performances, collaboration on the text is greater as the non-verbal effects become more important. In a musical, for example, the author is less in control of his text than in a play, while in a musical revue the identical show is not usually repeated for two performances in succession. In the production of movies, the writer ordinarily has little control over his text,

[35]"The Staging of a Play," *Esquire*, 51 (May 1959), 144–158.

[36]There is considerable evidence in Shakespeare's plays, for example, of revision for production. So far as the text is concerned, E. A. J. Honigman has maintained (*The Stability of Shakespeare's Text*, 1965) that we should not assume that there was a "finalized" text. He thinks that the texts are "instable," and the writers tended to alter their words every time they transcribed them.

[37]A vast amount of modern Shakespearean scholarship has been concerned with trying to infer which of these was the basis for the first printed edition of a given play. There seems to be a tacit assumption among some scholars that the earliest editors of Shakespeare were most interested in printing the words that he wrote. Alice Walker (with whom one fears to disagree) believes that Heminge and Condell "may have known that the *Lear* prompt-book better represented what Shakespeare wrote than the *Hamlet* prompt-book" (*Textual Problems of the First Folio*, Cambridge, Eng., 1953, p. 136). It seems a more plausible assumption that men of the theatre like Heminge and Condell would (unlike many modern scholars) have preferred the text which better represented the play in a good production.

must supply changes upon demand, and may be properly listed in the credits among the chief cameraman, electrician, and sound man. In the production of "Cleopatra" (released by Twentieth Century-Fox in 1963), the valuable properties were the female star and the assignational publicity, not the text. Three distinguished writers were successively employed to provide a scenario, and most of their work was scrapped.

It can be claimed that nearly every person involved in the transmission of literary works helps, in some sense, to shape the effect that a work will have on a reader. The designer, for example, can in some measure make the experience of reading the book a little more pleasant or easy or irritating by the appropriateness of the format, paper, binding, font and size of type. His work is not usually observed consciously. In order to realize something of the range of his effect, however, one has only to imagine reading *Tom Jones* in black letter throughout, on coated art paper, with the sheets printed alternately in red and black, in a tight binding with no inner margin, with illustrations by Willem de Kooning. On the other hand, influences which shape the intentions of the artist are sometimes advantageous. Few regret, I suppose, that James T. Fields (the publisher) was successful in persuading Hawthorne to make *The Scarlet Letter* into a full-length novel rather than finishing it (as Hawthorne had planned) as a long story for publication with half a dozen shorter ones.

So far, this discussion about the integrity of the work of art has emphasized its creation and the agents who are then at work in modifying the intentions of the artist. In fact, the work of art is also subject to alteration long afterwards. For nine plays by Euripides, the earliest manuscript—and the only one with any authority—is of the thirteenth-fourteenth centuries; thus any changes made in the text in the course of that transcription, some 1,750 years after the plays were composed, would have definitively altered the intentions of the author so far as the modern reader is concerned.

26

Emendation may be taken as an example of that range of editorial effort which modifies the works of the past in the hope of purging corrupt readings from them. Boswell tells of Johnson confronting him with a textual problem that required an emendation for its solution. "On the 65 page of the first volume of Sir George Mackenzie's folio edition, Mr. Johnson pointed out a paragraph beginning with *Aristotle*, and told me there was an error in the text which he bid me try to discover. I hit it at once. It stands that the devil answers *even* in *engines*. I corrected it to *ever* in *enigmas*. 'Sir,' said he, 'you're a good critic. This would have been a great thing to do in the text of an ancient author'."[38] Boswell here casts himself in the role of the clever schoolboy responding to the questions of the schoolmaster, who knows all the answers. In real life, however, nobody knows the answers, and it is impossible to say "I hit it at once."

As an expression of editorial preference, emendation is the exercise of textual decision. The corrupted readings in most of the manuscripts of the authors of Greek and Latin antiquity have made their works the happy hunting ground for ingenious editors. Since any plausible reading is preferred to one which is obviously corrupt, and since there is usually no way to validate conjectural emendations beyond the tests of meter and sense, our received texts are peppered with editorial guesses which have silently become indistinguishable from what textual scholars have agreed to consider the author's intentions.

This process of reconstruction by emendation has by no means been limited to writers of classical antiquity. Even such newcomers as English and American authors have also had these benefits conferred on them. The emendations suggested

[38]*Boswell's Journal of A Tour to the Hebrides With Samuel Johnson, LL.D.*, ed. Frederick A. Pottle and Charles H. Bennett (New York, 1936), p. 173. Entry for Wednesday, 15 September 1773. L. F. Powell, in his second edition of *The Tour To the Hebrides* (*Boswell's Life of Johnson*, ed. G. B. Hill and L. F. Powell, V, Oxford, 1964, p. 596) now maintains, in agreement with J. C. Maxwell, that the reading "engines" is in fact "perfectly correct." If so: alas, poor over-clever Boswell; alas, poor over-knowing Johnson.

by some eighteenth-century editors and critics to two lines in Milton are instructive. In the 1645 edition of Milton's *Poems*, lines 631–635 of *Comus* (the beginning of the "Haemony" passage) appear as follows:

> The leaf was darkish, and had prickles on it,
> But in another Countrey, as he said,
> Bore a bright golden flowre, but not in this soyl:
> Unknown, and like esteem'd, and the dull swayn
> Treads on it daily with his clouted shoon. . . .

It is the third and fourth of these lines that were thought to require emendation. Hurd said that "the passage before us is certainly corrupt, or, at least, inaccurate; and had better, I think, been given thus . . . 'Bore a bright golden flower, *not* in this soil / Unknown, *though light* esteem'd'." Seward proposed "*but* in this soil / Unknown and *light* esteem'd." Newton suggested that no change be made beyond the omission of either "but" or "not"; thus the reading could be "*but* in this soil / Unknown and like esteem'd" or else "*not* in this soil: / Unknown, and like esteem'd." Fenton printed "*little* esteem'd" rather than "*like* esteem'd," while Warburton proposed "*light* esteem'd" as the only change.[39] No one of these emendations is now accepted. The weight of the testimony in favor of the reading with which we began is apparently so overwhelming that no one now thinks to suggest any alternative. The same reading (minor variants in orthography and punctuation aside) is to be found in the Trinity College Manuscript (in Milton's hand), in the first (1637) edition of *Comus* (which derived from the Trinity College Manuscript), in the corrected copy of the 1637 *Comus* which Milton presented to the Earl of Bridgewater, and in the 1645 *Poems*; moreover, there is no shred of

[39]These various emendations are recorded in the notes to Henry John Todd's edition of Milton's poetical works (London, 1801, and many later editions). The most elaborate and extensive of all unnecessary emendations to Milton were undoubtedly those made by the great classical scholar Richard Bentley in his edition of *Paradise Lost* (1732).

28

evidence elsewhere that Milton's intentions were not carried out in this passage, which he reviewed so many times while he still had his sight. Each of the editorial emendations was thus (we may conclude) a temporary substitution of the intention of the editor for that of the author.

Very frequently, emendations are made in cases where there is not enough external testimony to confirm or reject them with any feeling of confidence. Sometimes they slide into the text and become the objects of our veneration on the principle that whatever is printed is right.[40] Such is the case in an indefinite number of passages in the works of writers of the past.

Emendation offers the appeal of a puzzle and the release of creation. Jack P. Dalton estimates that *Finnegans Wake* will require some 7,000 emendations, and his description of the task makes it sound like the work of more than one lifetime. "I think it is a task," he writes, "eminently worthy of all the erudition and passion that can be brought to it, for the understanding of this endlessly fascinating book depends upon it."[41] Samuel Johnson felt that "the allurements of emendation are scarcely resistible. Conjecture has all the joy and all the pride of invention, and he that has once started a happy change, is too much delighted to consider what objections may rise against it." Johnson offered a great many emendations to Shakespeare, most of them pure guesses sanctified by the supposition that Shakespeare wrote them. Unlike many critics and readers, however, he came to be aware that his own textual conjectures were likely to be mistaken; and he believed that the best any person can do is produce one of many plausible readings. He trusted conjecture less and less, and he congratulated himself on including none of his own emendations in the plays of Shakespeare that he latterly edited.[42]

---

[40]See, for example, the history of the reading "mid-May" in Keats's "The Fall of Hyperion," 1. 92.

[41]"Advertisement for the Restoration," in *Twelve and a Tilly*, pp. 129, 133.

[42]"Preface to Shakespeare," *The Works of Samuel Johnson, LL.D.* (Oxford, 1825), v, 151, 150, 149.

Johnson put a high value on the creative aspect of emendation. He described one change by Bishop Warburton as "a noble emendation, which almost sets the critic on a level with the author."[43] One can go further than Johnson: without praising either Warburton or the emendation, one can say that the critic who adopts an emendation of his own creation, without a genuine basis for showing it to be a recovery of what the author intended to write, has indeed become co-author of this portion of the work of art—he has in fact been set on a level with the author.

This brings us to a major point about the nature of authorship and of the integrity of the work of art. The literary work is frequently the result, in a pure sense, of composite authorship. We do not have to meddle with the unconscious, the preconscious, or the race consciousness in order to hold this view. In a quite literal sense, the literary work is often guided or directed or controlled by other people while the author is in the process of trying to make it take shape, and it is subject to a variety of alterations throughout its history. The intentions of the person we call the author thus become entangled with the intentions of all the others who have a stake in the outcome, which is the work of art. And yet we agree to say simply "*Two for the Seesaw*, by William Gibson." Not "*Two for the Seesaw*, by William Gibson, Henry Fonda, Fred Coe, Arthur Penn, Anne Bancroft, the elevator boy, wives, friends, and others. "*Jean Santeuil*, by Marcel Proust," not "by Marcel Proust and Bernard de Fallois." "*Look Homeward, Angel*, by Thomas Wolfe," not "by Wolfe and Perkins." "*J. B.*, by MacLeish," not

[43]This is the "god kissing carrion" passage in *Hamlet:* "For if the sun breed maggots in a dead dog, being a god kissing carrion–Have you a daughter?" (ii.ii.181–183). The folios and quartos concur in the reading "good," which Warburton emended (without any external evidence) to "god"–a reading which has been pretty generally accepted, although W. W. Greg objected, a little primly: "It is facile and plausible, but I think unnecessary. Hamlet's fancies are not always as nice as editors would have them" (*Principles of Emendation in Shakespeare*, London, 1928, p. 68). Johnson's observation appears in his edition of Shakespeare at the conclusion of his reprinting of Warburton's note to the passage.

"by MacLeish and Kazan." Our identification of the author is partly a convention for the sake of simplicity, partly a case of the Boss being given credit, whether he wants it or not, for all the work that the office (including volunteer workers) turns out.

Whatever complexities we agree to ignore in our daily encounters with works of art, it remains a fact that the literary work is a mingling of human intentions about which distinctions should be made. Its status as a work of art is not affected by whether these intentions all belong to the titular author; even collaborative authorship does not alter that status, however much it may endanger friendships. On the other hand, the integrity of the work of art depends very much on the work being limited to those intentions which are the author's, together with those others of which he approves or in which he acquiesces. When these intentions have been fulfilled, the work of art has its final integrity or completeness. It may be aesthetically imperfect or unfinished, and it is altogether possible that an indefinite number of people may be capable of improving it. But in the authorial sense it is already finished, it is already complete, it already has that final integrity which should be the object of the critic's chief attention. This is the final integrity which it is the business of the textual critic to identify as an order of words in fulfillment of the authorial intention, the business of the literary critic to understand as an order of words in the context of all literature.

We commenced this discussion with the question, put in the mouth of Emily Dickinson, as to how one can publish and still preserve the integrity of one's art. In a pure sense it is probably impossible, but anyone who is concerned enough to ask the question will undoubtedly realize that a good deal depends on the exercise of will: one must fulfill one's own intentions rather than the conflicting intentions of others, however valuable and well-meaning. Their desire to help is praiseworthy, and altruism is all the more appealing when it is self-effacing; but the dedication of such help to the improvement of others' works of art dissipates the integrity of those works.

III

In the conclusion to *Great Expectations*, Charles Dickens thought it necessary to have a final confrontation between the hero, Pip, and the greatest of his lost expectations, Estella. They meet casually in London. Estella has married a Shropshire doctor after the death of her first husband, the cruel Drummle. She sees Pip walk by on the street while she is sitting in her carriage. They shake hands, she wrongly assumes that the boy with him is his own child, he perceives that suffering has given her an understanding heart, and the book ends. This is the "unhappy," or at least unromantic ending; in less than three hundred words these ships pass one last time, saluting each other gravely all the while. Bulwer-Lytton was dissatisfied with this ending, and at his urging Dickens wrote another. This time Estella is free: she has been a widow for two years and has not remarried. They meet, not in impersonal London, but in memory's lane itself—the site of Miss Havisham's house, where they had first met, which neither has visited for some thirteen years. A silvery mist is rising, the stars are shining, and the first rays of the moon illumine the tears that course from Estella's eyes. They are full of forgiveness for one another, and understanding; they emerge from the ruins holding hands, and there is no shadow of another parting. This is the "happy," the romantic ending, accomplished in a thousand pulsing words. The ending which you read must to some degree affect your understanding of the entire novel. Which is the real *Great Expectations?*

The collection of W. H. Auden's sonnets and verse commentary which he entitled "In Time of War" concludes with these lines:

> Till they construct at last a human justice,
> The contribution of our star, within the shadow
> Of which uplifting, loving, and constraining power
> All other reasons may rejoice and operate.

It is an eloquent plea for men of good will to join together and "construct" a "human justice" for the benefit of all mankind. So the passage appeared in its first publication in 1939, in *Journey to a War*. Within a few years Auden's ideas about the right way to attain human justice—as well as his ideas about many other subjects—had changed markedly. When he came to reprint "In Time of War" in his *Collected Poetry* of 1945, he altered the concluding passage of the commentary as follows:

> Till, as the contribution of our star, we follow
> The clear instructions of that Justice, in the shadow
> Of Whose uplifting, loving, and constraining power
> All human reasons do rejoice and operate.

Instead of constructing human justice, man is now enjoined to follow Divine Justice.[44] Which is the real "In Time of War"?

Thomas Hardy printed four different versions of *The Return of the Native*, from 1878 to 1912. Between the first and second versions he made some 700 changes (of which 40 are major revisions), between the second and third about 350 changes, and between the third and fourth about 115. These changes substantially altered the characterization and plot. In his first manuscript version, Hardy envisioned Eustacia Vye as a literal witch, a demon; by the time he had finished his revisions, she had become a passionate, unconventional beauty with a surprisingly rigid sense of morality. An example of the change

---

[44]For an account of the very numerous revisions, excisions, and eliminations which Auden silently made in preparing his text for the *Collected Poetry* (New York, 1945) and *Collected Shorter Poems* (London, 1950), see Joseph Warren Beach, *The Making of the Auden Canon* (Minneapolis, 1957); his remarks on "In Time of War" are on pp. 5–10. Auden has continued to revise: the unsuspecting reader may be surprised to discover that there is a strong possibility of a significant change in any given poem reprinted in one of the "collected" volumes.

in plot may be found in Eustacia's plan to run away from her husband, Clym Yeobright. In the early versions, her moral problem was whether it was right to accept assistance and financial help from Wildeve since each was married to another; in the later versions, with Wildeve more forward, her problem was whether she could avail herself of his services or whether she also had to accept him as her lover and go away with him.[45] Which is the real *Return of the Native?*

I have asked this kind of question three different times, partly because the three situations are somewhat different, partly to suggest that the problem which I am now to treat is very widespread. That problem is the existence of the work of art in multiple versions, each created by the author. The principle which is involved touches the nature of composition: the work in process, the work in completion, the work in recompletion. Familiar examples of authorial revision abound in all periods: there are two distinct versions of *Piers Plowman*, two of Chaucer's Prologue to *The Legend of Good Women*, and two (possibly three) of *Troilus and Criseyde*, five of Gower's *Confessio Amantis*, two major versions of Sidney's *Arcadia*, two of Ben Jonson's *Every Man in His Humour*, several versions of Browne's *Religio Medici* and Walton's *Life of Donne*, two of Pope's *Rape of the Lock* and of *The Dunciad*, two of Keats's "La Belle Dame Sans Merci," four of FitzGerald's *Rubáiyát of Omar Khayyám*, seven of Whitman's *Leaves of Grass*, from two to five for each of Arnold's major prose works, and so on and so forth.

These are all familiar instances. To add a few other writers who have been notable revisers, within the limits (say) of nineteenth-century poetry, one might first mention Wordsworth, who spent forty-five years in tinkering with *The Prelude*, making the 1850 version in many ways a quite different poem from

[45]See Otis B. Wheeler, "Four Versions of *The Return of the Native*," *NCF*, 14 (1959), 27–44. See also John Paterson, *The Making of "The Return of The Native"* (Berkeley, Calif., 1960), particularly for Hardy's first intentions.

the 1805 version.[46] Or Tennyson, who was a devoted, continual, and minute reviser: he worked over his manuscripts (sometimes in as many as six versions), he altered the texts in the proofs for the first and later editions, and he made marginal changes in the printed editions. Sometimes there are as many as fifteen texts, all different, each armed with the poet's authority.[47] Or Emily Dickinson, who had second and third and fourth thoughts about what she wrote, and who sometimes could not decide which was the final form of a poem. For "Blazing in Gold and quenching in Purple," in the three fair copies she sent to friends, each time one line was different in the supposed final version; "the Otter's Window" in one is "the kitchen window" in another, which is "the oriel window" in a third. She wrote them all and meant each of them to be the poem.[48]

Recent scholarly investigations have revealed that authorial revision is embodied in multiple printed versions to an extent which seems to be almost limitless. I can at least hint at the spread of these findings through the mere mention of a sampling of the subjects, naming only those to whom I have not already alluded. For the twentieth century, Joyce, Faulkner, Yeats, Conrad, Lewis, Dos Passos, Lindsay, Cozzens, Fitzgerald, Ford, Lowell, Pound, Glasgow, D. H. Lawrence, Tennessee Williams, and West. For the nineteenth century, James, Twain, Crane, Pater, Clough, Hawthorne, Poe, Emerson, Thoreau, Longfellow, De Quincey, Blake, Irving, Meredith, and Coleridge. For the eighteenth century, Swift, Fielding, Richardson,

[46]See Helen Darbishire's revision of Ernest de Selincourt's edition (Oxford, 1959),pp. liv-lxxiv.

[47]See, for example, Edgar F. Shannon, Jr., "The History of A Poem: Tennyson's *Ode on the Death of the Duke of Wellington*," *SB*, 13 (1960), 149–177; or Shannon, "The Proofs of *Gareth and Lynette* in the Widener Collection," *PBSA*, 41 (1947), 321–340; or W. D. Paden, "A Note on the Variants of *In Memoriam* and *Lucretius*," *Library*, 5th Ser., 8 (1953), 259–273.

[48]See Thomas H. Johnson, "Emily Dickinson: Creating the Poems," *Harvard Library Bulletin*, 7 (1953), 257–270; or, more comprehensively, *The Poems of Emily Dickinson*, ed. Johnson (Cambridge, Mass., 1955), esp. i, xxxiii-xxxviii and 163–165.

Gibbon, Smollett, and Johnson. For the seventeenth and latter sixteenth centuries, Shakespeare, Drayton, Daniel, Burton, Crashaw, Lee, Rochester, Middleton, Shirley, Edward Taylor, and Dryden. The prize for revision should probably be awarded to Philip James Bailey. He wrote seven different versions of his poem *Festus*, which was, or were, published in thirteen British (and at least forty American) editions between 1839 and 1903. In the process it grew from a modest 8,103 lines (a little shorter than *Paradise Lost*) to a monstrous 39,159 lines.[49] Perhaps Robert Burton deserves honorable mention for the expansion of his *Anatomy of Melancholy* by some 180,000 words in the course of six editions.

The more of these scholarly studies one reads, the more one is impressed by the likelihood of authorial revision in any literary work where the writer had an opportunity to alter his work before communicating it to his public yet another time. What the scholar seems to need in order to demonstrate authorial revision in these cases is simply the good fortune to find that the evidence has not been destroyed. It seems logical to assume that revision may have taken place in other cases, wherever there was occasion for it, even though the editions, manuscripts, or letters to prove it are no longer extant.[50]

I am trying to make it clear that the examples with which I began, of works by Dickens, Auden, and Hardy, are by no means instances of authorial revision which can be dismissed because they are rare freaks. On the contrary, they seem to be examples of a fairly common phenomenon. The matters of principle which they raise will have widespread application.

When people write about literary works which exist in multiple versions, the question they commonly address is "Which is

---

[49]Morse Peckham, "English Editions of Philip James Bailey's *Festus*," *PBSA*, 44 (1950), 55–58.

[50]The consideration of this possibility will, of course, complicate the reasoning of the textual critic. On the whole, it is a possibility which has usually been disregarded unless the evidence to demonstrate the fact of revision has been overwhelming.

the best version?" About *Great Expectations,* for example, J. Hillis Miller writes that "the second ending is, in my opinion, the best. Not only was it, after all, the one Dickens published (would he really have acceded to Mrs. Grundy in the mask of Bulwer-Lytton without reasons of his own?), but, it seems to me, the second ending, in joining Pip and Estella, is much truer to the real direction of the story."[51] On the other hand, Edgar Johnson is somewhat contemptuous of the second ending as a "tacked-on addition of a belated marriage to Estella." "Both as art and as psychology," he informs us, "it was poor counsel that Lytton gave in urging that the shaping of a lifetime in Estella be miraculously undone. Save for this, though, *Great Expectations* is the most perfectly constructed and perfectly written of all Dickens's works." Johnson then proceeds to outline a third ending, of his own imagining, which he prefers to either of those that Dickens wrote. "It should close with that misty moonlight scene in Miss Havisham's ruined garden," but the final action should be that of Pip and Estella "bidding each other a chastened farewell."[52] Personally, I do not feel greatly assisted by any of these answers. The making of a choice between the versions may seem to be of a high order because it involves the exercise of taste; but it is not the first question to ask, and it turns out to be more of an innocently curious quest than a serious critical inquiry.

The first problem is to identify the work of art. The basic proposition which I submit about works created by authorial revision is that each version is, either potentially or actually, another work of art. It remains a "potential" work of art—it is in process, it is becoming—so long as the author is still giving

[51]*Charles Dickens: The World of His Novels* (Cambridge, Mass., 1958), p. 278.

[52]*Charles Dickens: His Tragedy and Triumph* (New York, 1952), II, 988, 992–993. Among the other people who have propounded answers are Monroe Engel (*The Maturity of Charles Dickens,* Cambridge, Mass., 1959, pp. 157–158, 167–168) and Martin Meisel ("The Ending of *Great Expectations,*" *Essays in Criticism,* 15, 1965, 326–331). Meisel affords us the relief of learning that "either ending works very well indeed" and that "in the total architecture of the novel neither ending is very important" (p. 326).

it shape, in his mind or in successive drafts or interlineations or in whatever manner he suspends those works which he is not yet ready to release to his usual public. On the other hand, the "actual" work of art is a version in which the author feels that his intentions have been sufficiently fulfilled to communicate it to the public, as his response to whatever kinds of pressure bear on him, from within or from without, to release his work into a public domain. The distinction which I am offering is a practical (rather than idealistic) way of separating the potential from the actual, the work of art which is becoming from the work of art which is. The distinction thus turns on the intentions of the artist: the work can have only such integrity, or completeness, as the author chooses to give it, and our only reasonable test of when the work has achieved integrity is his willingness to release it to his usual public. His judgment may not always be good, and he may release it too soon or too late or when (we think) he never should have; but it is his judgment not ours, his intention not ours, his work of art which he makes ours.[53]

The nature of the public differs for different writers. For Dickens—as for most writers since the invention of printing—it was the readers of a periodical or of a book issued by publishers to whom he had turned over a text. For Emily Dickinson,

[53]Lester A. Beaurline has objected to this view ("The Director, the Script, and Author's Revisions: A Critical Problem," in *Papers in Dramatic Theory and Criticism*, ed. David M. Knauf, Iowa City, 1969, pp. 86–87). He argues that my position does not take into account that some writers, because of youth or poverty or lack of experience, are understandably obliged to bow to pressures to alter their work to have it published or produced. Presumably Beaurline would like for the writer always to produce the best work of which he is capable, and so would I. But the writer cannot always do so, sometimes because of the very weakness (or strength) of his personality and of his human needs alluded to; the editor cannot venture to save the writer from himself (aside from the correction of inadvertences) by improving what he has chosen to make public. In my opinion, Beaurline's objection actually draws attention to a strength of my distinction. As I see it, editing is the practical task of recovering what the writer wrote and made public—not what he might have written, or was capable of writing, or could have been allowed or induced to write. The literary work as it exists in its public version or versions is the prime material of the editor.

however, her usual public might be her sister-in-law, Susan Dickinson, or Thomas Wentworth Higginson, or Helen Hunt Jackson. If she sent a fair copy of a poem to one of them, this action—as the equivalent of voluntary publication—can be taken as evidence that the work had achieved its integrity. For William Blake, the usual public might be anyone in the small circle of friends and kindly benefactors who accepted or purchased a copy of one of his books—written, designed, engraved, colored, and bound by Blake, with the assistance of his wife.

The application of this test is sometimes difficult, mainly when the evidence leaves obscure the question as to whether the artist intended to release the work to his public in the form in which we have it. Books which are published piratically or circulated surreptitiously are examples. Sir Thomas Browne "at leisurable houres composed" *Religio Medici,* as he says in his address "To the Reader," "for my private exercise and satisfaction"; "being communicated unto one, it became common unto many, and was by transcription successively corrupted untill it arrived in a most depraved copy at the presse. He that shall peruse that worke, and shall take notice of sundry particularities and personall expressions therein, will easily discerne *the intention was not publik.*" (I use italics to call attention to the key phrase.) There were two unauthorized editions issued anonymously in 1642, but Browne then proceeded to supply—to the same bookseller who had pirated his work—text for an authorized edition; he used a copy of one of the pirated editions, correcting some 650 errors (while overlooking many others), and adding four new sections, a dozen new passages, and many new errors.[54] However hasty and careless his alterations, *Religio Medici* was then a public work. With some writers, pirated (or even manipulated) publication has been used as an excuse to issue works (like Pope's publication of his own letters) which it might otherwise seem immodest to release to the usual public.

[54]Jean-Jacques Denonain, ed., *Religio Medici* (Cambridge, Eng., 1953), pp. xxiv-xxviii.

Sometimes a writer feels that publication puts an end to his freedom to revise. Guillaume De Guileville told, in the prologue to his *Pélerinage de la vie humaine,* of a wonderful dream he had in the year 1330 and of writing it down hastily "that I myht after, by leyser, / Correcte hyt when the day were cler." But before he had finished mending it, it was stolen from him and published abroad, "a-geyn my wyl & my plesaunce." Up to that time, he says, "fredam I hadde / To putte away, and eke to adde, / What that me lyst, lyk as I wende"; but after publication he lost that freedom. It was only after the passage of twenty-five years that he made a new version, by thorough revision, and was ready to send it forth into the world to replace the incomplete version which he had not wished published.[55]

The revisions which a writer makes while a work is in process —that is, before it becomes a version which he chooses to make public—constitute an intimate and complex view of that writer at work. "The minute changes made in their compositions by eminent writers are," in Edmond Malone's blunt dictum, "always a matter of both curiosity & instruction to literary men, however trifling and unimportant they may appear to blockheads."[56] The study of revisions can enlighten us, as Paul Valéry says, "about the secret discussion that takes place, at the time when the work is being done, between the temperament, ambition and foresight of the man, and, on the other hand, the excitements and the intellectual means of the moment. The strictness of the revisions, the number of solutions rejected, and possibilities denied, indicate the nature of the scruples, the degree of conscience, the quality of pride, and even the reserves and diverse fears that are felt in regard to the future judgment of the public." With a writer whose mind is reflective and rich in resonances, the work can only emerge "by a kind of accident

[55]EETS (Extra Series), 77 (1899), 6–8. (The Lydgate translation.)

[56]Quoted by James M. Osborn, *John Dryden: Some Biographical Facts and Problems* (New York, 1940), p. 131.

which ejects it from the mind."[57] The taste for making endless revisions is, according to Valéry, an occupational disease; "in the eyes of these lovers of anxiety and perfection, a work is never *complete*—a word which to them is meaningless—but *abandoned*."[58] Other writers have less difficulty with the creative process, and some find greater satisfaction in the results they obtain.[59]

In any event, the several verbal forms in which the literary work exists while it is being written are in the private province of the writer as part of his interior dialogue with himself. When extant documents preserve these variant forms, we must remember that they provide glimpses into the creative process and not a final form. Dickens never used the first ("unhappy") ending of *Great Expectations*; he wrote it, sent it to the printer, had it set in type, and read the proofs. But he allowed his mind to be changed and wrote the second ending, which he used in the serial and book editions of the novel. The first ending was preserved by his friend and biographer, John Forster; it was never printed as part of the novel until 1937, when it was used in the Limited Editions Club version, which carried the imprimatur of an introduction by George Bernard Shaw. The Rinehart Edition prints both endings, as if each reader could choose the one he preferred. As I read the evidence, the first ending never became an integral part of the novel in a public version; only

---

[57]"On Mallarmé" in *Selected Writings* (New York, 1950), pp. 217, 216.

[58]"Concerning *Le Cimetière marin*" in *The Art of Poetry* (New York, 1958), pp. 140–141. Even the abandoned work is often returned to, with the spirit of Anne Bradstreet in these lines from "The Author to her Book" in *The Tenth Muse:*

> I cast thee by as one unfit for light
> Thy Visage was so irksome in my sight; . . .
> Yet being mine own, at length affection would
> Thy blemishes amend, if so I could.

See Jeannine Hensley, "The Editor of Anne Bradstreet's *Several Poems*," *AL*, 35 (1963–64), 502–504.

[59]For discussion and examples of authorial revision of work in progress, see *Poets at Work*, ed. Charles D. Abbott (New York, 1948), and Robert H. Taylor and H. W. Liebert, *Authors at Work* (New York, 1957).

the second ending—no matter whether you think it better or worse—attained that status, and the only "real" *Great Expectations* by Charles Dickens is the one with that ending. Edgar Johnson's "third" ending, being of his own construction, could have status only if Johnson were considered a coauthor of the novel. The work of art cannot be judged by loading it with hypotheses of what it might have been or of what it could be made to be: the work of art has a radical integrity, and we must take that integrity, once discovered, as it is. The tactic of posing self-made alternatives is one which involves tremendous risks for a doubtful advantage.

When the literary work emerges as a public version it then has the integrity of its unique authorial form. Our suspicions about the sheer decency of contemplating more than one public version of a single literary work may be allayed if we think of the versions as separated in time, with something like five years between the two versions of Auden's "In Time of War," with about thirty-four years for insulation between the first and the last *Return of the Native*.

An analogy from sculpture may be persuasive in overcoming our reluctance to accept the view that different public versions of a literary work are in fact different works of art. If one sees, side by side, five versions of a bronze head of Jeanne Vaderin (Jeanette) by Henri Matisse—all distinctly different, each a new casting, yet all dating from 1910-1911—one will perhaps have no serious hesitation about recognizing them as five different works of art. They have the same subject and many similarities —and so do the many finished self-portraits by Rembrandt—but they are readily recognizable as different works of art.

"I cannot go back over anything I have written," said Valéry, "without thinking that I should now make something quite different of it."[60] If we consider the theory and practice of William Butler Yeats and Henry James, the status of multiple versions of a work of art will perhaps be clearer. Yeats under-

[60]"Concerning *Le Cimetière marin*" in *The Art of Poetry*, p. 144.

stood, with the utmost clarity, his drive to revise. When friends objected to his habit of returning again and again to his old poems and altering them each time, he replied with these lines:

> The friends that have it I do wrong
> When ever I remake a song,
> Should know what issue is at stake:
> It is myself that I remake.[61]

Yeats was an inveterate reviser because he was, quite simply, always trying to make his poems contemporaneous with his self as a changing human being. "This volume contains what is, I hope, the final text of the poems of my youth," he wrote in the Preface of January 1927 to the thirteenth reprinting and revision of his *Poems* of 1895; "and yet it may not be," he added, "seeing that in it are not only the revisions from my 'Early Poems and Stories,' published last year, but quite new revisions on which my heart is greatly set." To read his prefaces to the various editions of "The Countess Cathleen," for example, is to see more clearly what is involved in the making of a new public version of a literary work.

Yeats was always rereading his earlier poems, and always making new versions to issue to his public. He did not scruple to keep rewriting any of his previous work. Henry James, on the other hand, approached the revision of his earlier novels with anxiety, as a job that bristled with difficulties.[62] He had been at pains to dismiss his earlier work, to put it behind him, to become unacquainted with it. He was disinclined to exhume

[61]Untitled poem *ss*, in *The Variorum Edition of the Poems of W. B. Yeats*, ed. Peter Allt and Russell K. Alspach (New York, 1957), p. 778. (This poem is not included in the "definitive" edition.)

[62]The Prefaces to *Roderick Hudson* and *The Golden Bowl* (Vols. I and XXIII, respectively, in the New York edition) set forth James's central ideas on revision. In the collection of his Prefaces called *The Art of the Novel*, with an introduction by Richard P. Blackmur (New York, 1934), the passage about revision in the Preface to *Roderick Hudson* is on pp. 10–12 and the one in the Preface to *The Golden Bowl* on pp. 335–340. My exposition of James's views is based mainly on the latter passage and includes close paraphrase of what I take to be the major issues.

it, and very loath to start tidying it up for fear that he would become involved in expensive renovations. He had been accustomed all of his life to revising his work, it is true, to changing the periodical version for book publication, to altering the text from one edition to another; but those revisions were made in warm blood while the original vision of the story was still with him. What has made his revisions of special interest was this task that he approached with such reluctance, for the Definitive New York edition. The gulf of time which separated him from most of the novels to be included made him think of the idea of rewriting them as so difficult, or even so absurd, as to be impossible; it would not be a mere matter of expression, but of somehow harmonizing the man he then was and the man he used to be.

James resolved his dilemma by discarding the idea of rewriting altogether and by taking the task of revision in its etymological sense—to see again, to look over, to re-peruse. Thus he never thought of himself as rewriting a novel, but of seeing it again and recording the results of that re-vision in so many close notes that the pages were made to flower. James respected his novels and their characters as having an independent existence of their own, and he wanted to keep his hands off of them. By his own application of the term "revision," he made himself believe that he had done so. I take his argument to be an innocent but necessary piece of deception to avoid facing the fact of rewriting. However James looked on his job, the revisions for the New York edition resulted in new versions of the works. He made, for example, more than two thousand revisions in *The Reverberator*.[63] Voices rise and

---

[63]See Sister Mary Brian Durkin, "Henry James's Revisions of the Style of *The Reverberator*," *AL*, 33 (1961), 330–349. There has been, I dare say, more extensive scholarly investigation, in books and articles and theses, of the revisions by James for the New York edition than of those by any other writer on any occasion. The three novels in which the revisions have so far been examined the most thoroughly are, probably, *The American, The Portrait of a Lady,* and *The Ambassadors*. Such fertile fields are attractive to the husbandman, and we can expect every last one of the twenty-four volumes to be harrowed in e·cι direction.

fall as to whether James improved or debased his novels by revision, as to whether his later style is more tortuous and labored or clearer and more expressive, even as to whether the revision of a given novel makes a radical or minimal change in the effect of a certain character, like Newman in *The American.* The unarguable fact is that James supplied multiple versions of the novels which he revised.

The literary critic can afford enough detachment to observe the work of art as an historical phenomenon, as a part of the past from the moment of its creation. But few writers are able to take this view; for many of them the work continues, as for a possessive parent, a part of the self, as a child whose hair must be brushed into submission, as an adult who must be nagged into wearing more stylish clothes.

I suggested that our suspicion of multiple versions of the work of art may be allayed if we think of them as separated by long periods of time. Time is, however, only a practical convenience in envisioning why multiple versions may or must exist. No clock can measure the rate at which a man becomes different: a little, a lot, a little, a lot. Enough might happen in a day or even in a flash to require that the man rediscover his self and make a poem over in a new way, which is making a new poem. William Faulkner said that "no writer is ever quite satisfied with the work he has done, which is why he writes another one. If he ever wrote one which satisfied him completely, nothing remains but to cut the throat and quit."[64]

We come back again to the questions with which we began this discussion. The problem of identifying the "real" *Great Expectations,* we found, was simplified when we insisted on respecting the public version to which Dickens gave authorial integrity. The application of this basic test will not select one or the other of Auden's "In Time of War," however, since each

[64]*Faulkner at West Point* (New York, 1964), p. 49. "Probably the only reason the poet ever writes another poem is that the one he just finished didn't quite serve that purpose—wasn't good enough—so he'll write another one" (p. 48).

45

is a fulfillment of his intentions, and each was communicated to his usual public. From our review of what takes place in revision for private and public versions, I hope it is clear that the two versions of the Auden collection are equally "real." They stand, side by side, as two separate works, and each has every bit of the dignity and integrity with which an author can endow any work of art. So it is with Hardy, with Yeats, with James, with all multiple versions of works of art where each was given authorial integrity and communicated to the usual public.

This embarrassment of riches may make us restless to distinguish. Hence the critic asks "which is the best?" And the editor asks "which shall I print?" And the student asks "which shall I read?" Usually these three questions are the same, the latter two being applications of the first.

There is a conventional answer, made smooth by constant use. "It is generally accepted that the most authoritative edition is the last published in the author's lifetime." "The book collector may prefer to possess a first edition, however faulty the text, but an author's last revision must, as a rule, claim precedence in literature." This answer can be duplicated from the writings of most of the famous bibliographers and textual authorities: "I take it that the proper application of the critical editorial process is to produce a text that recovers the author's final intentions more faithfully than any preserved transmitted text." It is also the password when one is explaining one's terms in a footnote to a textual study: "By 'best text' I mean the text that represents the poet's own final choice among variants of the poem."[65]

---

[65]The first quotation is from R. W. Chapman, "The Textual Criticism of English Classics," in *English Critical Essays: Twentieth Century*, ed. Phyllis M. Jones (London, 1933), p. 274. The second is from Sir Harold Williams, *The Text of "Gulliver's Travels"* (Cambridge, Eng., 1952), p. 36. The third is from Fredson Bowers, "Old-Spelling Editions of Dramatic Texts," *Studies in Honor of T. W. Baldwin* (Urbana, 1958), p. 9. The fourth is from Zahava Karl Dorinson, " 'I Taste a Liquor Never Brewed': A Problem in Editing," *AL*, 35 (1963), 363, n. 1.

It is a bit puzzling to know why this dictum should for so long have passed unchallenged. For it is much like saying that an author's last poem (or novel, or play) is, as a general rule, his best one; it may be, and it may not be.

When several different works—or several versions of the same work—were written by the same author and communicated to his usual public, each is "authoritative." It is idle to try to solve an editorial problem, under these circumstances, by talking about which one is "the most authoritative." Likewise, any one of them might be said to "claim precedence." It all depends on where the procession is supposed to be going.

The rule of thumb of selecting the last version, when the choice is among multiple public versions of a work of art, is a desperate substitute for the whole process of critical understanding. Since that process is the only sensible way of trying to arrive at a sound evaluation of anything, it is that process which should govern the editor's selection of one version from among many.

IV

What is the aesthetic object with which textual criticism can deal? What constitutes the integrity of the work of art? When a literary work exists in several authorial versions, which is the real work of art?

These are the three questions which we have been addressing. The first invites us to consider the characteristics of the several types of phenomena which can be called aesthetic objects because they yield an aesthetic response. I have argued that the textual critic must limit himself to works of art: thus aesthetic objects which are the result of chance or nature are beyond his scope, however appealing or meritorious they may be, even if they improve the work of art. In being limited to the work of art, the textual critic is thereby limited to the linguistic intentions of the author. The basic goal of textual criticism is, therefore, the verification or recovery of the words which the author intended to constitute the literary work.

The second question asks us to explore the nature of authorship and of the literary work as an intricate entangling of intentions. Various forces are always at work thwarting or modifying the author's intentions. The process of preparing the work for dissemination to a public (whether that process leads to publication in printed form or production in the theatre or preparation of scribal copies) puts the work in the hands of persons who are professionals in the execution of the process. Similarly, the effort to recover a work of the past puts it in the hands of professionals known as textual critics, or editors. In all of these cases, the process must be adapted to the work at hand, and the work to the process. Sometimes through misunderstanding and sometimes through an effort to improve the work, these professionals substitute their own intentions for those of the author, who is frequently ignorant of their craft. Sometimes the author objects and sometimes not, sometimes he is pleased, sometimes he acquiesces, and sometimes he does not notice what has happened. The work of art is thus always tending toward a collaborative status, and the task of the textual critic is always to recover and preserve its integrity at that point where the authorial intentions seem to have been fulfilled.

The third question opens the nature of composition and seeks to define the authoritative quality of each work of art. Works which are in process can be called potential works of art, while the actual work of art is the one which fulfills the author's intentions. Our only practicable way of distinguishing is to observe whether the author does or does not communicate the work to his usual public. When the author provides us with multiple actual versions of what we commonly think of as a single literary work, he has in fact written separate works, among which there is no simple way to choose the best.

Throughout this discussion, the intentions of the artist have occupied a central position. It is his intentions which distinguish the work of art as an order within the class of aesthetic objects, which must be protected in order to preserve the work from becoming a collaborative enterprise, which give the integrity of completeness to the actual work of art. The inference for the textual critic is that the intentions of the artist are of controlling importance over textual work. While the textual critic should not neglect to carry out the more or less mechanical operations which his masters enjoin upon him, he must also undertake to discover all that he can, from whatever source, about the linguistic intentions of the artist. It is his interpretation of this evidence, within a consistent aesthetic, which plays the crucial role in giving his work value.

I would not wish to argue that these inferences simplify the task of the textual critic, nor that they supply him with a ready formula for solving hard cases, nor that they qualify him as a seer. They do, in fact, make his work more difficult. Whenever we deal with human motives and the operation of human intentions, we soon reach the point—if we do not have the advantage of being the omniscient author—beyond which the best we can suggest is probability, then possibility, then uncertainty. Whenever these stages are reached, the incidence of error is necessarily high. The main merit of establishing textual criticism on a consistent set of aesthetic assumptions is (I think) that it brings the real problems into the open and provides a fairer chance of producing results which will be fundamentally sound.

CHAPTER II

The Ideal of Textual Criticism

THE IDEAL of textual criticism is to present the text which the author intended.

This statement is easy to make, but its conditions are excessively difficult to fulfill. In order to reach a lively understanding of the ideal of textual criticism in actual practice, it might be advisable to recall the difficulties which naturally confront us and to recognize problems which we create.

The role of textual criticism is to provide essential mediation between the author and his audience, between the creator and the responder. The textual critic is a go-between. He is the agent of the writer to whom it matters what the reader reads. He is the agent of the reader to whom it matters what the writer wrote. (Otherwise, the textual critic is out of a job and this book is unnecessary.) The "text" can be of any amount: the whole body of an author's writings, a single work, a part of a work, a single word. It is what the author intended that matters; in most cases, this is identical with what he wrote, but sometimes slips and oversights that he allowed to stand can be identified and corrected in order to fulfill his intentions.

Thus, textual criticism has a place—though often a small place —in the preservation of our literary heritage. Whatever value it has derives from this service. Its practical importance hinges on one simple fact: the texts of the works which constitute our literary heritage become progressively corrupt. The process of the transmission of a text is full of chance for error at every step

50

of the way. The typist or the copyist cannot for long follow the text without making a mistake. The compositor, the proof-reader, the pressman, and the binder all err from time to time. Some people write additions, some make corrections, and some delete passages—all in the sweet name of improvement. These and many other people have a hand in the transmission of the text, with thousands of possibilities for change; every one of the changes that actually takes place without the knowledge or consent of the author can be only an error, only a corruption. A text is never self-correcting or self-rejuvenating, and the ordinary history of the transmission of a text, without the intervention of author or editor, is one of progressive degeneration.

This degeneration is not limited to the relatively trivial matters of spelling, punctuation, and capitalization. It may infect any feature of the work of art, and the work may be altered in the process by a little or by a great deal or to the point of being unrecognizable. *The Tragical History of Doctor Faustus* is an example of serious degeneration. It is now thought that a total of only about 825 lines of the two surviving versions of the play were written by Marlowe, but even this is no more than an acute guess. The earlier version, a quarto of 1604, contains around 1,500 lines; the other, a quarto of 1616, includes some 2,100 lines. The versions reflect revision and the writing of additional scenes by other persons, though the "additions" for which Samuel Rowley and William Birde were paid in 1602 are probably not included in either version and are thus no longer extant. Some passages were deleted in order to comply with the restrictions of censorship, and both versions were altered in the course of production; it has been argued that the earlier version is a reconstruction of one form of the play from memory, that the latter was extensively edited while preparing it for publication, and that the earlier is in fact a shortened version of a lost form of the latter. What remains is a play in two very crude forms, both of them undoubtedly very unlike what Marlowe wrote. Yet an emended and eclectic version of these two corrupt texts is the best that we have to mark the identity of that landmark of the Elizabethan drama, "Marlowe's *Doctor Faustus*."[1]

Decay inhabits the works of the past. We can easily convince ourselves that the vagaries of manuscript transmission from the distant past make ideal conditions in which mutability can flourish. There seem to be no authorial manuscripts for any of the classical Greek and Roman writers, nor any copies which were compared with them. The problems of the Synoptic Gospels have given occupation to generations of textual scholars. Even the major literary works in Middle English—*The Canterbury Tales,* for example, or *Piers Plowman*—are entangled in textual complexities too elaborate even to outline in a brief space. In all of these cases, and in hundreds more like them, it seems inescapable that what we can read is a very degraded form of what the author wrote, even though an intellectual discipline was created centuries ago to try to solve these problems.

But the touch of decay is not limited to times long past. It has been pervasive through the entire history of textual transmission, it has possessed many works of the nineteenth and twentieth centuries, and every literary work seems to come within its influence as soon as it is created and thus becomes a part of the past. The stories and novels of Joyce and Fitzgerald, for example, contain many textual errors, and the more thoroughly they are studied the more clearly one can see the ways in which the intentions of the author have become obscured. Until recently, it was commonly said that the works of only two American writers—Emily Dickinson and Sidney Lanier—had ever been "definitively" edited, and there are now murmurs of discontent about even those two.

The general difficulties with the text of many modern works—

---

[1]For a full statement of this textual problem, see *Marlowe's "Doctor Faustus" 1604–1616*, ed. W. W. Greg (Oxford, 1950). Although Greg's is the most extensive work on this problem, a great deal had gone before, some has come after, and without doubt much is yet to be. For a fairly recent recapitulation, see *Doctor Faustus*, ed. John D. Jump, The Revels Plays (London, 1962), esp. pp. xxiv-xxxvii.

poems, plays, and novels—may be exemplified by T. S. Eliot's *The Waste Land*. Eliot wrote the poem—or "sequence of poems," as Ezra Pound called the first complete version—while in Switzerland recuperating from a breakdown, and he sent it to Pound for revision. Pound reduced what Eliot described as a "sprawling, chaotic poem" to about half its original size, and Eliot accepted his editing with gratitude. It was published in four separate texts in 1922-23: in the United States in *The Dial* and in book form by Boni and Liveright, while in England it appeared in *The Criterion* and as a book from the Hogarth Press. All four texts are a little different in small details, even though Eliot certainly read proof for at least three of them and was pleased by the printing job of the fourth. The famous notes were not included in the two magazine prints but were written out and expanded in order to make the Boni and Liveright book a little less slim, "with the result," as Eliot said later, "that they became the remarkable exposition of bogus scholarship that is still on view to-day. I have sometimes thought of getting rid of these notes; but now they can never be unstuck. They have had almost greater popularity than the poem itself. . . . I regret having sent so many inquirers off on a wild goose chase after Tarot cards and the Holy Grail."

The text of *The Waste Land* has undergone considerable alteration since its first printed appearance. Most of the changes were in punctuation, spelling, and capitalization—matters which Eliot did not at all scorn—but some have been more substantial. In 1960, for example, he included in an autograph fair copy a new line which he said "was in the original draft but for some reason or other was omitted from the published text." In 1961, a signed edition was printed in Italy and published by Faber and Faber, and Eliot said that this was to be regarded as "the standard text"; the new line was omitted, but a few other small changes were made. The text of the 1963 Faber and Faber *Collected Poems* reprints most of those changes, but not quite all; on the other hand, the 1963 Harcourt, Brace and World

Collected Poems does not take any of the 1961 changes into account. So today exactly which *Waste Land* you read depends on which edition you pick up. The only editing that they have been given is by the author and by the publishers.[2]

Of course there is no absolute need for textual criticism or for definitive editing. But editing involves vision, and where there is no editing the texts perish. Those who read *Doctor Faustus* only in order to identify the outlines of the archetypal myth of the devil-compact will perhaps be content with a derivative or combined or corrupted text, or even with John Hersey's *Too Far to Walk*. But the validity of a detailed analysis of imagery or of other stylistic traits depends on using a text which is sufficiently accurate for the purpose at hand. A good deal of the analysis of Shakespeare's imagery appears to have gone wrong by reliance on texts which are adequate only for less sophisticated purposes. Since contemporary literary scholarship has proceeded so extensively through minute analysis, textual criticism provides a service of prime importance to many students, at least in preserving them from the gaping chasm of unnecessary error, at best in supplying a reliable basis for understanding.

Consider the ending of D. H. Lawrence's *Sons and Lovers*, for example. Paul Morel has been separated from his three loves: his mother is dead, thanks in some measure to the potion of milk and morphine that he gave her for her evening draught; Clara has chosen to take back her ailing but manly husband; and Miriam—never a very strong flame—flickers out of his life. He goes into the immense night, forced to decide whether he will follow his mother into darkness. " 'Mother!' he whimpered —'mother!' " . . . Or did he only *whisper?* Some editions have

---

[2]See Daniel H. Woodward, "Notes on the Publishing History and Text of *The Waste Land*," *PBSA*, 58 (1964), 252–269. For other examples of unrecognized variant readings in Eliot's poetry, see Robert L. Beare, "Notes on the Text of T. S. Eliot: Variants from Russell Square," *SB*, 9 (1957), 21–49; for the confusing variants in "Gerontion," see William H. Marshall, "The Text of T. S. Eliot's 'Gerontion,' " *SB*, 4 (1951–52), 213–217.

"whimpered" and some have "whispered," and I imagine that close readers ought to care which it was.

The textual critic enters the scene after the degeneration of the text has already taken place, after the damage has been done; he tries, with the aid of whatever evidence can then be assembled, to reconstruct the text as it was intended to be. Since his job is corrective in its nature, it may therefore be more appropriate to state the first principle negatively: the business of textual criticism is to try to identify and eliminate any corruptions which have subverted the author's intentions.

It would be cheerful to be able to report that a mastery of sound principles, an application of effective methods, and an exercise of conscientious care will enable the textual critic to reach the ideal which is incorporated in the first principle of his craft. But it would not be true. In textual criticism, the best that one can do is to cut the losses, to reduce the amount of error, to improve or clarify the state of textual affairs, to approach the ideal. After all has been done that can be done, however, the results of textual criticism still are necessarily imperfect.

The text of *Doctor Faustus* has engaged the attention of editors for a century and a half. In the last hundred years scholars have scrutinized the text with close attention, have looked for allusions in the play and to the play, and have ransacked the stores of literary, historical, and legal documents in search of new evidence about anything touching Marlowe. Even the tomb of Sir Thomas Walsingham, in the Scadbury Chapel of St. Nicholas' Church, Chislehurst, was opened on May 1, 1956, at the instance of a student who thought it possible that Marlowe's manuscripts might have been preserved along with his patron's remains. (No manuscripts were found.) One might expect that only the small details were still in doubt. In fact, the solution to such major issues as the relations of the two versions to one another and to manuscript material are (in the absence of conclusive evidence) based on elaborate hypotheses which are not very convincing even to their maker. "Were some miraculous revelation to prove all my guesses true," wrote Greg, "nobody would be more surprised than myself."[3] Moreover, it is pure guesswork, however expert, as to which lines in either version were written by Marlowe. The experts tend to assign the comic scenes to "the collaborator" or "the reviser"—but their main reason is, so far as I can see, that they dislike or (in my opinion) misunderstand those scenes. It is possible that we may at some time know more about the text of *Doctor Faustus* than we do now; there are certainly many things which are still quite unknown.

The imperfectness of the results is a hard fact of textual criticism. Most of us who have practiced the trade will allow ourselves to swell a little with pride upon hearing a description of the ideal of textual criticism; we, too, are of the company that performs those worthy deeds. But we are not equally willing to associate ourselves with the consequences of another principle: that, ultimately, the results of all textual criticism are necessarily imperfect. If we are doing a rigorously careful study of a literary work, we ought to feel suspicious about the text if (like *Sons and Lovers*) it has not been subjected to a careful textual examination. In general, we are made suspicious only by such nonsense as "I see that men make rope's in such a scarre" (in *All's Well That Ends Well*, IV.ii.38)—when all we can do is throw up our hands. Even if the text has been carefully examined, any given version may be remote from the author's intentions, either in large ways (as with *Doctor Faustus*) or in small ways (as with *The Waste Land*).

I realize that the imperfectness of the results of textual criticism is not accepted as a principle. If it were, it might sprinkle question marks over all textual scholarship and all texts, and thus it might undermine our confidence in ourselves, readers and textual scholars alike. The problems of textual criticism are thought of as difficult enough already, at least by textual schol-

[3]*Marlowe's "Doctor Faustus,"* p. viii.

ars, but it is usual, I believe, for them to assume that the ideal of textual criticism is in fact attainable.

Whether the ideal of textual criticism is or is not attainable in practice turns out to be a matter of some importance so far as a clear understanding of the nature of textual criticism is concerned. For the methods by which it must be fulfilled become a characteristic of its nature. I believe that there are two methods which are commonly adopted, on the assumption that these are the ways to attain that peace which the world cannot give. One is the scientific method for textual criticism, by which the realized ideal makes textual criticism a science. The other is the view of a text as a system of infinitely perfectible details, by which scrupulous attention to all details will ultimately yield ideal results.

The propositions which support these two methods are closely allied, and they are deeply woven into modern textual scholarship. But both are finally (I believe) insupportable. Since the position that one is free to take about the ideal of textual criticism depends on one's view of these two propositions, I will try to outline what is involved in looking on textual criticism as a scientific discipline or as a system of infinitely perfectible details.

II

The act of naming has no effect, I presume, on the inner nature of the thing named. But naming or classifying often alters our understanding. To call textual criticism "a science" or "scientific" is to begin the process of attaching the attributes— or even the metaphors—which go with the name. I suppose that "science" is the most honorific term that could be applied to any intellectual discipline in our times: the very name is taken as a guarantee that the results are (or can be) sound, forward-looking, and true even if we understand neither the results nor the process through which they came to pass. Anything that can cause a manned capsule to land on a predetermined spot on the moon can certainly solve any of our relatively trivial textual problems.

The great name of Science has, in fact, long been invoked to protect textual studies. The study of English and American literary texts rides in on the coattails of classical and biblical scholarship, which has long made claim that it is scientific. A modern biblical scholar, in reviewing the origins of textual criticism as a scholarly discipline, can even distinguish between the textual work on Homer in the fifth century B.C. and that in the third century B.C. by declaring that "a more scientific criticism of the text of Homer was developed in the Hellenistic Age"— particularly in that first great Center of Humanistic Studies, the Library in Alexandria.[4] This "more scientific criticism" has been dominant since the middle of the last century in both biblical and classical studies. A. E. Housman, a classical scholar with very nearly absolute confidence in his own authority, was careful to describe his work as being "within scientific bounds"; he could join the dominion of science and the power of that other great term of honor, "art," in his definition: "Textual criticism is a science, and, since it comprises recension and emendation, it is also an art. It is the science of discovering error in texts and the art of removing it. That is its definition, that is what the name *denotes*."[5] The hitching of these two stars to the bibliographical wagon has also been a frequent exercise in English studies, though one hopes that it is a practice more of the past than of the future.[6]

As a science, it was, in Housman's view, of a noble nature, to

[4]Bruce M. Metzger, *The Text of the New Testament* (New York, 1964), p. 149.

[5]"The Manuscripts of Propertius" (1892, 1894) and "The Application of Thought to Textual Criticism" (1921), in *Selected Prose,* ed. John Carter (Cambridge, England, 1962), pp. 71, 131. The purpose of Metzger's book, cited above, is "to supply the student with information concerning both the science and the art of textual criticism as applied to the New Testament" (p. v).

[6]"Bibliography is an art and also a science. The art is that of recording books; the science, necessary to it, is that of the making of books and of their extant record" (Arundell Esdaile, *A Student's Manual of Bibliography*, London, 1931, p. 13).

which most of us (who have, in his expressive phrases, pumpkins for heads and puddings for brains) need not aspire: "Textual criticism, like most other sciences, is an aristocratic affair, not communicable to all men, nor to most men. Not to be a textual critic is no reproach to anyone, unless he pretends to be what he is not."[7]

In the last fifty years or so, textual criticism of English and American literature has pretty often been described as a "science" or as "scientific," and this kind of description has been part of the larger movement through which bibliography—or at least analytical or descriptive or critical bibliography—has come to be classified as a science. Thus we have heard a great deal about "scientific editing," with its promise of indisputable accuracy through perfectly rigorous methodology.

The scholars who are generally counted as the brightest luminaries in the textual and bibliographical firmament of English literary studies during the first half of this century are A. W. Pollard, R. B. McKerrow, and W. W. (later Sir Walter) Greg. Their writings were of the first importance in extent, and in quality, and in influence. If one were to line up a dozen of their most important works chronologically, the list might go something like this. *Early Illustrated Books: A History of the Decoration and Illustration of Books in the 15th and 16th Centuries* (1893, Pollard); *The Works of Thomas Nashe* (1904–10, McKerrow); *Pastoral Poetry & Pastoral Drama: A Literary Inquiry, with Special Reference to the Pre-Restoration Stage in England* (1906, Greg); the first four parts of the *Catalogue of Books Printed in the XVth Century Now in the British Museum* (1908–16, Pollard, with others); *Shakespeare Folios and Quartos: A Study in the Bibliography of Shakespeare's Plays, 1594–1685* (1909, Pollard); *Printers' and Publishers' Devices in England & Scotland 1485–1640* (1913, McKerrow); *A Short-Title Catalogue of Books Printed in England, Scotland, & Ireland and of English Books Printed Abroad 1475–1640* (1926, Pollard,

[7]"The Application of Thought to Textual Criticism," in *Selected Prose,* p. 150.

with Redgrave); *The Calculus of Variants, An Essay on Textual Criticism* (1927, Greg); *An Introduction to Bibliography for Literary Students* (1927, McKerrow); *Prolegomena for the Oxford Shakespeare: A Study in Editorial Method* (1939, Mc-Kerrow); *The Editorial Problem in Shakespeare: A Survey of the Foundations of the Text* (1942, Greg); *A Bibliography of the English Printed Drama to the Restoration* (1939–59, Greg).

Even from these twelve books, some of the major tendencies evident in their work as a whole are suggested: that they were mainly concerned with English literature before the Restoration, and more particularly before 1640; that their interests centered on the drama, and more particularly on Shakespeare; and that the balance of emphasis between bibliography as description and bibliography as the basis for textual work tended to shift from the former toward the latter in the course of half a century. All of these tendencies have had a marked effect on the progress of later bibliographical and textual studies.

Moreover, all three of these scholars were also influential personally and officially. Pollard, for example, was Secretary of the Bibliographical Society for forty years, and edited the *Papers* for more than thirty-five, retiring from both positions in 1934 at the age of seventy-five; he was succeeded in both by McKerrow, who founded the *Review of English Studies* and edited it until the year of his death in 1940. Pollard seems to have been remembered with deep respect, McKerrow with deep admiration. It is Greg, however, whose influence is now most evident in the course of these studies, perhaps because he outlived his colleagues by two decades. And it was Greg, I believe, who did the most toward creating the image of bibliography and textual criticism as sciences, or at least as disciplines that proceed by scientific method.

In 1912, for example, in an important address before the Bibliographical Society, an address (entitled "What Is Bibliography?") which had a normative effect, Greg spoke of "the science of Textual Criticism or Critical Bibliography" and argued throughout that bibliography is a science. "It is a commonplace among those who have written on the subject," said he, "that bibliography has grown from being an art into being a science." It is "a science by which we co-ordinate facts and trace the operation of constant causes"; it is "the science of the material transmission of literary texts"; its mathematical nature is evident from the fact that "it aims at the construction of a calculus for the determination of textual problems."[8]

Attentive members who were old enough had heard this kind of talk before, however, as long before as 1892. The Inaugural Address of the first President of the Bibliographical Society, W. A. Copinger, sounded the clarion. "There can be no doubt," he asserted, "that Bibliography is now in process of development, and is fast becoming an exact science." And he concluded with an exhortation to action so that the New Day of Science could be made to dawn:

> The formation of the Society should mark an epoch in the literature of this country. It should raise the standard of excellence, and should labour with steady growth until Bibliography is established as an exact science, and occupies that proper position in the realm of literature from which it has been so long by ignorance excluded.[9]

I judge that Copinger's heady language appealed to Greg, as he several times quoted or paraphrased or repeated ideas from Copinger's Inaugural Address. He did so, indeed, in his own presidential address in 1932. The central argument of that paper was in support of the view that bibliography is "the science of the transmission of literary documents." One of his main conclusions was that of all the branches of bibliography, "the essence of the subject" is the bibliography which deals with textual transmission and "that alone justifies its claim to rank as a serious science." In his work, the textual scientist must think of books and manuscripts as material objects only, as "pieces of paper or parchment covered with certain written or printed signs. With

[8] *Transactions of the Bibliographical Society,* 12 (1911-13), 11, 39, 48.
[9] *Transactions of the Bibliographical Society,* 1 (1893), 33, 43.

these signs he is concerned merely as arbitrary marks; their meaning is no business of his."[10]

I believe that this address was the high-water mark of Greg's association of bibliography and science. Ten years later the tide had receded a good deal when he came to write his retrospective review of 1942, looking back on his forty years in the Bibliographical Society. He could still remark in passing about "the new and scientific study of Typography," and he could refer to the transformation of bibliography "from a study the main interest of which was artistic to one governed by the methods of scientific enquiry." But the old zeal had died down, and he felt it necessary to add:

> I am not in this trying to draw any controversial distinction. There is no necessary contradiction or opposition between art and science, it may not be possible ultimately to distinguish between their methods, but there is a vast difference in the attitude of the inquirer as the balance of interest sways between them.[11]

Scientific sentiments echoed in the United States as well. After describing George Watson Cole as "that patron saint" of the Bibliographical Society of America, one writer maintained that "it was he, who, as librarian of the Huntington Library, but more as the compiler of the great E. D. Church catalogues, did so much in the early part of this century to promote bibliography as a science."[12] It was left to Americans, mainly since World War II, to make the doubtful beam of these scales of art and science to

[10]"Bibliography—An Apologia," *The Library*, 4th Ser., 13 (1932), 114, 129, 122. It was also in this address that Greg created the multipurpose pensée that "Textual critics should praise God for the simple fool" (p. 125).

[11]"Bibliography—A Retrospect," *The Bibliographical Society 1892–1942: Studies in Retrospect* (London, 1945), pp. 26, 27. In 1950, Greg could even say (though in a footnote, as I repeat it here): "We have, moreover, come to recognize that those who rely most blindly on material statistics are usually those who know themselves incompetent to form an individual judgement of style and are most loud in decrying it. ... Thus for my part I would rather rely upon the impression of a critic in whose judgement I feel confidence than on an accumulation of mechanical tests" (*Marlowe's "Doctor Faustus,"* Oxford, 1950, p. 98n).

[12]Donald B. Engley, "George Brinley, Americanist," *PBSA*, 60 (1966), 465.

come to rest again, with science containing the heavy value. As late as 1942, so astute an observer as William A. Jackson could declare that "the greatest achievement of American bibliographical effort during the past fifty years has undoubtedly been the assimilation and organization of the vast quantities of books and manuscripts which have been brought to these shores."[13] Since that time, conditions have vastly changed: leadership in bibliography and editing has passed to the United States, and the talents of Greg's scientism have been increased tenfold.

The man who undoubtedly stands next in the succession after Greg is Fredson Bowers.[14] A learned man, a forceful writer, and an aggressive combatant in the lists of bibliography and editing, he has become preeminent partly through the sheer mass of his distinguished publications, partly through the journal *Studies in Bibliography* (which he founded in 1948 and has edited ever since), and partly through his voice in the councils of the academic mighty. Some of his works are examples of practical editing, such as the Cambridge Dekker or the Centenary Hawthorne or the 1860 *Leaves of Grass*. Many of them are normative in intent, like his *Principles of Bibliographical Description* (1949); or his Sandars Lectures at Cambridge published as *Textual & Literary Criticism* (1959); or his Lyell Lectures at Oxford, *Bibliography and Textual Criticism* (1964); or (perhaps most widely read of all) his essay on "Textual Criticism" in the Modern Language Association pamphlet entitled *The Aims and Methods of Scholarship in Modern Languages and Literatures* (1963; 2d ed., 1970). Much of his work consists of detailed studies of particular bibliographical or textual problems, lavishly scattered in learned journals.

His influence on American scholarship of the bibliographical or textual sort has undoubtedly been more profound and pervasive than that of any other individual. Even the Atlantic

---

[13]"The Study of Bibliography in America," *Studies in Retrospect*, p. 185.

[14]Bowers has many times acknowledged his debt to Greg and has called him "the greatest bibliographer of our times" (*Principles of Bibliographical Description*, Princeton, 1949, p. xi).

Ocean, which has generally displayed the unique property of limiting the transmission of scholarly influence to a westerly direction, has allowed part of his work to become known and admired by some persons in England.

Although Bowers' influence has been very great, not all of his work has been received with rejoicing, and all of it has been greeted (like Moses' message to the Israelites) with murmurings, murmurings on the part of some eminent scholars, particularly those who feel suspicious of bibliography as Bowers views it, as a way of life. Also, Bowers has been eager, it would seem, to insure that abuses are stripped and whipped; and some scholars feel a trifle uncomfortable when the lash is laid on with a heavy hand. Some reviewers have been irritated by one or two other features of his work and have noted a certain repetitiveness of observation and example, a sort of confidence that did not please them, and an occasional opacity of expression. These are all trivial in comparison with his permanent contributions to bibliographical studies, however. I would be distressed if the reservations which I feel obliged to make to his underlying theories were taken as obscuring the real distinction of his accomplishments.

It is in the context of Bowers' prodigious achievements and influence that his association of science with bibliography and textual studies must be understood. This association is one of the motifs of his writings, and a few samples from different periods may suggest the melody. "I do not see how one can escape the conviction that the 'scientific' is basic in true descriptive bibliography . . ." (1949). "Greg's procedure will undoubtedly yield a superior text both for accidentals and for substantives than can be assured by other less scientific methods" (1950). Critical bibliography is "the newer semi-scientific method," with methods which "at least parallel the scientific method" (1952). "I believe this method of comparison against a constant control is good scientific bibliography and is, in fact, the only safe method to employ" (1953). "Bibliographical analysis . . . provides a scientific method for the detection of error and the assignment of degrees of authority not ordinarily to be found in manuscript work" (1955). "Textual investigations . . . [are] now being made on a new and more scientific basis" (1959). "The purpose of the new scholarship that will produce tomorrow's texts is threefold: first, to evolve a more scientific and logically rigorous method to govern the critical choice of alternatives in respect to the words of the text . . ." (1964).[15]

Reviewers of his work often echo these sentiments. The text of the first volume of the Cambridge Dekker was described by Karl J. Holzknecht as a "bibliographically scientific, critical, old-spelling text." Cyrus Hoy felt, in connection with *Textual and Literary Criticism*, that "one is struck by the practical wisdom which the author brings to his highly scientific discipline." And F. B. Evans could describe *Bibliography and Textual Criticism* as "a stimulating review of what, when exactingly handled, this science [bibliographical analysis] can contribute to textual criticism."[16]

This "scientific" quality is by no means the private property of Bowers alone, of course, and it is sometimes described as emanating from a "school." In reviewing a volume of the Twickenham edition of Pope, Robert W. Rogers could write that "the new school of 'scientific' editing only found general acceptance after the edition had been organized." He added, however, as

[15]*Principles of Bibliographical Description*, p. 34n; "Current Theories of Copytext, with an Illustration from Dryden," *MP*, 48 (1950), 16; "Bibliography, Pure Bibliography, and Literary Studies," *PBSA*, 46 (1952), 207–208; "Purposes of Descriptive Bibliography, with Some Remarks on Methods," *The Library*, 5th Ser., 8 (1953), 6; *On Editing Shakespeare and the Elizabethan Dramatists* (Philadelphia, 1955), p. 95; *Textual & Literary Criticism* (Cambridge, England, 1959), p. viii. "Today's Shakespeare Texts, and Tomorrow's," *SB*, 19 (1966), 58. But Bowers also finds a little room for faith; in speaking of Theobald's famous emendation concerning the death of Falstaff, he says: "I have every confidence in *babbl'd*, but I accept it as an act of faith and not because the emendation has been 'scientifically' demonstrated" (*Bibliography and Textual Criticism*, Oxford, 1964, pp. 54–55).

[16]These reviews are all drawn, for the sake of simplicity, from the *Papers of the Bibliographical Society of America*, 48 (1954), 208; 53 (1959), 276; 59 (1965), 202.

if to provide reassurance that the edition does not actually fail
The Test, that "textually it attempts to satisfy some of the more
rigorous principles set for textual scholarship by W. W. Greg,
R. B. McKerrow, and Fredson Bowers."[17] For another example,
in a review of the *Transactions of the Cambridge Bibliographical
Society*, published in *The Library*, two articles are under scrutiny. "They present," it is observed, "an instructive contrast in
bibliographical techniques. Professor Berry [the author of one
of them] clearly allies himself with the school of Sir Walter
Greg and Professor Fredson Bowers, while Mr. Dawson's methods [in the other article] are those of an older, and less scientific,
generation of bibliophiles. . . . It is a great pity that it [Dawson's
work] has not been based upon a more exacting bibliographical
discipline."[18] The equations which run through these comments
are, I believe, usual among the more active bibliographers, at
least in the United States: with "scientific" work, the associations
are Greg and Bowers, rigor, exactitude, and modernity; with
"less scientific" work, the associations are bibliophile, lack of
rigor, and old-fashioned.

This attribution of value to work because it is scientific should
probably not be isolated from a number of related forms of literary study. For one, the translation of textual problems into quantitative form and the use of calculus to offer solutions: some
earlier examples are Sir Walter Greg's *The Calculus of Variants*
(Oxford, 1927) and Dom Henri Quentin's *Essais de critique
textuelle* (Paris, 1926); one later example is the work of Antonín
Hrubý.[19] Or, the use of statistical analysis in determining authorship: the most notable instance is the work on twelve disputed
Federalist papers, with the conclusion that they were written by

[17] *JEGP*, 62 (1965), 400–401.

[18] 5th Ser., 18 (1963), 230–231.

[19] Of Hrubý's work, the following two articles may be cited: "Statistical Methods
in Textual Criticism," *General Linguistics*, V, No. 3 (Supplement 1962), 77–138;
and "A Quantitative Solution of the Ambiguity of Three Texts," *SB*, 18 (1965),
147–182. Perhaps I should mention that the validity of the results of these methods
has not yet been established and that the methods themselves are more controversial than scholars in English seem to realize.

Madison rather than Hamilton. A statistical method was also used on such other problems as that of the authorship of the Junius Letters of 1769–1772, of Mark Twain and the Quintus Curtius Snodgrass Letters, and of the scansion of *Beowulf* and all the "hypermetric" lines in Old English poetry.[20]

Within the last generation or two, several devices (like the Hinman collating machine) have become available which can save much time in the process of carrying on research and others (like inexpensive reproduction through electrostatic or micro processes) which greatly aid in making rare material accessible to scholars. Most important of all, the computer is in the process of revolutionizing certain types of scholarship in the humanities. The value of the computer in preparing concordances and in machine translation is pretty well demonstrated by now. It is also evident that the computer can be useful in certain aspects of editing, in cataloging library material, in making comparative analyses for stylistic studies, and in storing many other kinds of information for retrieval or comparison or reorganization.[21] It is not yet evident just what the feasible limits of

[20]Frederick Mosteller and D. L. Wallace, "Inference in an Authorship Problem: A Comparative Study of Discriminating Methods Applied to the Authorship of the Disputed *Federalist* Papers," *Journal of the American Statistical Association,* 58 (1964), 275–309; Alvar Ellegård, *A Statistical Method for Determining Authorship: The Junius Letters, 1769–1772* (Stockholm, 1962) ; C. S. Brinegar, "Mark Twain and the Quintus Curtius Snodgrass Letters: A Statistical Test of Authorship," *Journal of the American Statistical Association,* 58 (1964), 85–96; A. J. Bliss, *The Metre of Beowulf* (Oxford, 1958). Actually, statistical analysis is not so new in literary studies as the dates of these works might suggest: it was in the 1880's and 1890's that Eduard Sievers examined Old English metrics on a statistical basis, and there were numerous studies in the early years of this century, on at least a quasi-statistical scheme, to determine who wrote which part of what Elizabethan and Jacobean play; literary scholarship has not yet quite recovered from the uncertain logic and evidence employed in reaching proofs.

[21]The *PMLA* Annual Bibliography for 1968 commenced to include a section on Computer-Assisted Literary Research. The more particular evidences may not quite be legion, but they are at least a motorized battalion. *Computers and the Humanities: A Newsletter* began publication in September 1966. A couple of symptomatic books are *Manual for the Printing of Literary Texts and Concordances by Computer,* by Robert Jay Glickman and Gerrit Joseph Staalman (Toronto, 1966), and *The Computer and Literary Style: Introductory Essays and Studies,* ed. Jacob Leed (Kent, Ohio, 1966).

data-processing machines are in literary studies, however, and it is undoubtedly true that there will be various extravagancies and inflated claims and false prophets to appear in the next decade or so before some practicable limits can be defined. Neither is it yet evident as to how extensive the use of machines will be to textual criticism. At least, I can see nothing in the present or future of textual criticism, however it is carried on, which will make it answerable to the term "science" or "scientific."

In short, I think that it is important to give up these terms as descriptions of textual criticism. In the humanities generally, when scholarship has sought to become objective in what are considered "scientific" ways, it has tended to lose its primary meaning and to retain only instrumental value. Then it is for others to make sense of it if they can, or to use it if they see how. I have noticed that when some of the greatest scientists I have ever met say that they don't know whether there is any useful end for their work, they seem to speak in thoughtful ignorance and perhaps even humility. I am afraid that when some of us humanists say that we have no knowledge of what use will be made of our work, we may incline toward thoughtless ignorance and pride. There is occasionally a dismissal of such a question with a superior wave of the hand. "Bibliography in this sense is akin to pure science. It is none of the business of the bibliographer or the pure scientist what use is made of his findings, and he ought not to be bothered with the trivial question 'Of what use is it?' "[22] In my way of looking at textual criticism, its value derives only from serving the useful purpose of helping to present the text which the author intended.

[22]This remark is, as I have given it, the most indirect (the most "unscientific" some would say) quotation that I know. It is said to be by S. L. M. Barlow (the nineteenth-century American collector) as quoted by Henry Harrisse (the bibliographer) as summarized by R. G. Adams (the collector) as quoted by Jacob Blanck (in "A Calendar of Bibliographical Difficulties," *PBSA*, 49, 1955, 6), as reproduced by me.

III

Nothing has turned literary scholars against textual criticism with more disgust than their belief that it involves excessive and pedantic attention to small details. It is a commonplace among academic oversouls that a young scholar who is thought deficient in imagination, taste, and literary sense may be safely recommended to carry on the dull duties of an editor. Among collectors and bibliophiles, as well as among those in more ordinary walks of life, various features of the entire modern bibliographical enterprise are contemned; one of the most gracious treatments was administered by Sir Geoffrey Keynes on the august occasion of his Presidential Address to the Bibliographical Society.[23]

Modern editorial practice makes remarkable demands on the native resolution and meticulous care of the textual scholar. These practices, often described as "principles," have come to characterize modern textual studies to such a considerable degree that it is worth inquiring into the limits of their efficacy in order to determine how far they can carry us in attaining the ideal of textual criticism. Since prescriptive comments and exemplary practice can be found in a large number of excellent modern sources, the samples to which I refer will be drawn from authorities which command wide, perhaps the widest, respect.

The *Statement of Editorial Principles* published by the Cen-

[23]"Religio Bibliographici," *The Library*, 5th Ser., 8 (1953), 63–76. Bibliography was, in his view, "what we had thought in our innocence was a pleasant, if sometimes exacting, pastime"; in the new "professional" hands it "was in fact a prime example of 'pure scholarship,' to be pursued with the mind of a detective, the spiritual temperament of an iceberg, and the precision of a machine" (p. 64). "It is impossible, however, not to feel some sympathy with the tendency we think we detect in academic bibliographers to exaggerate the claims of their craft. Finding themselves in the company of scholars, who need to be convinced that bibliography really has serious claims on their attention, they instinctively react by behaving as a small persecuted minority. They are forced to push their technical speciality in order to be taken seriously and to compel their institutions or universities to realize the necessity for acquiring first and early editions of the older books" (p. 66).

ter for Editions of American Authors (Modern Language Association of America, 1967) hails the "new era in editing the literary and historical texts of the United States" (p. iii) and tries to lay down principles to insure the accuracy and soundness of new texts, particularly complete editions of major nineteenth-century American writers. It has been called a "judicious statement of the problems of establishing an authentic text," a statement that recognizes differing opinions on the desirable degree of detail, and one that "indicates conscious decisions as to how far one should go."[24] In my opinion, this manual is mainly devoted to setting forth the mechanical tasks of the editor. He should, of course, assemble "all the potentially relevant forms of his texts"; "including the first posthumous edition as a possibly relevant form may seem merely finical: it is actually a guarantee of thoroughness" (p. 2). "To determine the relevant is a matter which must be decided by actual collations" (p. 2), and thus begins this process of comparing one form with another, word by word and character by character; the editor must "discover and somewhere describe all states and issues of the text in question, including concealed printings" (p. 3).

After the copy-text has been chosen, many examples must be collated to reveal internal variants; elsewhere we are told that "ordinarily five to six copies should begin to give an editor some notion whether press-correction will prove to be heavy or light,"[25] and for the Cambridge edition of Dekker's *Dramatic Works*—a work often cited as a model for editors—*all* copies were collated when no more than about a dozen were recorded as extant, and substantially all or at least the great majority (up to twenty-six copies) were completely collated when the recorded copies were relatively numerous. Sometimes

[24]*PMLA*, 82, No. 7 (December 1967), A4.

[25]Fredson Bowers, "Textual Criticism," in *The Aims and Methods of Scholarship in Modern Languages and Literatures*, ed. James Thorpe (New York, 1963), p. 33.

we are advised that it is necessary, ideally, to examine *every* extant copy of an edition.[26]

The *Statement of Editorial Principles* lays it down that, in the case of collating each later edition against the copy-text, "two or more independent readings are imperative for accuracy and completeness," and it adds in a footnote that "one experienced chief editor has found five readings necessary, and urges the value of one or more readings for substantive changes alone" (p. 6). It offers another method of collating these later editions, in a charming little vignette reminiscent of monkish scholars in a scriptorium:

> Alternatively, if a group of trained assistants is available and two copies of each authorized form can be assembled at one time, the editor may assign—for example—two copies each of six different editions to twelve readers, and collate the six texts in one careful reading operation. Either the editor himself or the textual editor will read the copy-text aloud, and a recorder will systematically tabulate textual variants as they emerge from the reading. (pp. 6–7)

When the long labors of collation cease, and when all the necessary tables of changes and emendations and end-of-line hyphenated words and the like have been prepared, and when the text has been finally established, then the proofreading begins. First, the text will be read twice against copy. When the printer starts his work, "the editor has a final obligation as weighty as any he has yet imposed upon himself—to proofread his galleys and page proofs, with the most scrupulous care, as they come to him from the publisher and to cooperate in the proofreading policy established by his own colleagues. . . . Proofs

---

[26]"The concern of the descriptive bibliographer . . . is to examine every available copy of an edition of a book in order to describe in bibliographical terms the characteristics of an ideal copy of this edition . . ." (Fredson Bowers, *Principles of Bibliographical Description*, p. 6). "A definitive bibliography, whether of an author, a press, or a *genre* should be based on the minute examination of every extant copy of the books in question" (James G. McManaway, in *Standards of Bibliographical Description*, Philadelphia, 1949, p. 65).

must be read at least five times against printer's copy..." (p. 11). Should a work be later reprinted by resetting, the text must be given three further careful proofreadings and a final check.

The *Statement* mentions three examples of "sophisticated disciplined theory and practice" (pp. iii–iv), and the first of these is the Centenary Edition of Hawthorne. That edition generally satisfies the conditions laid down in the *Statement*. To take *The Scarlet Letter* (the first volume issued) as an example, the editors did not stop with "the first posthumous edition as a possibly relevant form"; they collated the novel in all four of the posthumous collected editions (1875, 1877, 1883, 1900) which had a new setting of type (as well as the various "editions" which were printed from the plates of one or another of these), and they even collated a paperback edition published for students in 1960. Similarly, the number of copies collated was considerable: eight copies of the first edition, and as many as five or ten of some of the posthumous editions. So far as the proofreading of the Centenary *Scarlet Letter* is concerned, "all proofs have been read at least five times and by three or more editors." In short, the general practice of this edition seems to accord with the rules prescribed in the *Statement of Editorial Principles*.

These practices and "principles" raise several kinds of questions. The one most relevant to the present discussion is to know the extent to which the ideal of textual criticism will be attained by scrupulous attention to these matters. In the works and authors I have cited, there seems to me a strong inference, throughout, that adherence to these practices is the efficient cause of an ideal edition. In speaking of the Centenary *Scarlet Letter*, the textual editor observed that "the amount of collating and checking in such an edition as has been outlined is very heavy indeed; but only this editorial process scrupulously carried out will produce editions of American classics that will stand the test of time . . ."[27]—*only this editorial process scrupulously carried out will produce editions of American classics that will stand the test of time.* (Indeed, this process seems to be envisioned as part of an even larger movement: the same writer elsewhere reflected, for example, that "it may be that the discipline that will return us to an intellectually bracing critical vigor will come from the extension of the kind of reasoning mind that is now sweeping clean the bibliographical way.")[28] To return to the *Statement of Editorial Principles*—which would, in my opinion, be more accurately entitled "Statement of Editorial Methodology"—the center of gravity may be suggested by quoting again the warning to the editor that proofreading is "a final obligation as weighty as any he has yet imposed upon himself" (p. 11); as "weighty," one must assume, as a knowledge of the author's writings, or as the search for external evidence bearing on textual problems, or the like. Or, for another example, the advice that "to determine the relevant is a matter which must be decided by actual collations" (p. 2)—when, in my opinion, actual collations never provide more than some facts on which the trained intelligence can work, and often—usually, in my experience—those facts are of a kind from which it is not possible to determine what is and what is not relevant.

The application of these methods sometimes produces results which have debatable textual value. For example, the editors of the Centenary *Scarlet Letter* printed in their notes all of the textual variants that appear in all of the five posthumous editions which I have mentioned. Since none of these editions are "relevant forms," in that the changes possess no authority from Hawthorne, their textual value would seem to be zero and their interest mainly limited to historians of the

[27]Fredson Bowers, "Some Principles for Scholarly Editions of Nineteenth-Century American Authors," *SB*, 17 (1964), 228.

[28]*The Bibliographical Way* (Lawrence, Kansas, 1959), p. 34.

73

corruption of this text.[29] The Introduction includes a detailed discussion of the fact that two pages of *The Scarlet Letter* were set in duplicate (how to tell them apart, why it was done, how it was done), even though the two settings are without textual variant. One Appendix gives the "Variants in the First Edition," and these five variants "appear to be the result of loosened type"; another Appendix is devoted to "Variants in the Second Edition," from which it appears that one page number dropped out during printing and one comma is missing in the Preface in some copies.[30] (One may sometimes wish for the superior British attitude toward such details, as Helen Gardner's succinct statement in summing up the results of collating copies of the 1633 edition of Donne in search of press variants: "The variants discovered are not of much interest. They are noted in the apparatus."[31]) Yet another Appendix lists the words which are hyphenated in the Centenary Edition because they are divided at the end of a line and which were also hyphenated within the line in the first edition, as well as a list of words which were hyphenated at the end of the line in the first edition and the

[29]At least one large edition has been sharply criticized for a similar policy in the inclusion of variants. "I am still, however, not convinced that the full critical apparatus at the end of each volume will serve any important need among rational men—including bibliographers. In the apparatus printed beneath the text in the new volume there is much that is of dubious value: to provide a further six square feet of variant readings, likely by the end of the venture to amount to two volumes at £4 (or perhaps much more) apiece, is an expensive work of supererogation. It is a not unimportant part of an editor's duty to keep irrelevances to himself." James Kinsley, reviewing Volume III of the California Dryden in *RES*, 15 (1964), 87.

[30]Elsewhere the textual editor took occasion to discuss this comma and another example of "authoritative punctuation" with what might seem to one or two readers as high seriousness. "Here one typesetting has a comma that appears to be authoritative whereas the other omits it. An editor who neglected to collate a number of copies might have reprinted arbitrarily from the wrong typesetting. . . . Because an exclamation point dropped out very early in the printing of page 228 [of *The Scarlet Letter*], no edition before the Centenary recovered this original authoritative punctuation, for all editors were content to follow the second-edition comma that the later compositor inserted when he came to the blank space in his copy." Fredson Bowers, "Some Principles for Scholarly Editions of Nineteenth-Century American Authors," *SB*, 17 (1964), 225.

[31]*The Elegies and the Songs and Sonnets* (Oxford, 1965), p. xcv.

form in which it was decided to print them in the Centenary Edition. Since the author's manuscript is no longer extant, this meticulous care about the accidentals of printing can recover only the printing-house style; inasmuch as the printer of the first edition of *The House of the Seven Gables* (for which the manuscript *is* extant) imposed some fifteen changes per page in styling the text, it seems likely that the first edition of *The Scarlet Letter* represents a similar alteration of the manuscript and that the accidentals deserve consistent attention rather than veneration.[32] There is perhaps a little irony in recalling Hawthorne's own scorn for the meticulous care of the proofreader of *The Scarlet Letter*. While that book was being printed, Hawthorne wrote to Lewis Mansfield that "a small critic, (such as a certain proofreader whom I am, just now, afflicted with) might find many occasions, verbal, rhythmical, and rhymical, for carping at your poem; but these things are not broadly important, and I have not stopt to consider them."[33]

Moreover, it must be admitted that great care cannot always insure against calamity. No matter how many copies are collated in search of variants, there is always the possibility of another copy lurking in yet one more collection with a previously unknown variant. For example, Harris Fletcher reported that he had collated forty-two copies of Milton's 1673 *Poems* and found no variants; yet when William R. Parker looked into his own copy while reviewing Fletcher's facsimile edition, he spied two textual variants in *Elegia Prima*.[34] Similarly, Vinton A. Dearing reported that his collation of five of the seven recorded American copies of the first edition of Dryden's *Indian Emperor* disclosed six variants that had not previously been noted by Fredson Bowers in his collation of six of

[32]"One is foolish to prefer a printing-house style to the author's style. . . . When an author's manuscript is preserved, this has paramount authority, of course." Bowers, "Some Principles . . . ," p. 226.

[33]Feb. 10, 1850, MS in Berg Collection, New York Public Library. Quoted in the Centenary Edition of *The Scarlet Letter*, p. lxiii.

[34]"Fletcher's *Milton*: A First Appraisal," *PBSA*, 41 (1947), 35.

the seven recorded American copies.[35] As Bowers himself observed:

> Bibliographers sometimes exhibit the very human trait of believing that their examination of a considerable number of copies of a book has exhausted the probability of further variations coming to light, or that they have listed all the "important" variations. Experience shows the fallacy of this view. . . .[36]

In short, meticulous care does not in itself guarantee that the author's intended text will be reconstructed. It can more easily turn into pedantry, which I take to be sometimes characterized by emphasis on small details beyond any reasonably useful purpose. Of course, I do not wish to suggest that meticulous care is pedantry, nor that the examples I have cited of modern editorial principle and practice are pedantic. At times one may feel sympathy for Samuel Johnson when he said, speaking of Theobald, that "I have sometimes adopted his restoration of a comma, without inserting the panegyrick in which he celebrated himself for his achievement."[37] Some modern work does appear to be rather ceremonious in its self-concern, with the editor's name finally obscuring that of the author. Since there is no limit to the conceivable amount of detail that can be explored—and always someone is ready to point to more—weary years can pass while the process drags on. But it does not seem that great care is a cure for all the ills that texts are heir to.

The theory that scrupulous attention to all details will ulti-

[35]"The Poor Man's Mark IV or Ersatz Hinman Collator," *PBSA*, 60 (1966), 157–158.

[36]Bowers, *Principles of Bibliographical Description*, p. 22. Strangely enough, Bowers himself exhibited this trait in the Preface to the Centenary *Scarlet Letter:* "Although it is too much to hope that every minor variant in an impression has been discovered by the extensive multiple collation, one can state with some confidence that the majority have probably been noticed; unknown major variation, at least, is not likely to exist in unseen copies of the editions examined by this method" (p. xxx). There is, it would seem, no logical reason why a variant is likely to be minor because it has not been noticed.

[37]"Preface to Shakespeare," *Works* (Oxford, 1825), V, 138.

mately yield ideal results is sound only in a limited sphere. At the least, such a method—if perfectly done—will prevent the introduction of new mistakes. At the best, it will help to identify mistakes that were earlier introduced. But it cannot, ordinarily, offer much help toward a solution of major problems about texts. For an example, consider Sir Philip Sidney's *Arcadia* in the 1590 and 1593 editions. The latter introduces various major and minor changes in the text. The crucial question is whether these revisions are Sidney's work or not. No amount of meticulous care with collating or proofreading or the like can answer this question.[38] Likewise, a scholar has maintained that "there never can be established a 'reliable' text" of *Billy Budd*, however much meticulous care is expended, because Melville simply did not himself finish the work.[39]

Or consider the example of *The Waste Land*, which I spoke of at the beginning of this chapter. Let us suppose that a scholar tries to resolve the textual problems of this book in the year 2300—when *The Waste Land* is as far away in time as *Doctor Faustus* is from us, and when the external evidence about its publication has (let us assume) all been lost. Imagine that he has many copies of each of the four separate editions of 1922–23, the 1960 autograph copy with the "new" line, a dozen copies of the 1961 "standard" edition, and a large number of each of the two 1963 *Collected Poems*. Imagine that he tries to establish an authoritative text on the basis of this evidence, following the principle of meticulous care. He will collate all copies of each edition most minutely. In the process, he may learn a good deal about printing practices and perhaps develop theories about the differences in metallurgic qualities of the type that was used in British and American printing, in the way that scholars of our time have developed theories about casting off copy and

[38]The arguments put forward by various scholars on the revisions in the *Arcadia* are reviewed by William Leigh Godschalk, "Sidney's Revisions of the *Arcadia* Books III–V," *PQ*, 43 (1964), 171–184.

[39]Lawrance Thompson, rev. of *Billy Budd*, ed. Harrison Hayford and Merton M. Sealts, Jr., *AL*, 36 (1964), 76–79.

setting by formes and identifying compositors in early seventeenth-century printing through a minute study of (for the prime example) the Shakespeare First Folio. But I dare say that his Historical Collation would not lead him to decide accurately which of the changes were authorial and which were not, nor to reconstruct the history of the text properly, nor to determine whether the "new" line should be included or not. One can imagine the fine reasoning that would be devoted to these problems, and one can assume that the majority of the solutions would be wrong.

No matter how meticulous the care had been, the scholar would not (we are supposing) have the letters which do in fact clarify many of the obscure points—letters by Pound, Eliot, Gilbert Seldes, Leonard Woolf, John Hayward, Pamela Barker, Jeanne Robert Foster, and others, along with the newly recovered manuscript with alterations by Pound and Eliot, two early typescript copies of the poem, and various relevant comments in printed books by Clive Bell, Virginia Woolf, Hugh Kenner, William Wasserstrom, and others. Without this evidence, he would be left to speculate about material facts. Who would be lucky enough to guess that *The Waste Land* was, for example, at one important point a sequence of poems which were altered by Ezra Pound into the shape of a single poem?

Even now there are unanswered questions about the poem. There is still lost material of importance to the text (such as the manuscript notebook in which Eliot made early drafts of the poem), and there is always in textual studies an indeterminate amount of unsuspected evidence that might conceivably appear and alter one's conclusions about what the author intended to be the text of the work of art.

I should make it unnecessarily clear that I am certainly not against scrupulous attention or meticulous care in textual work. These qualities are not, however, a complete substitute for intelligence and common sense. If we allow them to be, it is a sign of confusing rules and standards, of mixing methods and principles. Moreover, a person who happens to lack intelligence and common sense will, unfortunately, sometimes be unable to distinguish between the trivial and the important: he will stoutly argue that the question of the authenticity of a casual comma in a long third-rate novel is equal in importance to that of a key word in a Shakespeare sonnet. He may imply that if the editor does not keep his finger in the hole left by the comma the enraged waters will wash our civilization away.

IV

It is doubtless permissible to argue, under some conditions, that textual criticism is a science and a system of perfectible details. One such occasion is the delivery of rhetorical exhortations in favor of sounder logic and greater care in textual studies. Certainly textual criticism requires logic and care, but these qualities cannot guarantee that the results will be perfect.

The ideal of textual criticism is to present the text which the author intended. The knowledge that this ideal is unattainable in any final and complete and detailed sense can perhaps help us to avoid the pedantry of vainly trying to attain it by a glorification of method. It is more advantageous to try to approach the ideal of textual criticism by attending to the basic principles and by exploiting every kind of relevant evidence that is available. Such a program is likely to give the largest return for the human effort expended.

CHAPTER III

The Province of Textual Criticism

THE GREAT MANSION of literary studies has many apartments, but what we are to call them is not always clear. Their names are subject to change, and their occupants move without notice.

Textual criticism has, through the long history of literary study, sometimes been regarded as the crown and summit of all scholarship, and sometimes as a subdivision of an auxiliary discipline. It has sometimes been described as one of the most important activities of the human intellect, and sometimes as one of the most trivial.

At the present time there is considerable controversy over the relation of textual criticism to bibliography, and over their respective provinces. The arguments put forward often sound like a jurisdictional dispute, with the officers trying to insure that their own union is given responsibility for the major part of the job. The bibliographers have had strong leadership; their spokesmen have agitated with some success for a closed shop, and their claims have been loud and frequent.

I would not be eager to undertake the role of a federal mediator in this dispute, even if I were asked. I am even less eager to try to tell the learned world what they ought to mean by the terms they use, or what terms they ought to use to mean what they appear to have in mind. Nevertheless, it seems a worthwhile task to try to sort out the current arguments that have a bearing on the province of textual criticism and to consider them (so far as I am capable, and without making any impudent claims for absolute impartiality) by some elementary

80

tests of logic, history, and utility. If it is possible to define the responsibilities of textual criticism with less confusion than now prevails, we can (I hope) come a little nearer to an understanding of the nature and principles of textual criticism. At least it is on such an assumption and with such a hope that I will examine the province of textual criticism.

II

Once upon a time, textual criticism was a central form of literary study. In the library at Alexandria, manuscripts were collected for the purpose of preparing critical editions, complete with variant readings. Several of the chief librarians there made textual studies: Zenodotus of Ephesus tried to restore the Homeric poems by collating many manuscripts, Aristophanes of Byzantium edited the *Iliad* and the *Odyssey,* and Aristarchus of Samothrace made two critical editions of those poems and also edited several other Greek authors.

The Church Fathers adopted the methods of textual criticism in use on Greek writers and devoted much attention to correcting and establishing the text of the Old and New Testaments. Philo Judaeus, Theodotus, Origen, and St. Jerome are only a few of the scholars who had, by the fourth century, practiced the skill of textual criticism very extensively. Even St. Augustine had the time and the knowledge to consider and judge textual problems.

In the Middle Ages, the tradition of textual study continued to be strong. One of the most important Greek scholars of the period, Eustathius, Archbishop of Thessalonica, studied corrupted texts extensively and tried to emend them. Some of the greatest Renaissance humanists, like Erasmus, were practicing textual scholars.[1]

[1]For an account of early classical scholarship, see J. E. Sandys, *A History of Classical Scholarship*, 3 vols. (London, 1908) . For a brief survey of the history of textual work on the Bible, see Bruce M. Metzger, *The Text of the New Testament* (New York and London, 1964), pp. 149–185.

The two subjects for earlier textual study were, of course, the literary works of classical antiquity and the Bible. In the first edition of Chambers' *Cyclopaedia* (London, 1728), for example, we are told (in the article on "Text") that "infinite Pains have been taken by the Cricks to restore, reconcile, settle, explain, etc. the *Text* of the Bible, and the Classic's." We should remember, however, that the practice of textual criticism was not limited to what we would call professional scholarship; it was, in fact, one of the major forms of private literary study as well.

Milton, for instance, left a good deal of evidence that one of his keenest scholarly interests was textual study. His annotations to the tragedies of Euripides may serve as an example.[2] He used the two-volume Stephanus edition of 1602, which contains the Greek text, a Latin translation, scholia, commentaries by four scholars, and a subject index. He made some 560 marginal annotations in his copy, and most of them reflect his interest in the text. He made many elementary corrections, such as in spelling, transposition, punctuation, and assignment of speeches. But he also suggested various emendations, supporting them by logical or metrical or grammatical arguments. Indeed, a number of his emendations have been incorporated in modern texts of Euripides. In some cases later scholars are given the credit, though often it seems that they got their ideas from a study of Milton's marginalia; in three cases, however, the emendations are attributed to Milton in modern scholarly editions.

This textual interest extended to private correspondence. In a letter to Milton in 1647, Carlo Dati devoted more than half of a long letter to an argument that the word *rapido* in Tibullus

[2] I am able to speak on this subject only because of the careful work of Maurice Kelley and Samuel D. Atkins, "Milton's Annotations of Euripides," *JEGP*, 60 (1961), 680–687. My statements are derived from this source and from those annotations printed in the Columbia Milton (New York, 1938), XVIII, 304–320; only 92 of the total of 820 annotations (not all of them Milton's) are there printed; of these 92, 12 are not by Milton and 17 are doubtful.

(*Elegies*, Book I, Elegy 2) should actually be *rabido*: "The adjective *rapido* applied here to the sea to me appearing to have little or no force, I would read *rabido,* by which term—simply by inverting a single letter—the greatest vigor is added to Tibullus' conceit, his desire being to depict Venus as relentless and cruel in punishing such a crime. To this emendation all the printed texts and all the commentaries on the aforesaid poet are opposed, all of them reading *rapido,* an epithet much more befitting the swift flow of rivers than the surge of the sea, but which is nevertheless applied to the sea by many poets. . . ." And on he flows for two more pages, arguing for his emendation, supporting it as best he can by many citations.[3]

George Crabbe, in "The Library: A Poem" (1781), summed up important methods of literary study that had been common to John Milton, Carlo Dati, and thousands of other scholarly readers up to that time:

> Our patient Fathers trifling themes laid by,
> And roll'd o'er labour'd works th'attentive eye;
> Page after page, the much-enduring men
> Explor'd the deeps and shallows of the pen;
> Till, every note and every comment known,
> They mark'd the spacious margin with their own;
> Minute corrections prov'd their studious care,
> The little Index pointing told us where;
> And many an emendation prov'd the age
> Look'd far beyond the rubric title-page.

These were gentlemen's methods of studying books that they regarded as important—as opposed to more casual reading. Both

---

[3]Milton, *Prose Works* (New Haven, 1959), II, 768. It is interesting to notice that the textual part of this letter—its central portion—has generally been omitted in translations of the letter. J. Milton French left out all of the textual part (*The Life Records of John Milton,* New Brunswick, 1950, II, 207–209); and David Masson left out most of it (*Life,* London, 1873, III, 680–683). They assumed, I believe, that such a passage had little bearing on Milton's *life;* but it is in just such ways that a man's life is foreshortened and a whole tradition is gradually set aside.

John Milton and the unremembered gentlemen kept a sharp lookout for corruptions in the text, and they tried to weed out the mistakes in whatever way they could, from the simple correction of typographical errors to the proposal of complex emendations.

It was fairly common to use the terms "critic" and "criticism" to mean what we would call "textual critic" and "textual criticism," and the context was apparently thought to suffice as an indication of the type of criticism being referred to. Samuel Johnson may serve as an example. "All the former criticks," he wrote in the "Proposals for Printing the Dramatick Works of William Shakespeare" (1756), "have been so much employed on the corrections of the text, that they have not sufficiently attended to the elucidation of passages obscured by accident or time."[4] In the earlier "Miscellaneous Observations on the Tragedy of Macbeth" (1745), Johnson had used the word in the same way: "I would not often assume the critick's privilege, of being confident where certainty cannot be obtained, nor indulge myself too far, in departing from the established reading."[5]

But it is probably in Johnson's "Preface to Shakespeare" (1765) that the terms appear most frequently. "The part of criticism in which the whole succession of editors has laboured with the greatest diligence, which has occasioned the most arrogant ostentation, and excited the keenest acrimony," he observed, "is the emendation of corrupted passages." Talking of conjecture as a way of improving corrupted readings, he said that "something may be properly attempted by criticism, keep-

[4]*The Works of Samuel Johnson, LL.D.* (Oxford, 1825), V, 99–100. In explaining his plan for the text, he said: "The corruptions of the text will be corrected by a careful collation of the oldest copies, by which it is hoped that many restorations may yet be made: at least it will be necessary to collect and note the variation as materials for future criticks. . . . The criticks did not so much as wish to facilitate the labour of those that followed them. The same books are still to be compared" (pp. 98–99).

[5]*Works,* V, 75. Or this example from the same Observations: "The line which I have endeavoured to amend . . . is, perhaps, the only passage in the play in which he [Hanmer] has not submissively admitted the emendations of foregoing criticks" (V, 92–93).

ing the middle way between presumption and timidity.... Such criticism I have attempted to practice, and, where any passage appeared inextricably perplexed have endeavoured to discover how it may be recalled to sense, with least violence." In speaking of those who were ignorant of textual work, Johnson said that he could not "promise that they would become in general, by learning criticism, more useful, happier, or wiser."[6] I can only suggest, by these few instances, the frequency with which the words "critic" and "criticism" and "critical" served for Johnson as an adequate indication, in the proper context, of the textual form of literary study.[7]

The terms "textual criticism" and "bibliography" seem to be of a somewhat later flowering. But ever since the origination of the former term it has been used in biblical studies with a definite and relatively comprehensive sense. "The Textual Criticism of the New Testament has for its primary object the reconstruction of the original text from the Greek mss. versions and quotations in early writers described above. A secondary object is to trace the history of the text, to identify and characterize the various editions or recensions current in different times or localities." This was the definition carried in the fourteenth edition (1929) of the *Encyclopaedia Britannica* in the article on the Bible, it is continued in later editions, and its substance had been more elaborately stated in the eleventh edition (1910). In an important recent handbook on the text of the New Testament, the scope of textual criticism is precisely

[6]*Works*, V, 146, 147–148, 149.

[7]Here are a few further instances out of the "Preface to Shakespeare": "The justness of a happy restoration strikes at once, and the moral precept may be well applied to criticism, 'quod dubitas ne feceris' " (V, 150). "I had before my eye so many critical adventures ended in miscarriage, that caution was forced upon me" (V, 150). "The criticks on ancient authors have, in the exercise of their sagacity, many assistances, which the editor of Shakespeare is condemned to want" (V, 151). ("Sagacity" is one of the favorite attributes which Johnson uses in praising a textual student.) "And Lipsius could complain that criticks were making faults, by trying to remove them ..." (V, 151). Works "which the criticks of following ages were to contend for the fame of restoring and explaining" (V, 154).

described at the outset as follows: "The science of textual criticism deals with *(a)* the making and transmission of ancient manuscripts, *(b)* the description of the most important witnesses to the New Testament text, and *(c)* the history of the textual criticism of the New Testament as reflected in the succession of printed editions of the Greek Testament."[8] In general, a similarly comprehensive view of the scope of textual criticism has been taken by students of the works of classical antiquity.[9] Moreover, textual criticism was highly, even extravagantly, valued by classical scholars. It was John Burnet, the Oxford professor, who maintained that "by common consent the constitution of an author's text is the highest aim that a scholar can set before himself."[10] To balance the accounts with a Cambridge view, A. E. Housman recorded the observation that "it has sometimes been said that textual criticism is the crown and summit of all scholarship."[11]

"Bibliography," on the other hand, had in earlier usage a more limited scope than it now enjoys. Samuel Johnson defined a bibliographer, for example, as "a writer of books; a transcriber." By the end of the eighteenth century, the *Encyclopaedia Britannica* could say of "bibliographia" that "the sense of it is now extended; and it signifies a work intended to give information concerning the first or best editions of books, and the ways of selecting and distinguishing them properly" (Edinburgh, 1797). By the ninth edition (Edinburgh, 1875), twenty-six columns were devoted to bibliography, and the author of

---

[8]Metzger, *The Text of the New Testament,* p. v.

[9]The articles on "Textual Criticism" by J. P. Postgate (Professor of Latin at the University of Liverpool and Editor of the *Classical Quarterly*) in the 11th and 14th editions of the *Encyclopaedia Britannica* exhibit this view. It is more bluntly evident in the article on the same subject in the *Encyclopedia Americana* (1964 edition): "Textual Criticism, the scientific study of the texts of ancient writings to determine their original wording, completeness, and authenticity."

[10]Quoted by R. C. Bald in "Editorial Problems—A Preliminary Survey," *SB,* 3 (1950–51), 3.

[11]"The Application of Thought to Textual Criticism" (1921), *Selected Prose* (Cambridge, England, 1962), p. 133.

the essay, E. Fairfax Taylor, found it appropriate to center his discussion on the history of printing, book collecting, typography, the rarity and price of books, the printing of the Latin classics, the problems of determining the authorship of anonymous and pseudonymous books, condemned and prohibited books, the book trade, systems for classifying books, and other similar topics. Since most twentieth-century writers on bibliography have presented the subject from a partisan viewpoint, it is particularly illuminating to read the informed remarks by Taylor—who of course was writing well before the time of what we call "modern" bibliography—on the history and development of bibliography up to 1875, and he calls attention to many interesting contributions which are now mostly forgotten. Although his topics are ranging, they all relate to his definition of bibliography "as the science of books, having regard to their description and proper classification." "Description" was not limited, for him, to the modern sense of physical makeup in relation to the process of its manufacture; it extended to the topics I have already mentioned, such as authorship, but it did not include textual criticism. Taylor tried to exclude all criticism of the literary work, in fact, and he observed, with perhaps justifiable consternation, that when the bibliographer "pronounces judgment on its intrinsic merits he usurps the office of the critic." In the last sentence of his article he enjoined bibliographers to "recognise the chief value of their science as the handmaid of literature."

III

It was toward the end of the nineteenth century that bibliography began to take a somewhat different course. It became more specialized in that ever greater attention has been given to the technical operation of the printing house, in such matters as compositor analysis, determination of the stints of pressmen, plate corrections, duplicate setting, concealed printings, variant formes, and the like. As a consequence, a considerable study of the craft of printing, binding, and auxiliary operations is necessary to qualify a student even as an intelligent reader of a great proportion of recent work. Bibliography has also, in the more advanced quarters, changed its province. There has been less interest in historical studies, with fewer articles on such topics as "The Will of an Old Dublin Bookseller" or "A Few Bindings Made in Winchester 1749-1789." Although book collecting has flourished, it has come to be of less concern to bibliographers as the division was more marked between bibliographers (as academicians) and book collectors (as amateurs); now there are few essays on topics like "Problems Encountered in the Collecting of Early Railway Time-Tables," and many collectors seem to feel increasingly diffident about writing on topics within their competence. Some trueborn bibliographers have contracted the habit of contemning, and wishing to withhold the title of "bibliography" from, check lists or descriptive catalogs or other examples of what are commonly called enumerative bibliography. Fredson Bowers has animadverted against the wicked practice of using the word "bibliography" to apply to any work that is not "a true bibliography," as well as against librarians and others who "have made too little effort to acquaint themselves with the demands of this new and peculiarly twentieth-century scholarly discipline, which is far removed from the enumerative bibliography taught in their profession."[12] Finally, I am inclined to say that bibliography has very largely taken over the task of textual criticism; or, in Taylor's terms, the bibliographer now "usurps the office" of the textual critic.

Of course a certain amount of provincialism creeps into most discussions of the scope of this or that form of scholarship, and

---

[12]*Principles of Bibliographical Description* (Princeton, 1949), pp. 15–18; *Bibliography and Modern Librarianship* (Berkeley and Los Angeles, 1966), p. 26. Also see Bowers, "The Function of Bibliography," *Library Trends*, 7 (1959), 497–510, in which librarians and librarian-minded folk are handled a little roughly.

we are all a little like those territorial birds that fight off invaders to protect their own area. Still, the process by which bibliography has taken over textual criticism seems worth recording, at least for historical purposes.

This development very closely parallels the twentieth-century association of science and bibliography. As I have already discussed this phenomenon at length (in Chapter II, section II), I will speak more briefly on the parallel extension of the scope of bibliography. Again, the three key English figures are Pollard, McKerrow, and Greg. Again, they look back to W. A. Copinger as a leader. Again, Americans took over about the middle of this century, with Fredson Bowers in the forefront of the large crowd.

Copinger's Inaugural Address in 1892 as the first President of the Bibliographical Society was mainly a plea for a comprehensive catalog of incunabula, and he went into such particular detail as to tell "what Mr. Burger has done toward the contemplated new edition. . . . He has cut up two copies of Hain, and each number has been pasted on a separate sheet of paper. In the same manner two copies of Campbell" and so forth have been cut up. Although Copinger's idea of the scope of bibliography seems to have been limited to the making of various bibliographical catalogs and indexes, the general influence of his address has been important, mainly because of one or two incidental metaphors that he loosed, along with the grand "scientific" cast to which I have previously alluded. One metaphor was the elaborate figure of bibliography as the mariner's compass which guides the student to his objective on the immense ocean of literature. The most significant one, however, was a simple sentence, which I quote in the context of the entire paragraph of which it is the beginning:

> Bibliography has been called the grammar of literary investigation. True are the words of Dr. Johnson: "Knowledge is of two kinds; we either know a thing or we know where to find it."[13]

[13]*Transactions of the Bibliographical Society*, 1 (1893), 34.

I believe that Copinger's maxim about bibliography as the grammar of literary investigation meant no more to him than that lists and indexes help you to find what you want to know. But the sentence has, like many metaphors, cast a mystic spell over later readers; as it conveys no readily definable meaning, it can be made to mean many things. And it has been, with and without reference to any source, by a number of later scholars, including Greg and Bowers.[14]

I believe that it was Greg, far more than any other person, who enlarged the limits of bibliography to encompass textual criticism. In his influential address of 1912 before the Bibliographical Society ("What is Bibliography?"), Greg followed the established tactic of classifying bibliography into branches. He spoke of "descriptive, or to use the wider term, systematic bibliography," but his main interest at that time was what he termed "critical bibliography." For a brief yet authoritative statement of what Greg meant this branch of learning to include, we can read his own summary of his paper, in which he asserted that "Critical Bibliography is very nearly what is commonly meant

[14]Here is an interesting example in which Greg quoted the key phrase out of context and converted it into an application of bibliography to textual criticism, making a moth into a butterfly: "There is a remark in Dr. Copinger's inaugural address before this Society that recently caught my attention. 'Bibliography' he said 'has been called the grammar of literary investigation.' It is an extraordinarily penetrating remark, but one which seems to me to have been strangely misunderstood. Bibliography has hardly ever attempted to be the grammar of literature; it has tried to be a dictionary. It has chronicled and described, sometimes it has even criticized, the books needed for the study of literature, and it has rendered valuable service in this line; but seldom if ever has it concerned itself with the methods of that study. By this, of course, I do not mean either the canons of criticism—if such exist—nor the methods of literary history, but I do mean what is antecedent to both these, namely the investigation of texts. Strictly bibliographical investigation forms three-fourths of textual criticism, and therefore of the work of the scientific editor" ("What Is Bibliography," *Transactions of the Bibliographical Society*, 12, 1911–1913, 47). The misinterpretation is more forthright, aided by an inadvertent (and later admitted) misquotation of Copinger, in Greg's summary of his own paper: "It is this branch of the science, Critical Bibliography, that best deserves the name of 'the Grammar of Literature,' which has sometimes been applied to the whole subject" (p. 11). Bowers has also been a user of Copinger's original "acute phrase," which he attributes to Greg only ("Some Relations of Bibliography to Editorial Problems," *SB*, 3, 1950–51, 37).

by Textual Criticism. It is, apart from the subject and language of his author, all that an editor requires for his work: a sort of calculus of the textual tradition."[15] His presidential address before the same society in 1932 is mainly an elaboration of his earlier paper on the scope of bibliography. He used Copinger's sentence as the basis for reasoning bibliography into the role of preeminence in literary investigation, and he reached the conclusions that "bibliography necessarily includes, as its most distinctive branch, the study of textual transmission, and that textual criticism, up to the point where it changes its nature and becomes metacritical, is essentially nothing but the application of bibliographical analysis."[16] Let me refer, finally, to Greg's conclusion, couched in something more like understatement, in his retrospective review for the Bibliographical Society: "Thus bibliography and textual criticism appear to interlock in a manner that makes it difficult if not impossible to separate their respective fields and leads one to wonder whether it may not in the end be necessary to bring most textual criticism within the province of bibliography."[17] Why, given this interlocking, most textual criticism should be brought within the province of bibliography rather than most bibliography within the province of textual criticism is a question that seems not to occur to bibliographers. This undersight is particularly out of place in a writer who set such store by rigorous logic; I believe that a careful examination of some of Greg's writings—like the passages cited in the two preceding footnotes—would reveal a large number of logical fallacies and false assumptions. The same might be the case with many of us, of course, and it may

[15]The article (cited above) occupies pp. 39–53 and the summary is on pp. 11–12.

[16]"Bibliography—An Apologia," *The Library*, 4th Ser., 13 (1932-1933), p. 136. The first two pages of this address contain some very curious reasoning. It appears that Greg—like many bibliographers before and since—felt it necessary to perfume the word "bibliography" and clothe it in silken garments; but the result will not stand close sensory perception.

[17]"Bibliography—A Retrospect," *The Bibliographical Society 1892–1942: Studies in Retrospect* (London, 1945), p. 30.

be pettiness of spirit to call attention to our common fault in one of the leading bibliographers because they have been so inclined to cry out against others with a loud voice on lesser provocation.

Several British voices were raised modestly in polite protest against Greg's position. Sir Geoffrey Keynes objected that the claims for bibliography had been exaggerated, and Alice Walker protested against the use of the term "critical bibliography" to include what had traditionally been counted textual criticism.[18] One or two people have undertaken to put all of these voices in tune. Lloyd Hibberd, for instance, tried to bring harmony to the bibliographers and textual critics by revising the terminology of the divisions of bibliography; indeed, his hope—visionary, it would seem, in the light of experience—was that the relations even among the various kinds of bibliographers "should be one not merely of toleration but of amicability." These qualities have been more uncommon among the interested parties than one might wish, and I have not observed any increase in them since the appearance of Hibberd's essay.[19]

IV

Greg's views have carried the day—or even, it would seem so far, the century—among the professional bibliographers and edi-

[18]Keynes, "Religio Bibliographici," *The Library*, 5th Ser., 8 (1953), pp. 63–76. "This tendency to exaggerate the claims of bibliography until it comes to be an end rather than a means is perhaps to be recognized as a psychological frustration" (p. 66). Walker, rev. in *The Library*, 5th Ser., 16 (1961), pp. 310–311: "I should like to take this opportunity of protesting against the use of the term 'critical bibliography.' It is, I suppose, generally agreed that the bibliographer is best qualified to construct a stemma for printed books; but, unless the recension provides an editor with a fool-proof text, it is the business of the textual critic to discriminate between true and false readings. Let us therefore use the traditional term 'textual criticism,' so that everyone knows what we are talking about, instead of 'critical bibliography,' which confounds what is strictly bibliographical (in the sense in which McKerrow used the word) and what is strictly the business of experts in other fields."

[19]"Physical and Reference Bibliography," *The Library*, 5th Ser., 20 (1965), 124–134. Among others who have essayed a similar task, Neal Harlow may be mentioned ("The Well-Tempered Bibliographer," *PBSA*, 50, 1956, 28–39).

tors. Such might not have been the case had it not been for Fredson Bowers. The situation closely parallels (let me say again) the claims for bibliography as science; since most of the same books and articles to which I referred in the preceding chapter are also relevant to this discussion—and since the pattern of development is almost identical—I will give a very condensed account of what seems to have come near the condition of dogma in the United States (and to a much lesser extent in England) since World War II.

Bowers has extended and elaborated Greg's basic view of the nature and scope of bibliography. It consists, in his presentation, of four branches: Enumerative (or Systematic), Analytical (or Critical), Descriptive, and Textual. "Textual bibliography," he writes, "is the backbone of textual criticism. It may be defined as the application of analytical bibliography to the three major specific problems of the textual critic: *(a)* the analysis of the physical characteristics of an extant manuscript; *(b)* the recovery of the characteristics of a lost manuscript from the details of the print; and *(c)* the study of the transmission of the text."[20] If the major problems of textual criticism are all to be treated by one form of bibliography which is in itself the application of yet another form of bibliography, one would be left to suppose that textual criticism is simply a term to describe some of the functions of bibliography.[21] And so it appears to be.

[20]*Encyclopaedia Britannica,* "Bibliography." This article seems to have made its first appearance in sets issued in 1958; it is current in the most recent set I have noticed, that dated 1967. Similar categories are set forth in various of his other writings, such as "The Function of Bibliography," *Library Trends,* 7 (1959), 497–510, and "Shakespeare's Text and the Bibliographical Method," *SB,* 6 (1954), 71–91. Earlier, he had also used the term "Critical Bibliography" in Greg's sense as applying to textual problems; one of the categories was called "critical or textual bibliography" in the article "Bibliography, Pure Bibliography, and Literary Studies," *PBSA,* 46 (1952), 186–208.

[21]So it seems to be in Bowers' article on "Textual Criticism" in the editions of the *Encyclopaedia Britannica* mentioned above. "Textual Criticism, a general term for the application of logical method to analyzing the relationship between preserved and inferential forms of a text, followed by the application of various techniques, including critical judgment, designed to establish what will ordinarily be the single definitive form of the text."

"When more than one authoritative version of a text is in existence," writes Bowers, "analytical bibliography takes over the tracing of the transmission of the text in all its details."[22]

Textual criticism stands, in Bowers' map of the past, somewhere between Bibliography and Literary Criticism. Bibliography attacks the problems with the scientific method, while criticism "works with meanings and literary values. . . . Bibliography endeavors to take as much guesswork as possible out of textual criticism, and the literary method endeavors to inform bibliography with value judgments as a check on mechanical probability."[23] Bowers seems to think of textual criticism not as a discipline but only as a job of work that others have to take on.[24] When representatives of these two other disciplines go about solving the problems of textual criticism, it sometimes happens that they disagree. There is, however, an easy solution to any such disagreement, for judgment that can be called "critical"—what Greg termed "metacritical"—is indeed a weak reed on which to put any weight. "When bibliographical and critical judgement clash, the critic must accept the bibliographical findings and somehow come to terms with them. Critical assumptions can never be so demonstrable as strict bibliographical interpretation from sound factual evidence. Indeed, this

[22]"Practical Texts and Definitive Editions," *Two Lectures on Editing* (Columbus, Ohio, 1969), p. 55.

[23]*On Editing Shakespeare and the Elizabethan Dramatists* (Philadelphia, 1955), p. 35. (The chapter is entitled "The Function of Textual Criticism and Bibliography.")

[24]"The relation of analytical to textual bibliography, and thence—immediately—to textual criticism, *is* subject to misinterpretation, principally because analytical bibliography thereby invades a field that has customarily been pre-empted by some form of literary criticism" (*Bibliography and Textual Criticism*, Oxford, 1964, p. 26). "Bibliography concerns itself with editorial problems not as a usurper of the functions of legitimate criticism, but instead as the necessary foundation on which, in certain investigations, textual criticism must be based and to which criticism must constantly refer for more or less definitive judgments" ("Some Relations of Bibliography to Editorial Problems," *SB*, 3, 1950–51, 37). One notices the recurrent protest that bibliography is not a usurper—but has come rather, one supposes, to clear the unweeded garden of things rank and gross in nature.

94

is not a question of degree: when a clash develops, strict biblio-graphical method must be assumed to be right, since step by step it rests on the impersonal interpretation of physical facts according to rigorous laws of evidence. And, correspondingly, criticism must be wrong, since its interpretation of evidence can ultimately rest only on opinion, or common consent in matters of taste governing judgement."[25]

The superiority of bibliography depends on Bowers' implicit definitions. The attributes of bibliography are (as we see in the preceding quotation) that it is strict, sound, factual, impersonal, rigorous; on the other hand, criticism is nothing more substan-tial than opinion, common consent, and taste. Evidence is what counts, and Bowers has been very fond of legal metaphors in extolling the beauties of bibliography.[26] Where bibliography provides a factual and scientific method to reach conclusions, criticism has to grope toward solutions impressionistically or imaginatively.[27] Bowers associates criticism with literary taste,

[25]*Bibliography and Textual Criticism*, p. 29. This passage is taken over, with minor changes, from Bowers' *The Bibliographical Way* (Lawrence, Kansas, 1959), pp. 20–21. He has expressed similar sentiments on numerous other occasions. The "bibliographical method . . . has provided a superior demonstration since it uses not an appeal to probability of opinion but instead the physical and inexorable evidence of the printing-house" (*On Editing Shakespeare*, p. 58).

[26]*The Bibliographical Way* is mainly in praise of bibliographical evidence. "This is evidence that could be taken into a court of law . . ." (p. 19). "The solu-tion is quite elementary" (p. 19). "Impersonal judgment is to be preferred to personal judgment" (p. 20). "An editor need not consult his private judgment in such a case . . ." (p. 20). ". . . his erroneous conclusion was reached on evidence nobody would hang a dog on . . ." (p. 23). ". . . bibliography by means of its par-ticular methods can determine, analyze, and interpret facts in a manner that leaves no room for critical option" (p. 27). I believe that the prize for the use of legal metaphor should be awarded to William B. Todd, however; in the course of one page he likens the bibliographer to a detective, the problem to a case for prosecution, the recorded accounts to depositions, the readers of the article to the court, and so on ("On the Use of Advertisements in Bibliographical Studies," *The Library*, 5th Ser., 8, 1953, 174–175). He does not, however, consider the hanging of a dog.

[27]Today's Shakespeare Texts, and Tomorrow's," *SB*, 19 (1966), 59; *Bibliog-raphy and Textual Criticism*, p. 37.

personal taste, and personal opinion.[28] He has frequently seized the occasion to make electrifying remarks about literary critics: "In contrast to the general uniformity among textual critics about ends and means, literary critics—as we might expect—hold diverse opinions about the operation of their discipline. . . . What sometimes seems to be a critic's almost perverse disregard for specific accuracy may offer the bibliographer a nasty shock."[29] Heaven help us in this need! One may hope, however, that heaven has provided some form of succor in addition to bibliography to relieve us in our distress.

It would greatly facilitate our choice of the daughters of light if bibliography could ordinarily fill our need with textual evidence which is strict, sound, factual, impersonal, and rigorous. Unfortunately, this does not seem to be the case. There are occasions when a piece of bibliographical evidence with textual implications is discovered, such as the misprint *tel's* caused by the light inking of the second *l* in the text being used as copy, and thus proving the order of editions. This exemplary discovery has been repeatedly cited to prove the triumph of bibliography,[30] but bibliographical evidence of this nature is not so common as one might be led to suppose. My experience as a textual editor has been that there is usually no bibliographical evidence to

[28]*Bibliography and Textual Criticism*, pp. 2, 23, 35. Also "Practical Texts and Definitive Editions": ". . . by critical, which is to say by merely tasteful, criteria" (p. 55) . F. W. Bateson has undertaken a refutation of what he calls "the Bibliographical Fallacy." One of his conclusions is that "analytical bibliography is a discipline in its own right, but its findings are likely to be of only marginal interest to the student of literature" ("Modern Bibliography and the Literary Artifact," *English Studies Today*, Bern, 1961, p. 76).

[29]*Textual and Literary Criticism*, p. 1. Many of his works are illuminated by sallies of wit directed at those who are ignorant of the mysteries of bibliography: at the librarian, for example, who can only "sit on his books like a hen on a clutch of eggs, but what he hatches will be less useful. China door-knobs, most likely" ("The Function of Bibliography," p. 506).

[30]It is cited by Bowers in, for example: "The First Edition of Dryden's *Wild Gallant*, 1669," *The Library*, 5th ser., 5 (1950–51), 52–53; "Some Relations of Bibliography to Editorial Problems," *SB*, 3 (1950–51), 57; "Textual Criticism," in *The Aims and Methods of Scholarship in Modern Languages and Literatures*, ed. James Thorpe (New York, 1963), p. 28.

96

use in trying to solve the most troublesome problems that I have encountered. An ignorance of the technical details of bookmaking may cause an editor to make serious mistakes, but the most extensive bibliographical knowledge will not solve non-bibliographical problems in dealing with texts. Moreover, there is a good deal of argument among bibliographers as to what constitutes a bibliographical "fact." It used to be a fact that half-sheet imposition was "a practice which was almost certainly not known in early days," and that "in the normal course the sheets will be perfected in the inverse order in which they were originally half-printed, so that the earliest state of the outer forme should be found on the same sheet as the latest state of the inner forme";[31] now these have ceased to be facts. The conclusions of some of the bibliographers who used to be held in high esteem are now controverted as erroneous.[32] Some bibliographers seem to approach verbal assault on one another, even in connection with a reading (like Hamlet's "solid" or "sullied" flesh) about which it is alleged that there is physical evidence, not subject to opinion, to reach an indisputable conclusion—though every conclusion reached by one bibliographer is disputed by another.[33] Occasionally, bibliographical conclusions are critically examined and the "overwhelming" evidence declared to be "non-existent," the application of results denied because "there is no result to apply," and fun poked at the claims made for the "inexorable evidence of the printing-house."[34] On other occasions, conclusions reached by great bib-

[31]A. W. Pollard and W. W. Greg, "Some Points in Bibliographical Descriptions," *Transactions of the Bibliographical Society*, 9 (1908), 42.

[32]See, for example, Bowers, *Bibliography and Textual Criticism*, pp. 3–7.

[33]There are, of course, numerous bibliographical disquisitions on this crux. These two articles (with their references to others) may serve as examples: Bowers, "Hamlet's 'Sullied' or 'Solid' Flesh: A Bibliographical Case-History," *Shakespeare Survey*, 9 (1965), 44–48; Sidney Warhaft, "Hamlet's Solid Flesh Resolved," *ELH*, 28 (1961), 21–30. F. W. Bateson has made a spirited attack on Bowers' view in "Modern Bibliography and the Literary Artifact," pp. 67–71.

[34]J. K. Walton, review of *SB*, 16 (1963) —specifically, the article by John Hazel Smith—in *MLR*, 59 (1964), 91–93.

liographers turn out to be wrong. Bowers maintained that G. I. Duthie was "able to prove beyond any question that the copy [for *King Lear*] is a makeshift prompt book reconstructed by a group of actors dictating to a scribe. The case is so completely convincing that its major thesis, one expects, will never be seriously challenged hereafter. This important matter is now settled, although some few details need filling in." It has turned out, of course, that the matter was very far from being settled; even Duthie later concluded that "my 1949 theory had better be abandoned."[35] Sometimes objection is made that conclusions which purport to be based on purely bibliographical evidence are in fact based on conjecture. E. A. J. Honigmann writes that

> Fredson Bowers, despite the acknowledged importance of his work, sometimes adds to the confusion by standing beside a textual crux and going through scientific bibliographical motions. The bibliographical part of the argument consists of "mechanical evidence," rigorous method, and irresistible logic, and yet its relevance to a specific crux may involve an awkward jump. All textual critics have to take the jump, of course, but not many will scrutinize their ground as meticulously, and then leap as daringly, as Bowers. Even at the purely verbal level one notices this habit, when the bibliographer looks beyond the mechanical evidence: "Dr. Williams is now able to *conjecture* on the bibliographical evidence that *Coriolanus* is *definitely* from a scribal copy." (p. 193, my italics)[36]

In view of these various uncertainties, one may do well to observe Bowers' cautionary advice: "Don't trust all the bibliographers."[37]

Bowers' central argument which I have been reviewing in these several pages is, let us say, that textual criticism—or, more

[35]Bowers, *MLQ*, 12 (1951), 363; Duthie, ed., *King Lear* (Cambridge, Eng., 1960), p. 132.

[36]Rev. of Bowers, *On Editing Shakespeare*, in *The Library*, 5th Ser., 23 (1968), 264.

[37]"Some Relations of Bibliography to Editorial Problems," *SB*, 3 (1950–51), 47.

generally, editing—properly falls within the province of bibliography. While he states his views with a certain bluntness which would not be employed by most scholars, I believe that his position has come to be widely accepted in the United States. Agreement is moderately general, I think, among most of the leading bibliographers who deal in any way with textual matters, and among virtually all of the scholars who are actively involved in major editorial projects. The validity of such a position is of interest chiefly because of the possible consequences. I believe that the consequences of this position are full of danger for sound editing.

V

If one wished to identify a single book which has, over a period of years, been the most basic volume for learning about modern bibliography, I suppose that the best candidate would be R. B. McKerrow's *Introduction to Bibliography for Literary Students* (1927). When I first read this estimable book, I kept wondering when the author was going to get to the part "for literary students"; I had the naïve idea that the phrase "for literary students" meant that the author would in due course offer applications that would have some relevance to the understanding of literary works. Probably I was puzzled because I am an American and was reading the book in 1940; had it been earlier, perhaps the question would not have occurred to me. Had I been English, perhaps the question would never have occurred at all—I might have known enough to take the expression "literary students" as a technical term defining persons who were arbitrarily required to pass an examination in bibliography in order to qualify for a degree in literature.[38] Anyone who had seen the first draft of McKerrow's book would doubtless have

[38]Charlton Hinman remarks in the opening lines of the preface to his *Printing and Proof-Reading of the First Folio of Shakespeare* (2 vols., Oxford, 1963) that, "like McKerrow's book, it is 'for literary students'." I have been unable to arrive at a satisfactory meaning for the expression in this context.

99

been less puzzled than I was. It was published (in the *Transactions of the Bibliographical Society,* 12, 1911-13, 211-318) under the accurate title of "Notes on Bibliographical Evidence for Literary Students and Editors of English Works of the Sixteenth and Seventeenth Centuries" and written on the assumption that "modern editorial methods demand some bibliographical knowledge"; the revision did not much alter the subject or the assumption. Sometimes we still find the title of McKerrow's book cited as a kind of symbolic proof that "literary study *is* the final goal of bibliography"; accordingly, we can be offered the comforting assurance that "there is no danger that the printing technicians will take over the guidance of bibliographical investigation. . . ."[39]

In the *Introduction to Bibliography,* McKerrow never tried to demonstrate the applicability of bibliography to literary study as I then understood the term. Rather, the inference throughout was that a knowledge of the mechanical aspects of book production was important to those who undertook to edit texts. In fact, McKerrow rather objected to the claims for bibliography which had been made even then—modest though they may seem by today's standards. At the outset of his book, he allowed that he was not sure "that the recent extensions of the term [bibliography] have been altogether justifiable" and he expressed the opinion that the "newer kinds of bibliographical investigation . . . belong rather to the sphere of textual criticism than to formal bibliography . . ." (pp. 2-3). If McKerrow had lived, it may be that the spokesmen for bibliography would not have been so successful in encompassing textual criticism.

[39]Fredson Bowers, "Bibliography Revisited," *The Library,* 5th Ser., 24 (1969), 98. About McKerrow: The "impact on bibliographical scholarship [of "association with the universities and their courses of instruction in literature"] by bringing in an entirely new breed of researchers can be traced directly back to the appearance in 1927 of McKerrow's *Introduction to bibliography for literary students.* The title alone is a sufficient indication of the change in direction that bibliography was thereafter to take in appealing to a broader public and receiving thereby a broader participation in its discipline" (p. 98).

I have alluded to those who would make textual criticism a branch of bibliography. This is a game that two can play. One can readily imagine the other party serving: the ambitious textual critic describes the four forms of textual criticism, with the fourth as "bibliographic textual criticism"—which is made to encompass all textual evidence that derives from an examination of the production of books and manuscripts as physical objects—and with bibliography as one branch of textual criticism. I might, under those circumstances, find myself writing about the way in which textual criticism was distorting bibliography.

It is true that only a small fraction of the sum of bibliography has a bearing on textual studies; it is also true that only a small fraction of the sum of textual studies has a bearing on bibliography. Alice Walker has observed that "the status of bibliography is not increased by belittling other studies which play an essential part in textual criticism and it will fall into disrepute if the claims made for it are exaggerated or ill-founded."[40] A similar stricture could doubtless be made about textual criticism if an ardent exponent of that discipline belittled other studies which play an essential part in bibliography.

On the basis of these facts and opinions, it would be possible to make a plea for tolerance and fair play, or to attack pedantry, or to express many other worthy sentiments. It might, indeed, seem that the issues which I have been outlining simply prove to superior beings that fleas have other fleas to bite them, or that a new Dunciad would be the only suitable method for putting us all in our places.

The way in which the province of textual criticism is envisioned does, in fact, have a direct effect on the practice of editing or of trying to solve textual problems. With the present

[40]Rev. of Bowers, *Textual and Literary Criticism*, in *RES*, N.S. 11 (1960), 449. "This book . . . is not, as a whole, agreeable work" (p. 449). "Indiscriminate tilting of this kind will do bibliography no good. . . . We have often been told that textual critics must learn to understand bibliographical evidence, but the bibliographer should try to understand linguistic and literary evidence" (p. 451).

emphasis on bibliography, a great deal of textual criticism is oriented toward the technical details of bookmaking. The result is that the edition of a novel, for example, involves an unusually careful examination of the book (in many copies, impressions, issues, and editions) as a physical object. Some irregularity in printing is often to be expected, and there may well be cancels or press corrections or other disturbances in the printing. Where these irregularities cause disturbances in the text, there is certainly need for the editor to call attention to the irregularity and point to the authoritative reading if he can do so. In practice, however, the bibliographically oriented editor tends to report very fully on every irregularity, even when it causes no disturbance in the text. We are obliged to hear as much about a page number inadvertently reversed in the printing as about a substantive change in the text; if the duplicate settings are textually identical, we must still be told the full speculations as to how and why the pages were set in duplicate; if the spacing alters in the course of printing through the slippage of type, it seems important to instruct us in the details of each instance. This list could be greatly extended, and examples can be found in many of the extensive American editions which are now in process or recently completed. In the meantime, the search for relevant evidence in letters, documents, books, and other sources may be passed over on the grounds that such sins of omission are venial.

The bibliographer's main concern is to treat books as tangible objects, and most of the leaders have emphasized the centrality of this idea. "I start then with the postulate," wrote Greg in his Presidential Address before the Bibliographical Society, "that what the bibliographer is concerned with is pieces of paper or parchment covered with certain written or printed signs. With these signs he is concerned merely as arbitrary marks; their meaning is no business of his." F. P. Wilson stated that "to a formal bibliographer a book is not the life-blood of a master spirit but a collection of pieces of paper with printing on them." Bowers has said that "the function of textual bibliography is to treat these imprinted shapes, their selection and arrangement, without primary concern for their symbolic value as conceptual organisms—that is, not as words that have meaningful values—but, instead, as impersonal and non-conceptual inked prints."[41] This view is, presumably, an article of religion with most bibliographers. If and when the bibliographer undertakes the task of textual criticism—by becoming an editor of a novel, for example—he must become a heretic to his bibliographical faith: the meaning of the words must be of primary importance to him.

The present practice of textual criticism in the United States reflects, in my opinion, its bibliographical orientation. One notable example is the normative statement issued by the Center for Editions of American Authors—*Statement of Editorial Principles: A Working Manual for Editing Nineteenth Century American Texts* (Modern Language Association of America, 1967). Since I have already discussed this work in some detail (Chapter II, Section III), I will only remark, in shorthand, on the strongly bibliographical cast that governs it and observe that the one-page list of recommended studies (of twenty-two items) consists almost entirely of works which are essentially bibliographical in nature, with the majority of those on editorial principle being by Bowers. By intention—or at least by reflection—most of the extensive American editions are being produced under similar principles and auspices.

I do not wish to minimize the importance of bibliography in the preparation of good texts. But I believe that we will not get the best texts by continuing to retain such a strongly bibliographical orientation to textual criticism. Some of the specific problems of a given text may be solved by bibliographical means, to be sure. But some of the problems may be linguistic

---

[41]Greg, "Bibliography—An Apologia," *The Library*, 4th Ser., 13 (1932), 121–122; Wilson, "Shakespeare and the 'New Bibliography'," *Studies in Retrospect*, p. 95; Bowers, *Bibliography and Textual Criticism*, p. 27.

in nature, and some may be problems of literary history or literary criticism, and many are likely to be simple problems in logic or common sense, and some will doubtless be problems that can be "solved" only by guesswork. The proportions of each type of problem will vary, of course, and each kind of problem must be approached in the way that scholars have learned to deal with that type most fruitfully.

Thus textual criticism cannot properly have a single methodology. When textual criticism is governed unduly by any one method, the results are likely to be distorted and incomplete as textual studies. As I have argued in Chapter II, the business of textual criticism is to correct errors: to try to identify and eliminate any mistakes or corruptions that have subverted the author's intentions. The tools of one trade will not repair every breakdown, and the special expertise that the textual critic ought to possess is that of a skilled and knowledgeable handyman. He is not a plumber or an electrician, but he must know how to deal with pipes and wiring.

The ideal of textual criticism is to present the text that the author intended. The province of textual criticism extends to all of the problems that arise in trying to reach that ideal. It has recourse to all of the methods that may be useful in trying to solve them; but it does not claim sole ownership of any of them, nor is it the property of any of them.

CHAPTER IV

Textual Analysis

JOHN DONNE'S "Holy Sonnets" are extant in the two earliest printed collections of his poems and in some fourteen early manuscripts. These texts differ among themselves for more than fifty passages. In "This is my playes last scene," some of the texts (or "authorities," or "witnesses") read, for line 7, "But my'ever-waking part shall see that face"; others read "Or presently, I know not, see y^t Face." In "Death be not proud," some texts read "we wake eternally" while others read "we liue eternally."

In each of these two poems, the differing readings ("variants") cause the poem to have a different meaning; various readers will take different views as to the degree of difference, depending on their own purposes and methods and standards. How shall we determine which reading was the one that Donne intended for that poem? Many people find it easy to decide on the reading which they prefer, or the one which makes (in their opinion) the better poem. I think that a judgment formed according to the taste of an acute, experienced, and well-informed reader is always a conclusion of consequence, and I believe that such a critical mind should be at work through every stage of the process of textual criticism in general and of textual analysis in particular. There was a time, in fact, when a judgment of that nature was thought to suffice in solving all textual problems. I confess that I generally feel rather uneasy when I reach a textual conclusion which does not accord with the judgment of what I conceive to be my considered taste or the taste of those whose views I have come to respect; on those occasions I contrive to linger over the possibility that I may be more than ordinarily mistaken in my textual conclusion.

On the other hand, we have to recognize that there are radical limitations to our ability to decide by the exercise of critical tact, even if our powers were to approach infallibility. Frequently the readings seem to serve equally well in the context of the poem. I have faced such alternate choices a multitude of times: I could think of arguments for each that seemed to me of equal weight so far as the quality of the resulting poem was concerned, and no way was revealed to me as a literary critic to make a choice between them without the exercise of self-hypnosis or of arbitrary selection. Moreover, it is not demonstrable that we can always identify the best, nor that the author always writes his work in the way that would strike us as the best, nor that the author is always capable of the best or even of his best. Authorial revision and the existence of various published versions indicate that different readings satisfied the author at different times. If the author cannot always make up his own mind as to which he prefers—as Emily Dickinson and a host of others could not—it is hopeless to think that the critic can do so, unless we assume that the critic is a seer.

In these uncertainties and doubts—which pervade much of textual studies—we have recourse to the help of textual analysis. What textual analysis does is to provide a way of testing the relative corruption of the texts among a group of differing texts which communicate a single literary work. If we think for the moment of the variations among these differing texts as a result only of errors in transmission, we can begin with the following series of simplified assertions.

The general purpose of textual analysis is to try to determine which text of a literary work most nearly fulfills the author's intentions; this general purpose is not the unique property of analysis, however, as it is shared with various other textual

106

procedures. The specific purpose of textual analysis is to try to establish the relationship among the various texts of a literary work in order to achieve the general purpose. The method of textual analysis is to examine the likenesses and differences in all of the available texts and to make inferences and draw conclusions from the facts which are assembled. The intellectual quality which is mainly exercised in the practice of textual analysis is logic. Although textual analysis seems to be an essential act when the occasion is apt, there is no guarantee that it will always be capable of solving the problem. In fact, my experience has been that a number of alternative conclusions frequently remain even after using all of the weapons of textual analysis. When several conclusions are logically possible, it is sometimes difficult to suppress the desire to chop down all except the most agreeable one, so susceptible are we of being convinced that the world is as we wish it to be.

In this chapter I will undertake to discuss four topics, which, as I see it, encompass the basic principles of textual analysis. First, the roles that analysis has played in the whole enterprise of textual criticism in the past, and what role it can play in the study of English and American literature. Second, the basic hypothesis, the main forms of textual analysis, and the principal objections to those forms. Third, the chief limitations to the practice of textual analysis. Fourth, a brief exposition of the useful role that textual analysis can take in dealing with the kinds of literary materials with which this book is concerned.

II

The role that textual analysis is given reveals a good deal about the chief problems of textual study and the nature of the material with which it must work. In the textual study of the works of Greek and Roman antiquity, analysis appears to be the most important procedure, and to have been so for more than a century. The three main processes of textual criticism

107

in those fields are sometimes described as recension (the selection of the most authoritative evidence for a text), examination (the determination as to whether the evidence yields the original reading), and conjecture (any necessary reconstruction of the original). The first two of these processes are carried on principally by analytical study of the interrelationships of manuscripts. This method had long been developing in classical studies, and it reached a high degree of sophistication in the work of Karl Lachmann (1793-1851), with his genetic arrangement of manuscripts into family trees, the provision for inferring lost copies, the reconstruction of archetypes, and the like.

The importance of analysis to classical textual studies has continued to be central. For example, the article on Textual Criticism (by a classicist) in the 11th edition of the *Encyclopaedia Britannica* (1910)—an article essentially repeated in the 14th edition (1929)—is mainly about families of manuscripts, constructing stemma, inferring the readings of the archetype, and the like. The little book by the noted classical scholar Paul Maas, entitled *Textual Criticism* (1958)—which seems to be admired by most breeds of textual critics, whatever their specialty—devotes about two-thirds of its space to what I have been calling analysis, what Maas calls "stemmatics."

Similarly, in textual work on the New Testament, analysis has also been central. The 11th edition of the *Encyclopaedia Britannica* (under "Bible: Textual Criticism") asserts that the object of the textual critic "is to discover and remove the various corruptions which have crept into the text, by the usual methods of the textual critic—the collection of material, the grouping of MSS. and other authorities, the reconstruction of archetypes, and the consideration of transcriptional and intrinsic probability" (III, 883A-B). In such current works as Bruce M. Metzger's *Text of the New Testament* (New York, 1964), analysis plays a central part in his outline of the practice of New Testament textual criticism.

It is natural that textual work on classical authors and on

the New Testament should have had to rely on analysis to such a large degree. For the main evidence—almost the only evidence—depends on the extant manuscripts, which have varying degrees of corruption. As Maas tells us, "we have no autograph manuscripts of the Greek and Roman classical writers and no copies which have been collated with the originals; the manuscripts we possess derive from the originals through an unknown number of intermediate copies, and are consequently of questionable trustworthiness" (*Textual Criticism*, p. 1). If there is usually little or no evidence aside from the varying manuscripts, there is sometimes an embarrassment of manuscripts. About 5,000 extant Greek manuscripts contain all or part of the New Testament, for example, and it has been necessary to classify them into various "family" groupings (Byzantine, Caesarean, Alexandrian) and to analyze their more complex relationships (ordinarily using sample passages only) in order to try to make some systematic decisions about the possible value of the variant readings that the differing manuscripts offer.

The situation which confronts the textual student of English and American literature since the medieval period is, of course, very different. There are still plenty of variant readings, but analysis generally plays a more modest role in trying to solve the problems. The difference is that there is frequently such a large amount of other evidence of the author's intentions: holograph manuscripts, the author's corrected proof sheets, letters from the author about the composition or revision or authority of a given text, authorial revisions, even sometimes an essay or a book by a writer about the composition and revision of one of his own works.

Since the ideal of textual criticism is to present the text that the author intended, the personal testimony by the author as to his intentions is plainly the most primary textual evidence that there can be. It would be a daydream for the ages if a classicist could imagine a parallel to what we have in William

109

Gibson's *The Seesaw Log*: perhaps an account by Euripides of *The Bacchae*, in which he tells in detail about the composition of the play, his rearrangements of the prologue, his story of a controversy about cutting Dionysus' last long speech and his three successive versions of what those verses (which now are lacking) should consist of, his arguments with the actors who insisted on altering which of his verses in what way in a preliminary version, and the like.

In addition to authorial testimony, we often have a vast amount of other textual evidence, as from wives, editors, publishers, friends, children, and others. The sources of information about *The Waste Land*, about which I have already spoken, may be taken as an example. Not to shortchange the New Testament scholar in daydreams, let us suppose that there existed a parallel within the field of his interest to the available evidence from a dozen sources about the text of *The Waste Land*: perhaps the letters and notes by the family and close associates and amanuenses of the author of the Fourth Gospel, telling which manuscripts he consulted, what he thought of the relative reliability of passages in "Matthew" and "Luke," why he included certain episodes and omitted others, who made what mistakes in which copies, and so forth.

With the kind of evidence that is so generally available for English and American literature since the medieval period, it is evident that the textual student should consider such testimony as of primary importance in trying to solve his problems. I believe that it is only a handful of scholars in these disciplines —scholars who have been particular specialists in analysis—who any longer think of textual analysis as the central procedure of textual criticism.[1]

There are, however, some literary examples within the scope of this book that call for moderately complex analysis. Let me

[1]One example is Vinton A. Dearing. His article on "Some Routines for Textual Criticism" (*The Library*, 5th Ser., 21, 1966, 309–317) limits textual criticism to textual analysis. It also presents a lofty view of the textual critic (analyst) that I am incapable of taking seriously: "The critic moved by this view of his tasks will

suggest, as a form of introduction, two categories. First, the sort exemplified by some poems of the latter seventeenth century which are extant in as many as a dozen manuscripts and printed texts, all relatively contemporary. Collation may reveal that half of them are derived by simple transcription from others and may thus be eliminated, thus leaving half a dozen versions with distinct and notable differences. These cases sometimes pose real difficulties. Second, the more common problem for analysis, which involves no more than three or four texts, with all (or most of them) printed books. Typically, the differences are minor, and the general relationship moderately easy to determine: analysis of a very elementary sort might reveal (for example) that the 1717 edition was set from the 1715, the undated edition from the 1717, the 1745 from the 1715, and that all variants from the 1715 appear to be typographical mistakes. (In this case, the result of analysis would be the elimination of all editions other than 1715 as a basis for the text.) My main concern in this chapter is with the principles that are relevant to problems of these two degrees of complexity.

The question is always which version—as a whole text, a passage, a word—most nearly fulfills the author's intentions. Obviously, the first effort is always to exhaust all testimony from the author or from others who have left worthwhile evidence on the matter. The need for textual analysis arises only when we can discover no such evidence or when it seems advisable to verify the evidence that we have.

III

Textual analysis is possible because a copy of a text can rarely ever be made, either in manuscript or by print, without introducing changes into the new copy. Sometimes the changes are

---

not conquer and come to his goal leaving the rest in the wild, but still turn and beckon the weary and give the dejected his hand. And this, surely, is the noblest kind of textual criticism, involving as it does an element of self-sacrifice in sharing the fruits of hard-won victories" (p. 309).

intentional and sometimes unintentional, but changes there will usually be. The changes—usually called variants, or variant readings—are discovered by a detailed comparison (collation) of the several forms of the text. Ordinarily, attention is given only to those details that are not commonly altered by copyists at their pleasure or convenience; thus, for a text copied at a time when spelling was highly variable and personal, common variations in spelling would not be regarded as useful variants. The variants which remain—usually called "substantive" when they affect the reading of the substance of the text—provide the material for textual analysis.

The basic hypothesis of textual analysis is that an examination of the variants can reveal the relationship of the copies which those variants represent. Variants are of two general kinds: errors of transmission (mistakes made by the copyist, compositor, editor, or the like) and intentional changes (readings introduced by the editor, author, copyist, or the like). It is assumed that when a new copy is made from an existing copy, the new copy will in general perpetuate the variants (both errors and intentional changes) that appeared in the version from which it was copied, and that it will itself also introduce new variants into the text. Thus the analysis of the variants may, ideally, reveal information about the order in which the copies were derived from one another.

Several kinds of conclusions are possible from analysis. At the least, it can indicate that one copy derives altogether from another copy: the importance of this information is that it proves the derivative copy to be of no independent textual authority and hence may be eliminated from further consideration in the establishment of the text. At the best, it can indicate the one copy from which all other copies derive: the importance of this information is that it identifies the one copy which is nearest to the author's original and hence the copy which is to be selected as the copy-text.

112

I think that the practice of textual analysis has taken three basic forms. Each of them is constructed, at least implicitly, on the assumptions I have been discussing, but each of them is different from the others in method and plan. I will first sketch the main lines of each of these forms, and then I will indicate the limitations and difficulties involved in the use of each.[2]

The earliest form—the one that might be called both classical and standard—is often termed the genealogical method and is associated, in origin, with the name of Karl Lachmann. This form undertakes to solve textual problems by trying to establish a family tree (or genealogy or stemma) of a group of versions of the same text. Its findings are often presented diagrammatically. Its method depends on a scrutiny of the textual errors in the different versions. To use Maas's terms, the critic focuses attention on the "indicative errors": an error which appears in one version but not in another is called a "separative error" in that it separates them and gives one kind of limit to their relationship (that the one without the error, for example, did not derive purely from the one with the error); an error which appears in two versions but not in others is called a "conjunctive error" in that it shows that they are joined together in a relationship (such as one having been derived from the other or from a common ancestor) which sets them apart from other versions. The analysis of a sufficiently large body of indicative errors should, in theory at least, reveal the detailed relationships of the various versions and thus permit the establishment of a stemma.

[2]Some recent accounts of the progress and state of textual analysis are contained in the following studies, which also provide further and detailed references to work of note: 1) Edward B. Ham, "Textual Criticism and Common Sense," *Romance Philology*, 12 (1958–59), 198–215; this article particularly emphasizes the state of criticism among medievalists. 2) Bruce M. Metzger, "Modern Methods of Textual Criticism," *The Text of the New Testament* (New York, 1964), pp. 156–185; this chapter, though it reviews all types of textual criticism, is the work of a scholar whose specialty is the New Testament. 3) Antonín Hrubý, "A Quantitative Solution of the Ambiguity of Three Texts," *SB*, 18 (1965), esp. pp. 147–155; the author of this article, a specialist in romance studies, writes from a mathematical (or statistical) point of view.

The genealogical form was developed for the purpose of trying to solve textual problems connected with the writings of classical antiquity, and with the New Testament. Ordinarily, the versions under analysis are manuscripts, and there is a large body of evidence with which to deal. This form has now been in intensive use for more than a century, and it is still generally accepted by classicists and by New Testament scholars. It allows much latitude to the textual critic; indeed, it demands the constant exercise of logic and aesthetic decision, and its application to a given problem is subjective to a considerable degree.

The second form I will mention—and call the "best-text" type—developed out of dissatisfaction with the genealogical method. It is associated with the name of Joseph Bédier. In 1913, he expressed strong skepticism about the validity of the genealogical method on the basis of his own experience. He observed that stemmata seemed always to be set up in such a way that all copies ultimately descend from two copies made from the archetype—which seemed to him highly improbable—and, furthermore, that in a given situation a number of different stemmata could be constructed which would accord equally well with a set of variants. From such practical tests he was convinced that the genealogical method embodied fallacies in its theory, and he repudiated it in favor of a method which involved selecting what he called the "best text." He was working with medieval French manuscripts. His choice of the best text depended on a comparison of the extant manuscripts of a given text, on such criteria as coherence of sense, regularity of spelling, and form of grammar. Moreover, various scholars have maintained that the identification of indicative errors is not usually possible in medieval French manuscripts; Alexandre Micha, for example, asserted that he had found no clear indicative error in any of the manuscripts of any of the romances of Chrétien de Troyes. The "best-text" form has been adopted pretty generally by scholars for their studies of medieval French texts, and it continues to dominate their work.

The third form can be called the statistical method. It is an effort to get away from subjective or qualitative criteria (which are admittedly crucial to the genealogical and best-text methods) in favor of quantitative criteria. Variant readings of the several versions of a text are classified and arranged into quantifiable form so that the entire body of variants can be subjected to statistical analysis. The information used will consist of statistical data derived from the different kinds of agreements and disagreements among the witnesses which have been compared, and the data are to be analyzed by the use of probability calculus. Quentin (through the use of elementary statistics) and Greg (through the use of mathematical logic) are usually thought of as the ones who formalized this method, in 1926 and 1927. Among scholars who have recently extended the system are Dearing and Hrubý; their hope has been to provide a formal procedure which is independent of opinion and which is capable of solving problems that apparently cannot be settled by the logic of the genealogical method. Hrubý has, for instance, spent considerable effort in trying to demonstrate a solution to the problem of four manuscripts belonging to the family of Jean Renart's *Le Lai de l'Ombre*, and Dearing offers (as the major illustration in his book on method) a study of the relationship of the four Synoptic Gospels through an analysis of ten manuscripts of the Greek text of Philemon.[3]

Such, in barest outline, are the three major forms of textual analysis. It has proved easy to raise serious objections to the theory or to the efficacy of each of them. Although I do not wish to give the impression that any one of them can be brushed off in a parenthesis, I would like to mention, in resumé, some characteristic objections that are frequently raised. These summaries are certainly not offered as confutations of important scholarly

[3]Hrubý's results are set forth in the article noted above, pp. 169–182, and in his "Statistical Methods in Textual Criticism," *General Linguistics*, Vol. V, No. 3, Supplement 1962, pp. 84–136; the work by Dearing is in his *Manual of Textual Analysis* (Berkeley and Los Angeles, 1959), pp. 86–102.

methods, of course, and it is never possible to make a fair presentation in a few sentences of a kind of complex work to which a multitude of scholars have devoted a lifetime of effort. Nevertheless, a review of some usual objections may lead us to general reflections about textual analysis.

With respect to the genealogical form, it is often pointed out that any complex body of variants can be "explained" by more than one arrangement of the several versions. Moreover, the identification as to which of two variant readings is the error and which the author's intention always depends on the experience or tact or taste of the analyst: in practice, a considerable part of the choices are marginal, some to the point of being virtually impossible to defend logically, whichever the choice. Since a small number of differences in these choices may require a radical change in the stemma which will explain the relationship of the texts, the results of the genealogical method applied to complex examples are very often uncertain and problematic. Most practitioners of the method are understandably cautious and tentative. I have sought help on complicated problems from some of the most eminent scholars of this persuasion, but I have rarely been able to elicit either objection to or verification of the stemma that I had constructed.

To the best-text form, it is obvious that the value of the results will depend entirely on the knowledge, experience, and taste of the analyst. When scholars with varying qualifications fall to the task of judging the relative coherence of the sense of several versions of a text, they can be expected to reach different conclusions. To settle on the best-text method as the best that can be achieved in textual analysis seems to many scholars to be a counsel of despair; to them, this method appears to be a repudiation of analysis as a way of trying to discover anything about what an author wrote.

To the statistical form, several kinds of objections can be made. One is that it has, in fact, proved unproductive—that hardly any worthwhile results have yet been produced in the more than forty years since the books by Greg and Quentin. The attempts have been various and extensive, and anyone who has ever looked at any single report must be impressed by the elaborate and burdensome labors that are involved in treating any problem, and by the form of presentation which makes the results available only to true adepts.[4] The best that one commentator could find to say about the work of Greg and Quentin was that "each author has a fascinating game to offer for the reader with a weakness for unambitious mathematics as well as for textual criticism."[5] As long ago as 1911, A. E. Housman—in speaking of editing, in his Inaugural Lecture—observed that "while the English fault is to confuse this study with literature, the German fault is to pretend that it is mathematics."[6]

Some of the recent followers of Greg and Quentin have themselves recognized that the statistical method has, at best, severe limitations. As Hrubý observes, the method serves well "with relatively simple cases of genealogies," but that the success "decreases rapidly with increasing complications" so that there is an inherent difficulty "which no method shall ever be able to overcome completely. The theoretical analysis has shown that not even the stemmata without any convergences are soluble in the strict, mathematical sense of the word"; consequently, we must expect that many problems "will prove simply insoluble and that the critic will then have to assume the full responsi-

[4]One may sympathize with a reviewer of Hrubý's "Quantitative Solution" article when he said that it "illustrates a statistical solution using probability calculus and is an impressive exercise in logic, although I must admit that I got lost about half-way through Professor Hrubý's exposition" (R. Donaldson, *The Library*, 5th Ser., 21, 1966, 160).

[5]Ham, p. 203. Or F. M. Salter, who called Greg's *Calculus* "only a rather unproductive means of eschewing idleness" (*RES*, 13, 1937, 350).

[6]*TLS*, May 9, 1968, p. 476. Again, after likening the textual analyst to the dog hunting for fleas, he went on: "If a dog hunted for fleas on mathematical principles, basing his researches on statistics of area and population, he would never catch a flea except by accident. They require to be treated as individuals; and every problem which presents itself to the textual critic must be regarded as possibly unique" ("The Application of Thought to Textual Criticism," in *Selected Prose*, ed. John Carter, Cambridge, Eng., 1962, pp. 132–133).

bility of a subjective interpretation, determined only by the reliability of his philological insight."[7]

Another objection is that the effort to be objective results in a repudiation of judgment on points that have been thought to require it. One practitioner of the statistical method writes that "in textual analysis . . . all the evidence is of equal weight. In the event that two or more solutions to a problem are equally satisfactory, a choice may be made between them, but that is all. . . . Judgment is not necessary, and indeed is forbidden, during the analysis proper."[8] We may sometimes be urged to stick to the rules even when we go wrong. One reviewer of the book from which I have just quoted observed that on those occasions one may be "blandly told by the textual critic that everything is really quite satisfactory because he went wrong *by rule.*"[9] This view may remind one of the landlady who chides Susan the maid, at the Inn at Upton in *Tom Jones*, for saying that she saw Tom leap out of a woman's bed. " 'Well,' says Susan, 'then I must not believe my own eyes.'—'No, indeed, must you not always,' answered her mistress; 'I would not have believed my own eyes against such good gentlefolks. I have not had a better supper ordered this half-year than they ordered last night' " (Book X, Chapter III). Finally, one must remember that decisions arrived at by statistical probability are essentially educated guesses. While they may be the best that one can do, they may also be wrong in a given case. To the lover of system and method, the decisions may be "right" by definition; to the lover of evidence and logic, they may be unverifiable by nature. And so scholars make dispute.

In short—and at best—the statistical method seems to produce a very small mouse for a very large mountain of effort.

[7]Hrubý, "Statistical Methods," pp. 132, 134, 135.

[8]Dearing, *Manual*, p. 8.

[9]David Vieth, in *JEGP*, 59 (1960), 556. Or Metzger (pp. 166–167) on Archibald Hill: "To a scholar trained in the classical tradition, such a doctrinaire approach to the problems of textual criticism appears to be tantamount to saying that when theories and facts disagree, so much the worse for the facts!"

118

IV

These various kinds of objections to the three forms of textual analysis suggest serious questions about the fundamental limitations to textual analysis in general. Since the useful application of textual analysis to any problem depends on an awareness of its limits, I would like to set forth four difficulties in the theory and practice of analysis. While other people would perhaps formalize these limits somewhat differently, I think that the essential problems fall within these four areas.

First, there is the essential difficulty in distinguishing the reasons for variants. It is true to say that some variants are accidental and some are intentional, and that some intentional variants are authorial in origin and some are (in a broad sense) editorial. For textual analysis to be definitively successful, it is necessary to be able to make all of these distinctions in practice, and to make them unfailingly. Many of the problems in distinction which face the critic can be easily resolved, but a host of witnesses proclaim the truth that it is sometimes impossible to select readings which are demonstrably authorial. Should one choose the "lasie pacing cloudes" of the first quarto of *Romeo and Juliet*, or the "lazie puffing Cloudes" of the second quarto, or the "lazy-passing clouds" of an emender?[10] Someone stands ready to argue in favor of each possibility on the grounds that the image created by the word of his choice is appropriate or visually effective or compatible with the context or consistent with the author's usage—or that it possesses some other equally desirable quality. Is it logically more plausible to think that the Ghost of Hamlet's father talks about the "fretfull Porpentine" or the "fearefull Porpentine"? In my experience, I have found it frequently impossible, when faced with two variant readings, to decide which is the error and which is the "right" (that is, authorial) reading, or whether they are both errors or both au-

---

[10]G. I. Duthie reviews several of the possibilities for this crux in "The Text of Shakespeare's *Romeo and Juliet*," *SB*, 4 (1951–52), 24–25; he himself argues in favor of "pacing."

thorial. I believe that this dilemma (or multilemma) is likely to confront all textual critics with relative frequency in all but the simplest kind of work. Under these circumstances, it would seem that a statistical analysis of a body of variants which include doubtful and undifferentiated readings is more likely to succeed in masking guesswork than in supplanting human judgment. Moreover, there is a great temptation to indulge in circular reasoning as a way of (seemingly) solving some kinds of hard problems: to put it crudely, one may first establish a stemma by systematizing the errors that one has identified through distinguishing which variant readings are authorial (or intentional) and which are errors (or accidental); then one may feel free to use the stemma to determine which variant readings cannot be authorial. The difficulties in making the crucial distinctions between intention and error are inescapable and, alas, in some cases the problems are unsolvable.

Second, there is the essential difficulty (or even impossibility, often) of resolving relationships among texts in which conflation has taken place. When an editor or copyist conflates two or more versions of a text—that is, takes some readings from one and some from another—the problems of analysis are greatly complicated, at the least. The practice of conflation (or contamination, as it is sometimes called) seems to have been not uncommon in the preparation of classical, biblical, and other early texts. To take one specific example, the treatise by St. Cyprian (the third-century Bishop of Carthage) called *De ecclesiae catholicae unitate*, extant in at least 160 manuscripts: there is actual evidence that the Cistercian manuscripts of the twelfth century were prepared by combining the evidence of different earlier manuscripts; the modern editor, Maurice Bévenot, has found it necessary to suppose that similar conflation took place in the ninth century, and he believes that conflation among the families of manuscripts (which presumably had already come into being by the third and fouth centuries) had also happened in earlier centuries as well. As a result, an unusually careful study of these manuscripts leads to a conclusion that it is impossible—because of conflation—to draw up a conclusive stemma even of the families of the manuscripts. If contamination has taken place on a large scale in any body of texts being analyzed, Bévenot asserts, "the construction of such a stemma becomes impossible. To overlook the fact of contamination or to treat it as negligible, and to construct a stemma in spite of it, is to print a stemma that is positively misleading. 'Contamination' among the MSS upsets all our calculations."[11]

We may hug ourselves with joy that these problems are the lot of other scholars. But the practice of conflation, having persisted, makes problems for us too. The laudable scholarly impulse to try to reproduce the best possible text has led—and continues to lead—copyists, amateur editors, friends of the author, and other interested people to combine readings from different versions of a work of art without warning readers that what they are perusing is in fact an edited text. In the latter seventeenth century, for example, professional copyists seem regularly to have conflated the texts of poems that they distributed. Modern Shakespeare scholars frequently find it necessary to hypothesize that conflation must have taken place while texts of plays were being prepared for the first folio and for various quartos. Examples of conflation exist in all modern periods, and the possibility of conflation in a complicated set of relationships should chasten the lust for certainty.

Third, there is the inescapable fact that the more complex the relationship of the witnesses, the nearer analysis approaches the state of being either impossible or useless. There are many reasons for complexity of relationships. One is lack of evidence. For example, numerous variant readings are necessary in the witnesses in order to establish, with any reasonable confidence, one stemma which can be logically preferred to other possibilities. For a more oppressive example, when some versions of

[11]Bévenot, *The Tradition of Manuscripts: A Study in the Transmission of St. Cyprian's Treatises* (Oxford, 1961), pp. 132, 6.

a text do not survive, it is often necessary to postulate missing versions in order to present a stemma which is logically possible; the greater the proportion of missing versions, the more unverifiable and arbitrary the hypothesis will become until at last it enters the realm of pure speculation. Consequently, the value of a stemma for textual purposes depends in part, so far as the evidence of witnesses is concerned, on the proportion of the total texts which are extant or textually recoverable. Other common reasons for complexity of relationships are conflation (about which I have just spoken) and authorial revision (which I have discussed at length in Chapter I): in both of these cases, the sources of the variants are usually difficult to perceive, and the choice of an hypothesis soon becomes arbitrary. If human ingenuity were set loose alone on the scents of a pack of foxes—to reverse the common conditions of the hunt—it is unlikely that it would be the patriarch fox which would chance to become the one caught.

One acme of complexity would be the situation in which every existing text represents a different version, each derived from a text which at some earlier time had taken readings from every other version: under these circumstances any reading might be authorial, and analysis is of no textual value. Complexity does not have to proceed that far, however, before the analyst feels inclined to throw in the towel. G. Blakemore Evans, when confronted by two printed and seven manuscript texts of *MacFlecknoe*, concluded that the construction of "some kind of genealogical tree" was "impossible" and that "the establishment of any order of descent or even any temporal priority" was "quite impossible."[12] George Kane, after a full and detailed study of the seventeen extant manuscripts of the A version of *Piers Plowman*, reached the conclusion that "recension is not a practicable method for the editor of the A manuscripts. Nor is the creation of a hierarchy, with some one copy elevated to a

[12]"The Text of Dryden's *MacFlecknoe*," *HLB*, 7 (1953), 44–45.

rôle of authority: while some of these manuscripts are certainly more corrupt than others, all are corrupt to an indeterminate but evidently considerable extent." Such eminent scholars as J. B. Bessinger, J. A. W. Bennett, and John Lawlor have reviewed Kane's methods and evidence, and they have commended him for reaching this conclusion.[13] Sometimes intractable evidence can be impressed into the shape of a logically possible stemma which may (or may not) be correct, but which is not helpful in establishing the text because its complexity allows almost any given reading to be authorial.[14] Analysis can be practiced for its own sake, to create a stemma which comes as close as may be to indicating the order of transmission of a text. To be useful textually, however, analysis must serve some purpose in the establishment of the text: to eliminate witnesses which are purely derivative, to indicate which text (or texts) are nearest to the archetype, to be helpful in indicating which of the variant readings in several texts is most likely (by virtue of its place in the transmission) to be authorial.

Fourth—and last among these fundamental difficulties in analysis—there is the more subtle danger of avoiding the other difficulties by adopting assumptions which place the hard problems in forbidden territory. The greatest practitioners of the art of analysis follow this system openly and explicitly. One of the two assumptions on which Paul Maas proceeded in his standard book is "that no scribe has combined several exemplars (*contaminatio*)." Antonín Hrubý excluded all mixed gene-

---

[13]*Piers Plowman: The A Version* (London, 1960), p. 115. Bessinger, *JEGP*, 60 (1961), 571–576; Bennett, *RES*, NS 14 (1963), 68–71; Lawlor, *MLR*, 56 (1961), 243–245. "What is deceiving in the application of genetic recension, as this process was developed by Lachmann in the first half of the nineteenth century, is the appearance of exactitude in mere rigidity, with the improper extension of subjectivity to the construction of genealogical patterns and the treatment of textual cruces; yet of course editing must begin and end with judgments" (Bessinger, p. 573).

[14]The simplest final textual diagram which Dearing can offer for the four Gospels (*Manual*, pp. 86–102) has to include conflation and lost intermediaries with the result that it will not definitely resolve a great part of—or any?—particular textual problems that arise.

alogies from his consideration and assumed that all extant manuscripts of a given work are derived by transcription from a
single original, that the archetype could have no recognizable
errors, and that there could be no conflation or contamination.[15] Both of them explicitly recognized that their assumptions
do not correspond to the facts as we often find them. Maas
adopted his assumption because, without it, the process of
eliminating worthless witnesses "is greatly hindered, if not made
impossible"; "where contamination exists the science of stemmatics in the strict sense breaks down," for "no specific has yet
been discovered against contamination." Hrubý sought to "eliminate, at the outset, extreme logical and technical complications"; yet, concerning his assumptions, he knew that "none of
them is necessarily true, and every critic knows that especially
the last one [about contamination] has very little chance to
correspond to the reality; their only function thus is to permit
us to create a scale of hypothetical norms."[16] These assumptions
severely limit the area in which analysis can operate, and it is
only the most experienced and rigorous mind that will be constantly careful not to invade the areas which have, by assumption, been proscribed. In fact, it may be felt in practice that
there is so little room left that the assumptions keep one
crowded into a corner. Or, to utter the objection from another
position, there seems to be little merit in truths of analysis so
fragile that they fall to pieces when applied to ordinary problems. Those of us who are less careful (or more ambitious) may
forget the limits which the assumptions impose and proceed
gaily to solve whatever problems come to hand, while some of
us may even contrive assumptions so imaginative that they will
spirit us across impassable frontiers.

Of course there are many other assumptions or rules of
thumb which may lead the unwary analyst astray. One is the
notion that the reading which is repeated in the largest number

[15]Maas, p. 3; Hrubý, "Quantitative Solution," pp. 155, 157.
[16]Maas, pp. 7, 48, 49; Hrubý, p. 157.

of witnesses is the right one; of course those numerous witnesses may all derive from one single source—and that source a corrupt one—while two or three others may be independent confirmations of the authorial reading. Another is the belief that the oldest version is the most nearly authorial; there are many examples where a much later manuscript preserves a better text from a lost original that was much nearer what the author wrote. A third is the idea that the most "correct" witness is the best one; but the "correctness" may be the work of later editors or revisers, and the integrity of an unadulterated text is of much greater value to the textual scholar.[17]

V

I commenced this chapter with an account of what, ideally, textual analysis can do. I reviewed its role within the whole enterprise of textual criticism, concluding that for ancient writings it has been central and primary but for literary works since the medieval period it is an important but secondary procedure. With this background, I summarized the basic hypothesis and the conclusions possible from analysis, outlined three major forms of analysis, and reviewed the major objections that are made to each of these forms. Finally, I outlined four major limitations to the theory and practice of analysis. It is probable that I have circumscribed textual analysis to a degree greater than most writers on the subject—who tend to speak as advocates—usually do. I do not give this emphasis accidentally, and at least I can say that it reflects my own reading and experience in this line of work. Analysis is that branch of textual criticism which—more than any other, it seems to me—generates the noble impulse to set forth Great Truths. With a smattering of mathematical logic and a touch of calculus, with a comfortable

[17]For the sake of simplicity, I will cite passages from works of a single writer, A. E. Housman, for discussions and examples of all three of these erroneous ideas. See his *Selected Prose*, pp. 58, 87–88, 88.

recollection of early success in making proofs for geometry and in solving problems in algebra, we analysts often feel impelled to emit a memorable truth about the relationships of texts. A. E. Housman put us all in our places when he uttered his own memorable truth saying that the textual analyst "engaged upon his business is not at all like Newton investigating the motions of the planets: he is much more like a dog hunting for fleas."[18]

Under these circumstances, it seems prudent for me to limit an attempt to define the effective role of textual analysis in two ways; first, to the study of problems in English and American literature since the medieval period, and second, to the kinds of problems on which analysis has in fact shown itself capable of providing useful assistance.

A form of analysis which is usually very simple yields essential results in determining the order and relationship among the various early editions of (for example) nineteenth-century novels. The Centenary Hawthorne provides an excellent analysis of the editions of each novel treated. From collation and simple analysis of *The Blithedale Romance*, for instance, it is revealed that the plates for the first American edition of 1852 served for more than a dozen later impressions, some of them called new editions; a new typesetting was based on the 1852 plates for the Little Classics Edition of 1876, and many further "editions" were manufactured from these plates with occasional alterations; another new typesetting was based on a late state of the Little Classics text and issued as the Riverside Edition in 1883, the plates for which in turn served for other "editions"; the Autograph Edition of 1900 was set from a late state of the 1883 plates; and so forth. The first English edition, of 1852, was set from uncorrected proof sheets of the American edition of 1852, and the second English edition, of 1854, was set from its predecessor. Thus the textual analyst concludes that, of the printed editions, the 1852 American edition is the primary text,

[18]"The Application of Thought to Textual Criticism," in *Selected Prose*, p. 132.

with two straight lines of successive derivation from it: the 1876, 1883, and 1900 in one line; and the English 1852 and 1854 in the other. It remains to examine the variations from edition to edition and among the states of each set of plates to discover (if possible) whether any of the changes are authoritative; to simplify the careful answer supplied in the Centenary Hawthorne, there is little reason to think that any of the changes came from the author, and each new setting introduced further corruptions to the text. Still, there are manuscripts to be reckoned with: a holograph manuscript is extant, which proves (upon analysis) to be the printer's copy from which the earliest edition was set; one leaf only is extant of the manuscript in an earlier stage. These conclusions about *The Blithedale Romance* may not seem earthshaking, but they are absolutely essential. It is only on the basis of such analysis of the relationship of all the existing witnesses that scholars can proceed soundly with the detailed work of editing the novel. The basic task of analysis, in dealing with works since the medieval period, is to eliminate derivative versions and thereby identify the version which comes nearest to conveying the author's intentions. Next most fundamental is the task of analyzing all of the variants with a view toward determining, as nearly as may be, which are authoritative and therefore deserve inclusion in at least some version of the text.

A slightly more complex example of analysis that may be useful is the arrangement of the early editions of Dryden's *State of Innocence*. From analysis, it appears that the Second Quarto (Q2) was set from Q1, Q3 from Q2, and Q4 from Q3; but Q5 was set from Q3, and Q6, Q7, Q8, and Q9 from their immediate predecessors; F1 was set from Q7. To this information must be added, of course, any facts or inferences about which editions include authorial changes.[19]

[19]Marian H. Hamilton, "The Early Editions of Dryden's *State of Innocence*," *SB*, 5 (1952–53), 163–166.

Sometimes it is possible to deduce the text of a missing original by analysis. In 1677 Dryden wrote his important critical notes called "Heads of an Answer to Rymer" on the blank leaves of a copy of Rymer's *Tragedies of the Last Age,* but the book was destroyed by fire in 1786 or 1787. From an analysis of the two extant transcripts (one as preface to Tonson's 1711 edition of Beaumont and Fletcher, the other as appendix to Johnson's life of Dryden), George Watson was able to conclude that the order of Tonson's was probably correct and to use Johnson's text to correct some misreadings in the other.[20]

Sometimes it is possible to show for the first time, by analysis, that an undated manuscript is to be preferred to the first printed text; L. A. Beaurline has made a pretty demonstration of this possibility in connection with his work on Suckling.[21]

It is often difficult to determine the order of two witnesses. When they are printed from the same type—as was the case with the two issues of Upton Sinclair's *The Jungle,* 1906—the decision can usually be made by analyzing type wear and damage.[22] In the case of new settings of type, it is sometimes difficult to determine which is printed from the other; Arthur Friedman solved the problem of the two 1765 editions of *Essays by Mr. Goldsmith*—and made it possible to ignore the readings of 1765B—by comparing them with the periodical text being reprinted.[23] The solution to the priority between two witnesses is not always easy, however, and even so experienced a scholar as J. Milton French was reluctant to decide which of two Vlacq editions of Milton's "Second Defence" was set from the other.[24]

In a complex problem of analysis involving authorial revi-

[20]"Dryden's First Answer to Rymer," *RES,* NS 14 (1963), 17–23.

[21]"Suckling's *A Session of the Poets,*" *SB,* 16 (1963), 43–60.

[22]Jacob Blanck, "Bibliographical Jungle," *Antiquarian Bookman,* 6 (1950), 579–580, 1419–1420.

[23]"The First Edition of *Essays by Mr. Goldsmith,* 1765," *SB,* 5 (1952–53), 190–193.

[24]"An Unrecorded Edition of Milton's 'Defensio Secunda' (1654)," *PBSA,* 49 (1955), 262–268.

sion, editorial revision, and several manuscript and printed texts, David M. Vieth has supplied a model solution in the case of Rochester's "To a Lady in a Letter." He has been able to identify three versions of the poem with remarkable clarity; but this degree of success is more than could ordinarily be expected.[25]

The recovery of important versions of a text is often crucial to making an analysis which will have useful conclusions. One scholar, in trying to distinguish between errors and Joyce's intentions in *Finnegans Wake,* made a list of passages which had been omitted from *Finnegans Wake* (in error, he generally assumed) despite their appearance in *Work in Progress.* Another scholar analyzed the manuscripts which are intermediate between the two printed versions and noted that it was Joyce himself who had deleted six of the passages which had earlier been thought of as omitted in error. Without the availability of the intermediate manuscripts for analysis, it was logical to reach a different conclusion.[26] John T. Shawcross has noted that a totally erroneous stemma would probably be constructed for *Comus* if one failed to consult the Trinity College manuscript.[27]

Finally, the usefulness of textual analysis depends on availing oneself of bibliographical evidence which is relevant. T. M. Parrott, in editing Chapman's *The Conspiracy of Byron,* usually retained the readings of the 1608 edition as the original and uncorrupted text, taking occasional readings from the 1625 edition, which he thought generally filled with errors and alterations by the proof corrector. Actually, as John Butler Gabel has shown, the 1608 edition has corrected and uncorrected formes, the 1625 was set from uncorrected formes, and the 1608

[25]"A Textual Paradox: Rochester's 'To a Lady in a Letter'," *PBSA*, 54 (1960), 147–162, and "An Unsuspected Cancel in Tonson's 1691 'Rochester'," *PBSA*, 55 (1961), 130–133.

[26]The earlier work was by Fred H. Higginson, "Notes on the Text of *Finnegans Wake*," *JEGP*, 55 (1956), 451–456; the latter work is by Clive Hart, "Notes on the Text of *Finnegans Wake*," *JEGP*, 59 (1960), 229–239.

[27]"Certain Relationships of the Manuscripts of *Comus*," *PBSA*, 54 (1960), 38–56.

129

edition that Parrott used consisted of corrected formes. Thus Parrott's choices were just the opposite of what he thought: what he considered original and uncorrupted was actually corrected, and what he considered corrected was actually the original.[28]

Textual analysis of moderately elaborate or fairly complex data is made possible by a knowledge of principles and by experience, but it is not made simple. It is commonly a difficult task. The expert cannot do what some people expect: glance at collation notes and announce the order of the witnesses. The advantage he does enjoy is in knowing ways in which to proceed, not being at an absolute loss, and knowing what conclusion is defensible from the degree to which it has been possible to verify an hypothesis. He should be able to establish the relationships among a group of witnesses when all (or almost all) of the witnesses are available for analysis and they have not been conflated or subjected to authorial revision. After establishing a set of relationships, he ought in most (but not all) cases to be reasonably confident as to which variant readings are errors of transmission. Through experience, the expert can more easily spot the work of the professional copyist, and suspect editorial manipulation or authorial revision, and distinguish errors of transmission, and solve particular problems.

Beyond these kinds of problems he can sometimes offer useful help, because of the possession of crucial bits of information or of a favorable situation or of luck. The present state of the principles of textual analysis is far from secure enough, however, to assure solutions to the manifold difficulties which befall the transmission of texts.

[28]"Some Notable Errors in Parrott's Edition of Chapman's Byron Plays," *PBSA*, 58 (1964), 465–468.

CHAPTER V

The Treatment of Accidentals

It is a truth universally acknowledged that the greatest human effort is spent on the least important details.

Textual students appear not to have risen above this state of nature. Indeed, the recorded life of our mystery testifies to our support of providence in sharing a special concern for mites, motes, and mustard seed. As early as the fifth century, St. Jerome set our standards: when a woman asked him for advice on raising her young daughter, the textual scholar within him suggested that her treasures be manuscripts of the Holy Scriptures and that the daughter concern herself with the correctness and the punctuation of the text.[1]

As we are fond of reminding ourselves, the lowly comma is capable of moving mountains of meaning. William Butler Yeats's "The Statues," for example, includes one crucial line which has been given four different forms and four different meanings by the successive withdrawal and shifting of commas. "We Irish," the poem says, were "thrown upon this filthy modern tide,"

And by its formless, spawning, fury wrecked . . . .

Or so the line appeared in the first printing in *The London Mercury* of March 1939. In the next month, however (in *The Nation* for April 15, 1939), one comma is eliminated and the meaning changed:

[1]Bruce Metzger, *The Text of the New Testament* (New York, 1964), p. 4 n.

131

And by its formless, spawning fury wrecked . . . .

In *Last Poems* (Dublin, 1939) the shifting of the remaining comma converts parts of speech:

And by its formless spawning, fury wrecked . . . .

Then in *Last Poems* (London and New York, 1940) the comma is eliminated and the reader is left greater latitude in the sense he can make of the line:

And by its formless spawning fury wrecked . . . .

It has not yet been established what the "right" reading is— Yeats had died two months before the poem first appeared—but the changes in meaning are evident.[2] "The Folly of Being Comforted" offers another Yeats example in which a change in punctuation alters the sense more clearly. In the 1903 edition, the greying hair of a woman caused this response:

> Time can but make her beauty over again
> Because of that great nobleness of hers;
> The fire that stirs about her, when she stirs
> Burns but more clearly.

In 1913, however, the concept is altered by the shift of a semi-colon:

> Time can but make her beauty over again;
> Because of that great nobleness of hers
> The fire that stirs about her, when she stirs
> Burns but more clearly.[3]

[2]For fuller details about this example, see Marion Witt, "Yeats: 1865–1965," *PMLA*, 80 (1965), 312.

[3]There were several other changes in the punctuation of these lines. For an interesting brief account, see Russell K. Alspach, "Some Textual Problems in Yeats," *SB*, 9 (1957), 64–65.

Parody can make any possibility absurd: by taking the province of the editor to include punctuation and the conversion of one word to another word with a similar sound, John Frederick Nims has rendered the first two lines of Joyce Kilmer's "Trees" as follows:

> *I* think? That I shall never, see!
> Up, owe'em love. Leah's a tree.[4]

I am afraid that some emendations which have been seriously proposed are not much less absurd.

It is certainly true—as everyone old enough to know the difference between restrictive and nonrestrictive clauses is aware —that a change in punctuation can change the meaning. In the last half century, one of the main preoccupations of textual scholars has been with punctuation, along with spelling, capitalization, and italicization—the features of the formal presentation of a text which have come to be known as the "accidentals" of the text, as opposed to the "substantives" or verbal readings that directly communicate the essence of the author's meaning. The deep concern for accidentals is plainly evident, for example, in work on English plays of the latter sixteenth and early seventeenth centuries, and in editions of American fiction of the nineteenth century. In order to center attention on one area, I will limit my references in the remainder of this introductory section to scholarly reflections which mainly treat Shakespeare and his contemporaries.

It is no longer possible to take the lofty view that Samuel Johnson did in his "Preface to Shakespeare": "In restoring the author's works to their integrity," he wrote, "I have considered the punctuation as wholly in my power; for what could be their care of colons and commas, who corrupted words and sentences?

---

[4]"The Greatest English Lyric?—A New Reading of Joe E. Skilmer's 'Therese'," *SB*, 20 (1967), 1–14. Nims also parodies close reading, and (as a parody of textual criticism) he "reconstructs" Shakespeare's Sonnet 129 from fragments ("The expense of spirits is a crying shame!").

Whatever could be done by adjusting points, is, therefore, silently performed, in some plays with much diligence, in others with less."[5]

Nowadays it seems to be thought by some people that the good deed of Shakespeare's punctuation will shine through the naughty work of the compositors and bring us some kind of aesthetic light. As there is almost no direct evidence concerning Shakespeare's spelling, punctuation, and the like in his manuscripts that lay behind the printed plays (at how many removes?), speculation has reached a peak of sophistication in supplying answers to the question of what Shakespeare's manuscript was like. In reading passages on this subject, I have sometimes had the unsettling feeling, from the sense of confidence with which the writer proceeded, that he was describing an extant manuscript.

The desire to discover the form of spelling and punctuation and capitalization in Shakespeare's own manuscript derives, I imagine, from the altogether laudable ambition to know the intentions of the writer to the maximum extent that this is possible, and to know it in the smallest details. "Authority resides in some part in the accidentals of a text as well as in its substantives," writes Fredson Bowers, "and it is even possible that the most authoritative edition in respect to the accidentals may not be the same as the most authoritative edition in respect to the substantives."[6]

Another motive—the one most frequently cited, in fact—can be described as the effort to achieve, through these details, some sense of the individuality of the author and the flavor of the period. "So long as there is any chance," says W. W. Greg, "of an edition preserving some trace, however faint, of the author's individuality, the critic will wish to follow it: and

[5] *The Works of Samuel Johnson, LL.D.* (Oxford, 1825), V, 148–149.

[6] "Established Texts and Definitive Editions," *PQ*, 41 (1962), 4. Accidentals "may have a significant authority" if "the print's accidentals have been transmitted faithfully from the author's original" (p. 2).

134

even when there is none, he will still prefer an orthography that has a period resemblance with the author's. . . ." Greg applies the same argument to the retention of the other accidentals. "Just as the language of an Elizabethan author is better represented by his own spelling than by ours," he writes, "so the flow of his thought is often more easily indicated by the loosely rhetorical punctuation of his own day than by our more logical system."[7] Literary students ought to have—or so the argument runs—an interest in the flavor of the period as communicated by the accidentals of printing. "I feel that for a student of literature," writes Arthur Brown, "any spelling from a text of this period [that of Shakespeare], whether it be authorial or compositorial, should have an intrinsic interest of its own."[8]

This view that the accidentals convey the right flavor is very popular, but not universally accepted. C. J. Sisson observed that "with regard to spelling, we have occasionally met with what seems to me to be a somewhat sentimental desire to represent the text of Shakespeare in its original spelling. An 'Old Spelling' Shakespeare suggests a Shakespeare in Elizabethan costume, as it were, bringing us nearer to intimacy with text and mind alike. This, of course, has its attractions, as have also half-timbered houses or thatched cottages. But we should not delude ourselves with the belief that we should have a replica of Shakespeare's spelling."[9] Some people feel that the flavor of early spelling is real but irrelevant. "The 'Elizabethan flavour' of an old-spelling text is a modern phenomenon," writes John Russell Brown, "(as the term 'old spelling' is itself), and its dissemination can do no service to the original authors or their work."[10]

[7]*The Editorial Problem in Shakespeare*, 3rd ed. (Oxford, 1954), pp. li–lii.

[8]"The Rationale of Old-Spelling Editions of the Plays of Shakespeare and His Contemporaries: A Rejoinder," *SB*, 13 (1960), 74–75.

[9]*New Readings in Shakespeare* (Cambridge, Eng., 1956), I, 35–36.

[10]"The Rationale of Old-Spelling Editions of the Plays of Shakespeare and His Contemporaries," *SB*, 13 (1960), 61.

However, the main argument against the retention of earlier accidentals seems to turn on the difficulties that they create for general readers (undergraduates mostly, I assume). "The most powerful argument for modernization, so far as I am able to see," writes S. Schoenbaum, "stems from concern for the un-specialized reader's convenience. This reader has trouble enough (so the argument runs) coping with the plays themselves, with-out the added burden—or should I say *burthen*—of old spelling. Also, by imparting a quaint look to the text, such spelling widens the gap between the modern reader and the literature of an earlier age." A good many scholars feel that this argu-ment is fallacious. Schoenbaum himself maintains that "there is much to be said in behalf of old-spelling texts, even in the undergraduate classroom. Surely the illusion of quaintness fades very quickly as the reader settles down to the material at hand. Surely, too, we underestimate the calibre of the present generation of undergraduates when we assume that old-spelling texts will be a trauma for them. Most of these students will be upperclassmen and English majors." He observes that "in other courses they will be asked to read Chaucer and Spenser in the original. They will tackle willingly, and even with eagerness, difficult modern works like *The Waste Land, Ulysses,* or *The Sound and the Fury.* Why not old spelling?"[11] G. Blake-more Evans deplores the attempt, by means of modernization of accidentals, "to appeal to that *ignis fatuus,* the so-called com-mon reader, who, in fact, for a publication of this kind [minor Restoration poetry], does not exist."[12]

One matter on which most scholars with a special interest in texts are agreed is that there are serious difficulties for the editor whether he decides to modernize or to prepare an old-spelling text. Either plan involves compromise, ambiguity, and the risk of misleading considerable groups of readers. John

[11]"Editing English Dramatic Texts," in *Editing Sixteenth Century Texts,* ed. R. J. Schoeck (Toronto, 1966), pp. 22, 23.

[12]Review of *Poems on Affairs of State,* vol. I, in *JEGP,* 63 (1964), 789.

Russell Brown and Arthur Brown write from different textual points of view, but they both set forth, in the two essays which I have cited above, these difficulties with examples and details, no matter which plan one follows. Arthur Brown concludes that "any form of reproduction of a sixteenth or seventeenth century play, whether it be by photography, by type facsimile, or by an edition in old or modernized spelling, must involve some degree of compromise" (p. 69); John Russell Brown concludes that "a perversion of Elizabethan English is inevitable in both old-spelling and modern-spelling texts" (p. 61). Many other scholars have spoken, sometimes melodramatically, of the difficulties involved in making a clear, consistent, and reliable text of either sort. If one extends either of these two methods far enough, problems of some degree of importance inevitably arise. Scholars feel free to set the degree of compromise tolerable in accordance with their own position; likewise they can trumpet the egregious faults which naturally arise from the simple act of following the other method. Before being persuaded in favor of one method on the strength of several choice examples, it is wise to remember that similar examples can be produced to support the other method.

In the light of these alternatives, it is not surprising to discover that some scholars conclude in favor of modernization, and some in favor of old-spelling. "There will always be, one hopes," writes R. C. Bald, "editions in modern spelling of the major English authors since Spenser." He concludes that "if ever the day comes when no modernized editions of Shakespeare and Donne and Milton are available to the general reader, our cultural heritage will be in a sad state."[13] In a similar vein, Clifford Leech believes that "a word should be said in favour of modern-spelling editions of Elizabethan and Jacobean plays." He points out that, since students will read Shakespeare in modernized form, it is a disservice to Shakespeare's contemporaries not to offer modernized texts for them

[13]"Editorial Problems—A Preliminary Survey," *SB*, 3 (1950–51), 7–8.

too; otherwise, "we are immediately suggesting that Shakespeare is still 'contemporary' and they are buried in an antique mist. For his sake and for theirs, we need to get this mist out of the way." Secondly, says Leech, modern-spelling editions of plays are essential because "we want our texts to be used in the theatre, and they will not be so used if they are in old spelling."[14]

On the other hand, the most eminent textual scholars of our time have settled firmly against modernization, at least wherever possible. W. W. Greg felt that "the former practice of modernizing the spelling of English works is no longer popular with editors, since spelling is now recognized as an essential characteristic of an author, or at least of his time and locality."[15] Or, on another occasion, Greg asserted that "whatever practice may be thought desirable in a popular or reading edition, in a critical—that is, a critics'—edition modern opinion is unanimously in favour of preserving the spelling and punctuation of the original authority, at least so far as they are not actually misleading."[16]

Fredson Bowers holds the same general views. "By its nature," he writes, "no modernized text of an Elizabethan play can be trustworthy enough to satisfy the requirements of a serious critic"; or, to put it the other way round, "such an edition must be in old spelling."[17] To move to the nineteenth century for a moment, Bowers holds that "the first problem that faces any editor of a text from the nineteenth century, or earlier, is whether to modernize. For nineteenth-century American books there is only one answer: no gain results from modernizing, and much is lost that is characteristic of the author. . . . Indeed, one may flatly assert that any text that is modernized can never

[14]"A Note from a General Editor," in *Editing Sixteenth Century Texts*, p. 25.

[15]"The Rationale of Copy-Text," *SB*, 3 (1950–51), 21.

[16]*The Editorial Problem in Shakespeare*, p. 1.

[17]"Old-Spelling Editions of Dramatic Texts," in *Studies in Honor of T. W. Baldwin*, ed. D. C. Allen (Urbana, 1958), pp. 13, 12.

pretend to be scholarly, no matter at what audience it is aimed."[18] As he sees the world of the textual scholar, "at present," he says, "opinion seems to be hardening that early texts for popular general reading had better be modernized, despite the inevitable inconsistencies that result, whereas editions of literary works intended for scholarly use had better remain in old-spelling. . . . At least as early as the beginning of the nineteenth century, and sometimes before, the advantages of modernization largely disappear and its disadvantages multiply even for popular texts."[19]

When confronted by contraries, the race of politicians among men will commonly strive to achieve a settlement through compromise. If there is much to be said on both sides, surely it is wise policy to unite as much as possible from each. As one might expect, this principle has been applied to textual studies as well as to virtually every other area of human inquiry; the result in the topic under discussion is called "partial modernization." The results have, so far, not been notably successful in pleasing scholars of either persuasion. The Yale edition of the works of Samuel Johnson, for example, retains the spelling and the punctuation found in the copy-text but modernizes the capitalization and the use of italics. This modest venture into compromise has been strongly condemned. F. W. Bateson (who describes himself as "no lover of original spelling editions") vigorously criticized this practice as a "curious textual formula" and an "irrational compromise."[20] Fredson Bowers (who *is* a lover of old-spelling) condemned it with even greater severity, calling it "a half-hearted compromise between a popular reading edition and a trustworthy scholarly text" with the result that "this edition is not thoroughly satisfactory for either

[18]"Some Principles for Scholarly Editions of Nineteenth-Century American Authors," *SB*, 17 (1964), 223.

[19]"Textual Criticism," in *The Aims and Methods of Scholarship in Modern Languages and Literatures*, ed. James Thorpe (New York, 1963), p. 26.

[20]*RES*, NS 17 (1966), 328.

purpose."[21] The reviewer in the *Times Literary Supplement* called the partial modernization a "ludicrous convention" and added, "I have not heard of anyone apart from a Yale editor who was prepared to defend it."[22]

Perhaps scholarly opinion is hardening—as Bowers says it is—about when to modernize and when to retain old spelling. If so, it may now be all the more timely and important to examine any principles which govern accidentals before opinion takes an absolutely rigid position. It seems to me that two principal considerations have heretofore been taken into account. One is the practical matter as to whether the resulting edition will be convenient or inconvenient for readers. The other is the assumption that the recoverable accidentals that may be the author's work will aid in communicating the intentions of the author.

The status of accidentals has, I think, been examined only in a cursory fashion before deciding that only one type of edition alone can merit the name of "scholarly" or a "critic's edition." We all like to have easy rules of thumb, and it would be convenient if we could rightly conclude that scholars and critics require old-spelling texts while other readers are adequately served by modernizations. I cannot help feeling that deeper principles should be consulted before drawing any conclusions. I would like, in the sections that follow, first to review briefly the attitudes that writers have in fact taken toward the accidentals of their own work. It is, after all, the intention of the writer that counts for most in textual studies. Secondly, I will consider the degree to which the writer's accidentals have or have not been respected in the transmission of texts and the likelihood of recovering them. I hope that an exploration of these two topics will provide a basis for reaching sound conclusions about the treatment of accidentals.

[21]*MP*, 61 (1963–64), 300.
[22]May 22, 1969, p. 547; June 19, 1969, p. 662.

II

A good many writers have taken occasion to complain, sometimes bitterly, about inaccuracies in the published form of their works. For example, Dryden tells his publisher, Jacob Tonson, that "the Printer is a beast, and understands nothing I can say to him of correcting the press." Or, later, that "you cannot take too great care of the printing this Edition, exactly after my Amendments: for a fault of that nature will disoblige me Eternally." Dryden had other threatening remarks at his disposal: "I vow to God, if Everingham takes not care of this Impression, He shall never print any thing of mine heerafter."[23] Likewise, John Evelyn felt that the common calamity of those who had their work printed was that they were "at the mercy of Sotts & Drunkards; that can neither print Sense nor English, nor indeede any other language, thô it lie never so plainely before them."[24] It is a rare writer whose tolerance extends to the committer of errors in his book.[25]

It does not necessarily follow, however, that complaints against printers signify a concern about accidentals. Ben Jonson is, with some justice, considered the most meticulous of our early writers when it comes to correctness of text, and he appears to have the name for being much concerned with accidentals. The main evidence is the care that he took in preparing the text for the 1616 Folio, and *Sejanus* and *Cynthia's Revels*

---

[23]*The Letters of John Dryden,* ed. Charles E. Ward (Durham, 1942), pp. 97, 98, 99.

[24]For the full letter, see the Earl of Crawford and Balcarres, "Gabriel Naudé and John Evelyn: With Some Notes on the Mazarinades." *The Library,* 4th Ser., 12 (1931–32), 392.

[25]The only example I know is Damas van Blyenburg, who collected a large number of misprints in his book, *Cento Ethicus* (1599), and observed (in Latin) that "it makes no sense—which even a child might see, or somebody unskilled in poetry (perhaps the proofreader was such a person). But typographical compositors should be pardoned for two reasons: first, because they may be ignorant; secondly, because it is hard for them to follow manuscripts written in hasty, cursive fashion. I myself have had such difficulty; but I manage to get the sense of a passage from the context...." R. H. Bowers, "Blyenburg Corrects His Book," *PBSA,* 55 (1961), 382–383.

may serve as examples. It is true that he revised some minutiae of spelling and punctuation, often into a peculiar system of his own devising. But it is also true that he was, at the same time, making major corrections in substantives. When it came to proofreading, he was careful with his more important corrections; but he did not insist that the printer comply with what he had called for in abbreviations and metrical punctuation, for example.[26] Jonson's most celebrated revision is probably *Every Man in His Humour;* a recent study of that revision makes it plain, however, that Jonson's main concern was for the structure of the play—particularly to integrate the "humours" business into the action by reshaping the play—and not much for the accidentals.[27]

One other seventeenth-century writer who has been thought to have had grave concern for accidentals—spelling, in particular—is Milton. John T. Shawcross's studies have now for the first time put these matters into perspective. "We see," he concludes, "that Milton cared less about spelling than has previously been thought. He did not write certain words or groups of words in any rigid way, and even those which seem to be consistent do not give evidence of a grand scheme of improved spelling." Milton did not make exacting demands on scribes and compositors; at least, he "was not particularly concerned with obtaining from them texts which were rigorous in mechanics."[28]

When scholars begin to examine closely the evidence that is available about the interest of seventeenth-century writers in accidentals, they often come to such a conclusion as Roger Sharrock did about Bunyan: "There is no evidence that he was interested in the exact preservation of the minutiae of his original copy; nor does it appear that he felt strongly about the attempts of editors and printing-house correctors to improve

[26]*Ben Jonson,* ed. C. H. Herford and Percy Simpson, IV (Oxford, 1932), 335–340, 6–17.

[27]J. A. Bryant, Jr., "Johnson's Revision of *Every Man in His Humor,*" *SP,* 59 (1962), 641–650.

[28]"What We Can Learn from Milton's Spelling," *HLQ,* 26 (1963), 361, 352.

on his provincial English and loose grammar."[29] Some scholars who are widely acquainted with authorial practice in the seventeenth century can generalize more broadly, and they do so along similar lines. Bowers observes that compositors commonly superimposed their own characteristics on the accidents of the copy; "the usual experience of textual critics suggests that in the sixteenth and seventeenth centuries, at least, many an author accepted with indifference the accidents of a print and would make slight effort to improve them except in cases of egregious error."[30] Similarly, John Russell Brown notes that authors who, like Jonson, took special care with spelling "were exceptional in Elizabethan and Jacobean times and most authors and readers (each of whom always spelt to please himself) must have accepted the irregular spelling of their printed books with something close to the unthinking ease with which we accept modern, regular spelling."[31]

In the eighteenth century, there is a little more direct evidence from writers themselves about their attitude toward accidentals. Thomas Gray, for example—fastidious Thomas Gray —had very little interest in punctuation. When the Glasgow edition of his poems was about to be printed by the Foulis Press in 1768, Gray wrote as follows about the printing: "Please to observe, that I am entirely unversed in the doctrine of *stops,* whoever therefore shall deign to correct them, will do me a friendly office: I wish I stood in need of no other correction."[32]

[29]*Grace Abounding to the Chief of Sinners,* ed. Sharrock (Oxford, 1962), p. xxxviii.

[30]"Established Texts and Definitive Editions," p. 13.

[31]"The Rationale of Old-Spelling Editions," p. 60. Further generalizations along the same line are made in Percy Simpson's *Proof-Reading in the Sixteenth, Seventeenth, and Eighteenth Centuries* (London, 1935), which still has value despite its age and despite the modifications that more recent work has indicated. Simpson reviews a large quantity of relevant authorial and printing practice. Virtually all of his examples of corrections by authors to proof concern substantives; in his view, modern students who champion "the spelling of the poets," if they had looked into it, "would have learnt that, with rare exceptions, they were championing the spelling of the printers" (p. 52).

[32]Undated MS letter, to Mr. Beattie in Aberdeen, now in the Robert H. Taylor Collection. These sentences were quoted in "Letters of English Authors: From the Collection of Robert H. Taylor," *PULC,* 21 (1960), 212–213.

(And the sentence is itself splendid testimony to his unversed condition.)

Henry Fielding's younger sister, Sarah, made several remarks which reveal her attitude toward these details. "I am very apt when I write," she observed, "to be too careless about great and small Letters and Stops, but I suppose that will naturally be set right in the printing." Or, these comments to an unnamed man when she asked him to see a book of hers through the press: "I beg that you will be so very kind to cast an eye on the printing of it if your Health will permit without injury and pray be not scrupulous to alter any Expressions you deslike, but if this will do you any hurt and you are overloaded with other business I will trust it to your Nephew, and the proof sheets not being sent about will prevent the stoppage of the printing if it is necessary."[33]

The eighteenth-century record may be balanced, however, by citing the arrangements undertaken by Matthew Prior for the publication of his *Poems on Several Occasions* (1718). He engaged two "colon and comma men" to help him prepare copy for the printer and to assist with proofreading. They conferred on such matters as the spelling of the word "Compliment"; Prior said he was "plagued with commas, semicolons, italic and capital"; and this "wretched work" consumed at least six months of time. I mention this book as the work of an author interested in accidentals; but I have to add the melancholy fact that all of the volumes except those in the presentation size turned out to be less perfect than he had intended them to be and than he had assumed that they were.[34]

In the nineteenth century, there is a great deal more direct evidence from writers about their attitude toward the acci-

[33]Both quotations are from MS letters in the Robert H. Taylor Collection. The first, dated Dec. 14, 1758, is printed in "Letters of English Authors," p. 212; the second is dated only Dec. 14, from Bath to an unnamed correspondent.

[34]For full details, see H. Bunker Wright, "Ideal Copy and Authoritative Text: The Problem of Prior's *Poems on Several Occasions* (1718)," *MP*, 49 (1952), 234–241.

dentals of their own work. Wordsworth is a prime example. He seems to have dictated a good deal of his poetry, and the manuscript versions tend to be heavy with multipurpose dashes. He did not show much interest in putting the accidentals into any order himself. When the manuscript for the second edition of *Lyrical Ballads* was being made ready for printing, he sent part of it to Humphry Davy—a man whom he had never met, a chemist, a lover of poetry recommended by Coleridge—and asked Davy to correct the punctuation and send the manuscript directly on to the printer: "So I venture to address you," wrote Wordsworth, "though I have not the happiness of being personally known to you. You would greatly oblige me by looking over the enclosed poems and correcting any thing you find amiss in the punctuation a business at which I am ashamed to say I am no adept. . . . You will be so good as to put the enclosed Poems into Mr Bigges hands as soon as you have looked them over in order that the printing may commence immediately."[35] (It seems usual for writers to demonstrate their inability to punctuate by the manner in which they write their pleas for assistance in punctuation. Sometimes the resulting plea seems to verge on parody of a plea.)

Byron repeatedly called for help with the punctuation of his poems. "Do you know any body," he writes to John Murray, "who can *stop*—I mean *point*—commas, and so forth? for I am, I hear, a sad hand at your punctuation." He cheerfully accepted the punctuation inserted by others. "Mr. Hodgson has looked over and *stopped,* or rather *pointed,* this revise, which must be the one to print from." Or, later he writes to Murray, "Correct the *punctuation* of this by Mr. G[ifford]'s proof." Or, as a general exhortation to Murray, "Do attend to the punctuation: I can't, for I don't know a comma—at least where to place one."[36]

[35] *The Letters of William and Dorothy Wordsworth,* ed. Ernest de Selincourt, 2d ed. rev. by Chester L. Shaver (Oxford, 1967), pp. 289–290.

[36] *Works: Letters and Journals,* ed. R. E. Prothero (London, 1898–99), II, 252; II, 283; III, 3; II, 284. I am indebted to Leslie A. Marchand and to Thomas L. Ashton for calling my attention to these passages.

Shelley also had little concern for accidentals. Scholars reach such conclusions as these about him: "It appears that the poet purposely left the burden of such matters to Mary as copyist, to the printer, or to the proofreader. The punctuation, if present, is frequently careless." Aside from the use of the question mark, at line endings Shelley "was quite likely to omit any pointing, or to indulge his favorite substitute, the dash, which he used in place of normally expected punctuation."[37] Or, as another scholar sums it up, "Like Keats, Clare and other poets of his day, Shelley expected to have his accidentals regulated for him by somebody else, the printer if no other."[38]

Many authors have been content to leave the handling of the accidentals (and many other things as well) to their publishers. James Fenimore Cooper asked John Murray, his English publisher, to improve his text of *The Pioneers*; Cooper went so far as to say that "if you find any errors in grammar or awkward sentences you are at liberty to have them altered."[39] Charlotte Brontë (as C. Bell) returned thanks to her publisher, Smith, Elder, and Company, for punctuating *Jane Eyre*: "I have to thank you for punctuating the sheets before sending them to me, as I found the task very puzzling, and, besides, I consider your mode of punctuation a great deal more correct and rational than my own."[40] As for Trollope's *The American Senator*, Bentley (the editor of *Temple Bar*) punctuated it, adding about 4,500 commas and other marks in proportion.[41]

Some writers leave the choice of accidentals to their readers. Perhaps no one ever did so with the explicitness of Timothy

[37]Lawrence John Zillman, ed., *Shelley's "Prometheus Unbound": The Text and the Drafts* (New Haven, 1968), pp. 7–8.

[38]Neville Rogers, "Shelley's Spelling: Theory and Practice," *The Keats-Shelley Memorial Bulletin*, No. 16 (1965), 25.

[39]*The Letters and Journals of James Fenimore Cooper*, ed. James F. Beard, I (Cambridge, Mass., 1960), 86.

[40]*The Brontës: Their Lives, Friendships and Correspondence*, ed. Thomas J. Wise (Oxford, 1932), II, 142.

[41]Robert H. Taylor, "The Manuscript of Trollope's *The American Senator* Collated with the First Edition," *PBSA*, 41 (1947), 123–139.

Dexter. In *A Pickle for the Knowing ones,* he says: "fourder mister printer the Nowing ones complane of my book the first edition had no stops I put in A nuf here and thay may peper and solt it as they plese." There follow thirteen lines of punctuation marks, including three lines of commas, two of semicolons, one of colons, one of periods, four of mixed periods and exclamation points, one of commas, and one of mixed periods and question marks.[42]

A few counter examples are required, however, to present the nineteenth-century situation fairly. Keats sometimes showed an interest in accidentals. When he received an advance copy of *Endymion,* he sent a list of errata to the publisher immediately; half of the twenty-one items were corrections in the punctuation ("place a comma after *dim,*" "dele comma").[43] Tennyson was also particular with his proofs, and once wrote to Moxon, his publisher, saying "I think it would be better to send me every proof twice over—I should like the text to be as correct as possible."[44] Mark Twain's comment to William Dean Howells about *A Connecticut Yankee* is, I think, regarded as a classic (and I suppose comic) remark: "Yesterday Mr. Hall wrote that the printer's proof-reader was improving my punctuation for me, & I telegraphed orders to have him shot without giving him time to pray."[45]

[42]I have used the Boston, 1838, edition, p. 42. This passage is said to derive from the second edition, 1805, which I have not seen; the passage is not in the first edition, Salem, 1802.

[43]*The Letters of John Keats,* ed. Hyder Edward Rollins (Cambridge, Mass., 1958), I, 270–273.

[44]"Letters of English Authors," p. 222.

[45]*Mark Twain—Howells Letters,* ed. Henry Nash Smith and William M. Gibson (Cambridge, Mass., 1960), p. 610. Twain thought punctuating was a special art. In an essay in the *Atlantic Monthly,* 45 (1880), 849–860—identified as Twain's by Charles Neider in *Harper's Magazine* for June 1952, pp. 52–53—he wrote: "Some people were not born to punctuate; these cannot learn the art. They can learn only a rude fashion of it; they cannot attain to its niceties, for these must be *felt*; they cannot be reasoned out. Cast-iron rules will not answer, here, any way; what is one man's comma is another man's colon. One man can't punctuate another man's manuscript any more than one person can make the gestures for another person's speech" (p. 850).

For the twentieth century, a brief review of writers who alleged little interest in accidentals may begin with William Butler Yeats. In 1915, Yeats wrote as follows to Robert Bridges: "I chiefly remember you asked me about my stops and commas. Do what you will. I do not understand stops. I write so completely for the ear that I feel helpless when I have to measure pauses by stops and commas."[46] Bridges was certainly not the only person to whom Yeats gave permission to punctuate for him. In 1932 he wrote to his publisher's editor, T. Mark, "I have never been able to punctuate properly. I do not think I have ever differed from a correction of yours in punctuation. I suggest that in the remaining volumes you do not query your corrections."[47] Mrs. Yeats testified similarly about her husband's punctuation. G. D. P. Allt reported that she spoke to him as follows: Yeats "always said 'I know nothing about punctuation.' He once said to me, 'I never know when I should use a semi-colon or a colon. I don't like colons.' He also disliked a dash, and detested brackets. He did use brackets a good deal in *later* work (himself in MSS.). But punctuation, apart from a comma and a full stop, were, I think, mainly outside influence."[48]

To return to the end of the nineteenth century, Stephen Crane is one writer who had a splendid indifference toward accidentals. He wrote to Ripley Hitchcock of Appleton and

[46]*The Letters of W. B. Yeats*, ed. Allan Wade (London, 1954), p. 598.

[47]Unpublished letter, quoted in Jon Stallworthy, *Between the Lines* (Oxford, 1963), p. 12.

[48]"Yeats and the Revision of His Early Verse," *Hermathena*, 64 (1944), 96–97. Allt added that his own examination of the printed texts and of the manuscripts had led him independently to form a similar conclusion about Yeats's punctuation.

I should add that in 1954 Mrs. Yeats told Russell K. Alspach that "in later years W. B. had become very irate several times with a publisher who had taken it upon himself to change the poet's punctuation. Perhaps Yeats became more careful and more knowing as time went on" (*The Variorum Edition of the Poems of W. B. Yeats*, ed. Peter Allt and Alspach, New York, 1957, p. xv). Marion Witt has expressed the opinion that "Yeats's protestations that he was never able to punctuate properly may be one of those proudly humble statements which he was fond of making to avert or parry criticism" ("Yeats: 1865-1965," *PMLA*, 80, 1965, 312).

148

Company that "the proofs make me ill. Let somebody go over them—if you think best—and watch for bad grammatical form & bad spelling. I am too jaded with Maggie to be able to see it."[49] T. E. Lawrence expressed outright contempt for small details of the printing of his writings. The proofreader raised various questions about inconsistencies and apparent slips in *Revolt in the Desert*. The proofreader writes "Bir Wahei*da*, was Bir Wahei*di*," and Lawrence comments, "Why not? All one place." When the proofreader notes "The Bisaita is also spelt Biseita," Lawrence responds "Good."[50] The greater Lawrence also expressed indifference about the accidentals which give such concern to textual scholars: "What do I care if 'e' is somewhere upside down, or 'g' comes from the wrong fount? I really don't."[51] Winston Churchill thought it important for the accidentals of his writings to be "correct," but he wanted others to make them so. "I am above all things anxious," he wrote to his publisher, in connection with his biography of his father, "that the grammar and punctuation should be strictly correct. In these circumstances I suggest to you that the book should be read for punctuation solely once again before it goes to press. I am incompetent to do this, for I know the book nearly by heart and cannot concentrate my attention by reading." He suggested that an outside reader might make the corrections. When it was done, he wrote that "Mr. Frank Harris has now completed fully his revise of the proofs of my book. He has taken a great deal of trouble over them, and I now feel some confidence in submitting it to the public so far as grammar, construction and punctuation are concerned."[52] As for Sherwood Anderson, Waldo Frank gives a vivid account of his punctuation: "I read *The Untold Lie* and wrote back to Ander-

[49]*Stephen Crane: Letters*, ed. R. W. Stallman and Lillian Gilkes (New York, 1960), p. 122.

[50]Preface by A. W. Lawrence to *Seven Pillars of Wisdom* (New York, 1935), p 25.

[51]D. H. Lawrence, Introduction to *A Bibliography of the Writings of D. H. Lawrence* (Philadelphia, 1925), p. 9.

[52]*Letters to Macmillan*, ed. Simon Nowell-Smith (London, 1967), pp. 258, 259.

149

son how luminous and exciting I found it. But . . . I said . . . before I bought his story, would he mind throwing in a few commas? and I returned the manuscript which was virtually free of punctuation. It came back to me with a savory note in which the author hoped he had provided enough punctuation; if not, would I please suit myself? What he had done was to thrust a comma after each half dozen words or so, irrespective of sense." [53]

On the other hand, the twentieth century has been inhabited by several writers with notable solicitude for the minutiae of the texts of their works. A. E. Housman was very reluctant to let his publisher make a typewritten copy of his poems to send to the printer for fear that a minor slip should be introduced. He hurried his *Last Poems* into print for the reasons that he gave in the Preface: "What I have written should be printed while I am here to see it through the press and control its spelling and punctuation." Even so, the result was not what he had wished for; opposite these words in his own copy of the book, he wrote the words "Vain hope!"[54] Max Beerbohm also took considerable interest in the accidentals of his work. In returning the corrected proofs of two stories to the editor of *The Century Magazine,* he deplored the unnecessary trouble that had been imposed on him by the printers and proofreaders. "It is due merely," he wrote, "to their crude and asinine interference with my punctuation, with my division of paragraphs, and with other details." He mounted his platform and delivered a little lecture on the subject in general: "Details? No, these are not details to me. My choice of stops is as important to me—as important for the purpose of conveying easily to the reader my exact shades of meaning—as my choice of words." He went on to fulminate against those who ventured

[53]Waldo Frank, "Sherwood Anderson: A Personal Note," *The Newberry Library Bulletin*, Second Series, No. 2 (December, 1948), 40.

[54]Tom Burns Haber, *JEGP*, 65 (1966), 740, and Haber, "A. E. Housman's Printer's Copy of 'Last Poems'," *PBSA*, 66 (1952), 70–77.

to alter his accidentals: "It is most annoying for me to find my well-planned effects repeatedly destroyed by the rough-and-ready, *standardizing* method of your proof-readers. These methods are, no doubt, very salutary, and necessary, in the case of gifted but illiterate or careless contributors to your magazine. But I, personally, will none of them. And if, at any future date, you do me the honour to accept any other piece of my writing, please let it be understood that my MS. must be respected, not pulled about and put into shape in accordance to any schoolmasterly notion of how authors ought to write."[55]

In reviewing the attitudes of writers of the last four hundred years toward accidentals, it is of course impossible to do more in a few pages than to offer a small sample of the possibilities. I hope that this sample is a fair cross section of all who might have been cited. I think that I have a little overemphasized writers who have concern about the accidentals of their text; I have done so, I suppose, because those remarks have been more popular with editors and have thus been given greater prominence. In any event, I could much more readily multiply the examples of writers who were, to varying degrees, indifferent about accidentals. And it is usually true that people do not write about what they do not have much concern for.

The most obvious conclusion to this review is that some think one thing and some another, with the great majority being of the indifferent persuasion. What this—and its less obvious corollaries—signifies should await a consideration of the degree to which accidentals have been respected in the transmission of texts.

III

One assumption underlying the preceding pages is that the attitudes which writers have taken toward the accidentals of their own work have a bearing on the attitudes which we should

55 Unpublished letter, dated March 6, 1916, in the Robert H. Taylor Collection. Excerpt printed in "Letters of English Authors," pp. 232–233.

take toward those accidentals. Of all of the intentions of the writer, however, the intention with respect to accidentals is the most fragile. In the transmission of texts, it is the accidentals that are the most likely to be altered and those alterations that are the most likely to pass unnoticed. Through almost all of the period which is the scope of this book, it has been the printers (particularly the compositors and proofreaders) who have mainly exercised this control over the text in the process of transmitting it. In practice, therefore, it is crucial to note their attitudes toward accidentals in order to understand the limits that this practice imposes on our ability to recover the author's accidentals. To that end, I offer a short review of those attitudes. As the craft of making and distributing books has changed in the last two or three hundred years—with first the bookseller and then the publisher taking over some of the tasks earlier performed by the printer—the location of the editorial function has of course shifted consequently. I will not attempt in this brief space to extend the discussion to include the role of the editor nor of twentieth-century practice but will limit this short review to the attitudes of printers from Elizabethan times to the twentieth century.

The first extensive printer's manual which sets forth English practice did not appear until 1683, in the form of Joseph Moxon's celebrated and valuable treatise, *Mechanick Exercises on the Whole Art of Printing*. It is possible to deduce the earlier practice of printers with some confidence, however, by observing what actually took place in a printing shop. Perhaps the most famous (and closely-studied) example of an extant Elizabethan manuscript which served as printer's copy is the autograph of Cantos XIV–XLVI of Sir John Harington's verse translation of Ariosto's *Orlando Furioso*. The translation was printed by Richard Field in 1591, and a comparison of the book and the copy from which it was printed reveals the degree of freedom that Field took with the accidentals of this clear and meticulous manuscript, which includes instructions from the translator to the printer. Field's work was extremely careful, but the liberties he took with the accidentals were considerable. On a single page he made as many as seventy changes in spelling (not counting the expansion of contractions and changes in medial "u" and "v"), and a dozen changes in punctuation on a page. Harington's spelling was, for example, archaic and irregular, and Field and his workmen did not scruple to make it modern and regular; similarly, for example, they took out and inserted colons (or changed them to semicolons), and they took out and inserted commas as desired.[56]

Another notable example from the same period is the fifth book of Richard Hooker's *Lawes of Ecclesiasticall Politie,* printed by John Windet in 1597. The printer's copy is extant, a clear and careful piece of work which Hooker corrected in preparing it for the press. Even so, the printer "freely modifies the spelling and the use of capital letters"; while the printer mainly followed the careful punctuation, he changed even some of that, particularly the use of the comma. In reviewing other examples, the verdict is frequently similar. ("Taylor's spelling the printer freely altered, and he filled in defects in the punctuation.")[57]

Scholars who have studied the habits of printers of the sixteenth and seventeenth centuries in dealing with their copy have generally reached similar conclusions. Fredson Bowers has written that "of all features of an author's manuscript the Elizabethan compositor seems to have followed the punctuation the least faithfully, even when it existed—as mostly it did not."[58] F. P. Wilson concluded that "normally the printer considered the regulation of spellings and capitals to be within his own province."[59] I am aware of some controversies among scholars

[56]See Simpson, *Proof-Reading,* pp. 71–75. This relationship had earlier been discussed in detail by W. W. Greg in "An Elizabethan Printer and his Copy," *The Library,* 4th Ser., 4 (1923), 102–118.

[57]Simpson, pp. 76–79, 86.

[58]"Today's Shakespeare Texts, and Tomorrow's," *SB,* 19 (1966), 48.

[59]"Shakespeare and the 'New Bibliography'," *Studies in Retrospect* (London, 1945), p. 128.

concerning Elizabethan punctuation—such as the degree to which the First Folio may preserve Shakespeare's punctuation, or the precise meaning of punctuation; since they concern refinements in detail and not the general issue, however, it seems inadvisable to pursue them here.[60]

When we come to the latter seventeenth century, we have available the first in a long series of important printers' manuals. These manuals, mainly for the instruction of apprentices and others learning the craft of printing, describe the practice of their time. Since printing was one of the more conservative crafts, a given manual tends to embody the practice of earlier times as well; moreover, the amount of acknowledged and unacknowledged quoting and paraphrasing in one manual from its predecessors draws them together into a relatively unbroken progression.[61] In view of these facts, one can take seriously the statements of practice in these manuals, particularly when they are repeated in successive manuals. (As a reminder of this common practice, I will cite one or two similar statements from more than one manual; and I assure the reader that most of the remarks I quote could be matched in other sources.) Though printers' manuals are moderately well known, they have not been carefully examined for the purpose of defining the practices of printers with respect to accidentals. Consequently, this review must, to be useful, go into sufficient detail about an adequate number of examples so as to make clearly evident what those practices were. As the attention of readers is much shorter than the length of the substance I would like to offer from each, I will limit these remarks to what seems to me only the barest suggestion of their contents.

[60]For one review, see Vivian Salmon, "Early Seventeenth-Century Punctuation as a Guide to Sentence Structure," *RES*, NS 13 (1962), 347–360. A shorter and earlier comment is made by F. P. Wilson in *Studies in Retrospect*, pp. 126–127.

[61]For a summary review of the relations among English and American manuals, see Lawrence C. Wroth, "Corpus Typographicum: A Review of English & American Printers' Manuals," in *Typographic Heritage*, Typophile Chap Books, 20 (1949), 55–90.

Moxon's book is not only the earliest but also (I believe) the most influential of all English and American manuals. It is, even among textual scholars, one of those books more known about than read, and very short phrases taken out of context often seem to have satisfied any floating curiosity. (F. P. Wilson could limit his evidence from Moxon about correctors to the remark that they ought to be "very sagacious in Pointing," and to quote even that from a secondary source.[62]) As with all such manuals, the material of greatest interest to us is set forth in the instructions to the compositor and, secondly, to the "corrector" of the press. In his Preface to the Compositor's Trade, Moxon begins with the hallowed statement, clung to by printers as if it were their most valuable defense against a hostile world, that *"by the Laws of* Printing, *a* Compositor *is strictly to follow his* Copy, *viz. to observe and do just so much and no more than his* Copy *will bear him out for; so that his* Copy *is to be his Rule and Authority."* As soon as that statement of theory is out of the way, however, Moxon proceeds with practical matters:

> *But the carelessness of some good Authors, and the ignorance of other Authors, has forc'd* Printers *to introduce a Custom, which among them is look'd upon as a task and duty incumbent on the* Compositor, *viz. to discern and amend the bad* Spelling *and* Pointing *of his copy, if it be English....*
>
> *Therefore upon consideration of these accidental circumstances that attend* Copy, *it is necessary that a* Compositor *be a good English Schollar at least; and that he know the present traditional* Spelling *of all English Words, and that he have so much Sence and Reason as to* Point *his Sentence properly: when to begin a Word with a* Capital Letter, *when (to render the Sense of the Author more intelligent to the Reader) to Set some Words or Sentences in* Italick *or* English Letter, *&c.*[63]

[62]"Shakespeare and the 'New Bibliography'," p. 127.

[63]Joseph Moxon, *Mechanick Exercises on the Whole Art of Printing* (1683-4), ed. Herbert Davis and Harry Carter, 2d ed. (London, 1962), pp. 192–193.

Moxon has, for the compositor, a good many specific instructions which reveal the degree to which he is in fact responsible for punctuation, capitalization, and the use of type to indicate the author's meaning:

> If his *Copy* be written in a Language he understands, he reads his *Copy* with consideration; that so he may get himself into the meaning of the *Author*, and consequently considers how to order his Work the better both in the *Title Page*, and in the matter of the *Book*: As to how to make his *Indenting, Pointing, Breaking, Italicking, &c.* the better sympathize with the *Authors* Genius, and also with the capacity of the Reader. (p.212)

The particularity of Moxon's instructions on these matters makes plain the scope of the responsibility that the compositor is supposed to feel:

> As he *Sets* on, he considers how to *Point* his Work, viz. when to *Set*, where; where: and where. where to make ( ) where [ ] ? ! and when a *Break*. But the Rules for these having been taught in many Schoolbooks, I need say nothing to them here, but refer you to them. . . .
>
> And as he considers how to Point, so he considers what proper Names, either of Persons or Places, he meets with in his *Copy*, as also what Words of great Emphasis, and what Words of smaller Emphasis, what Obsolete Words, and what Foreign, *&c.*
>
> When he meets with proper Names of Persons or Places he *Sets* them in *Italick*, if the Series of his *Matter* be *Set* in *Roman*; or in *Roman* if the Series of his *Matter* be *Set* in *Italick*, and *Sets* the first *Letter* with a *Capital*, or as the Person or Place he finds the purpose of the Author to dignifie, all Capitals. . . .
>
> Words of great Emphasis are also *Set* in *Italick*, and sometimes begin with a *Capital Letter*. . . .
>
> Words of a smaller Emphasis may be *Set* in the running Character, viz. *Roman*, if it be the Series of the *Matter*; or *Italick*, if *Italick*, but begun with a *Capital*. (pp. 215–217)

These passages may suggest the considerable degree to which the compositor was made to feel personal responsibility for the accidentals; or, to put it another way, the considerable degree to which he was made to feel personally free to change, add to, or subtract from the accidentals which the author had in his copy.

The other agent of the printer in a regular position to alter the accidentals was the corrector of the press. This person read the proof; ideally he was learned in several languages and had an important responsibility in correcting errors, but actually it was only the larger printing offices that had correctors before the middle of the eighteenth century. Moxon describes the larger printing offices of his own time when he says that "a *Corrector* should (besides the *English* Tongue) be well skilled in Languages. . . . He ought to be very knowing in Derivations and Etymologies of Words, very sagacious in *Pointing,* skilful in the *Compositers* whole Task and Obligation, and endowed with a quick Eye to espy the smallest *Fault.*" While watching the proof as copy is being read to him, the corrector also "considers the *Pointing, Italicking, Capitalling,* or any error that may through mistake, or want of Judgement be committed by the *Compositer*" (pp. 246–247). It is plain that in those offices that had correctors—and in virtually all offices after the middle of the eighteenth century—correctors were expected to exercise considerable control over the accidentals of printing with a view toward regularizing them to the "correct" current style.

The practice of the middle of the eighteenth century can be represented by John Smith's manual, entitled *The Printer's Grammar* (London, 1755). There is no intervening book between Moxon and Smith of comparable importance, and Smith gradually took over Moxon's place and was widely influential for three-quarters of a century. There is a certain tartness in his observations, and he exhibits a strong sense of loyalty to printers as a band of long-suffering men, who are more sinned against than sinning. Smith first exhorts authors to regard it as their essential duty to punctuate their copy—though few authors might be reasonably expected to study and obey a printer's manual. With which, Smith quickly proceeds to his instructions to compositors as to how they must do what is neglected by authors, who "point their Matter either very loosely, or not at all: of which two evils, however, the last is the least; for in that case a Compositor has room left to point the Copy his own way; which, though it cannot be done without loss to him; yet it is not altogether of so much hinderance as being troubled with Copy which is pointed at random, and which stops the Compositor in the career of his business more than if not pointed at all" (pp. 86–87).

Smith recommends a rough and ready punctuating to compositors. "When we compare the rules which very able Grammarians have laid down about Pointing," he says, "the difference is not very material; and it appears, that it is only a maxim with humourous Pedants, to make a clamour about the quality of a Point; who would even make an Erratum of a Comma which they fancy to bear the pause of a Semicolon, were the Printer to give way to such pretended accuracies. Hence we find some of these high-pointing Gentlemen propose to increase the number of Points now in use" (p. 87). Printers must take a firm stand with these "high-pointing Gentlemen." "For these several reasons," Smith later writes, "it will appear how material it is not to make an Erratum of every trifling fault, where the sense of a word cannot be construed to mean any thing else than what it was designed for; much less to correct the Punctuation, unless where it should pervert the sense" (p. 223).

After reciting "the Laws of Printing"—from Moxon, of course —that the compositor should follow copy and not vary from it, Smith proceeds immediately to a statement of present practice:

> But this good law is now looked upon as obsolete, and most authors expect the Printer to spell, point, and digest their Copy, that it may be intelligible and significant to the Reader,

which is what a Compositor and the Corrector jointly have regard to, in Works of their own language, else many good books would be laid aside, because it would require as much patience to read them as books did, when no Points or Notations were used; and when nothing but a close Attention to the sense made the subject intelligible. (pp. 199–200)

That was then the situation confronting printers, in Smith's view. How should printers meet it? First he sums up the need and then lays down his solution:

Pointing, therefore, as well as Spelling and Methodizing some Authors Copies being now became part of a Compositor's business, it shews how necessary it is for Master Printers to be deliberate in chusing Apprentices for the Case, and not to fix upon any but such as have either had a liberal education, or at least are perfect in writing and reading their own language, besides haveing a taste of Latin, and some notion of Greek and Hebrew; and, withal, discover a genius that is capable of being cultivated and improved in such knowledge as contributes to exercise the Art with address and judgment. Had this been always the aim and object of the Planters and Nurses of our Art, Printing would make a more respectable figure, and be more distinguished from mechanical business. (p. 200)

Smith proceeds then to his instructions to correctors. He advises correctors to review copy before it goes to the compositor and make their changes in the manuscript. Thus the compositor will not be bothered by having to change in proof the alterations which the corrector has to make to the author's copy, "especially if they are of no real signification." Such, for example, as the compositor being obliged to correct a manuscript in which the author has indulged in "far-fetch'd spelling of Words, changing and thrusting in Points, Capitals, or any thing else that has nothing but fancy and (perhaps pettish) humour for its authority and foundation" (pp. 273–274).

Smith is very precise about the main duty of the corrector, however. "What is chiefly required of a Corrector," he says, "besides espying literal faults, is to Spell and to Point after the prevailing method and genius of each particular language." Smith admits that these tasks present difficulties which will "always afford employment for pedantic Critics." The corrector, therefore, "ought to fix upon a method to spell ambiguous words and compounds always the same way," and to this end Smith urges the making of lists and catalogs and other aids to consistency (p. 274).

Smith thus leaves no doubt about the role of the printer in handling accidentals. However much one may think them the responsibility of the author, they are almost always left to the printer. It is therefore the usual and ordinary duty of the printer —through the compositor and corrector—to take complete charge of these matters, which he regards as of relatively little importance.

Smith's heart is with the compositor. Charles Stower followed Smith in many large and small details—even to the title, *The Printer's Grammar* (London, 1808). But the corrector enjoys a larger role in Stower—thanks, no doubt, to the fact that he enlisted the help of Joseph Nightingale, who is introduced as "Reader in one of our largest printing-offices" as well as "author of a 'Portraiture of Methodism'." Stower's book asserts that the reader or corrector of the press "should make it a rule never to trust a compositor in any matter of the slightest importance— they are the most *erring* set of men in the universe" (p. 397). It is the corrector who has to assume major responsibility, as with punctuation. "The duty of punctuation is often made to devolve on the corrector; and what has been disregarded as a matter of little consequence, by the author, becomes an important part of the corrector's business. Let him discharge the duty with propriety and uniformity" (p. 391).

The first American printer's manual—C. S. Van Winkle's *The Printer's Guide: or, an Introduction to the Art of Printing*

(New York, 1818)—was based on Stower. Van Winkle takes the position that "correct pointing most certainly depends upon printers" (p. vi). Accordingly, the book commences with a long section on punctuation, and this is succeeded by a long section on spelling. His description of the role of the proofreader—quoted and paraphrased from Stower in passages that had earlier appeared in Luckombe in 1770 and in Smith in 1755—gives the same charge to alter and amend matters in the author's manuscript, "especially if they are of no real signification; such as far-fetched spelling of words, and thrusting in capitals, or any thing else that has nothing but fancy and humour for its authority and foundation" (p. 148).

John Johnson's *Typographia* (London, 1824) and T. C. Hansard's book of the same title (London, 1825) are both based on Smith and Stower and repeat those authorities in full measure. Johnson reiterates the "laws of printing" passage (about the compositor abiding by copy, from Moxon and his successors) and similarly reminds his readers that this law is now considered obsolete and that "most writers expect the printer to spell, point, and digest their copy, that it may be intelligible and significant to the reader. . . ." Therefore the printer must choose apprentices who can do this "pointing, therefore, as well as spelling and methodizing" (II, 127). Likewise, Johnson repeats the well-worn remarks about correctors revising copy before it goes to the compositor, especially when the follies of the authors "are of no real signification; such as far-fetched spelling of words, changing and thrusting in points, capitals, or any thing else that has nothing but fancy and humour for its authority and foundation." The corrector's chief duty, after noting typographical mistakes, "is to spell and point after the prevailing method" (II, 209).

Hansard is almost equally conventional. He lays the same responsibilities for accidentals on compositor and corrector, and he gives them the authority to make all necessary changes. One passage in Hansard was apparently of special appeal to other writers of manuals. Since it appears in several other manuals, I will quote enough of it here to suggest its main drift and the source of its appeal to printers:

> The late Dr. Hunter, in reviewing a work, had occasion to censure it for its improper punctuation. He advises authors to leave the pointing entirely to the printers, as from their constant practice they must have acquired a uniform mode of punctuation. We are decidedly of this opinion; for unless the author will take the responsibility of the pointing entirely on himself, it will be to the advantage of the compositor, and attended with less loss of time, not to meet with a single point in his copy, unless to terminate a sentence, than to have his mind confused by commas and semicolons placed indiscriminately, in the hurry of writing, without any regard to propriety.[64]

And so Hansard proceeds, always careful to see that the best interests of the printers are uppermost, commonly quoting or paraphrasing the familiar ideas and passages that were the staple of earlier books.

This short review may be brought toward a close with Thomas Mackellar's *The American Printer: A Manual of Typography* (Philadelphia, 1866). Mackellar's book was influential and popular; it reached its eighteenth edition by 1893. "The world is little aware," writes Mackellar, "how greatly many authors are indebted to a competent proof-reader for not only reforming their spelling and punctuation, but for valuable suggestions in regard to style, language, and grammar—thus rectifying faults which would have rendered them fair game for the petulant critic" (p. 180). Throughout, Mackellar carries on the tradition of the printer exercising substantial control over the accidentals. "The compositor," he says, "is bound to 'follow the copy,' in word and sentiment, unless, indeed, he meets with instances of wrong punctuation or false grammar (and such instances are not rare), which his intelligence enables him to

---

[64]Pp. 434–435. Among other manuals which include this passage are the following: C. H. Timperley, *The Printer's Manual* (London, 1838), p. 4; Joel Munsell, *The Typographical Miscellany* (Albany, N.Y., 1850), pp. 27–28.

amend" (p. 183). The proofreader has his role, too, but "the duty of amending the punctuation should be generally confined to one reader" (p. 183). At the same time, Mackellar's book is transitional in that it gives less latitude to the printer and has more understanding for the wishes of the writer. Mackellar admits that "sentiments in print look marvellously different from the same ideas in manuscript; and we are not surprised that writers should wish to polish a little" (p. 183); but he also makes it plain that writers can expect to have all second thoughts reflected on their bill. ("How unreasonable—nay, how transparently unjust—the expectation that the printer should give gratuitously the time and trouble requisite for the radical changes in the type which an author's whim or taste may demand!" (p. 184). Moreover, the printer ought to feel free to alter the accidentals only if the writer allows him to do so; "when an author gives him the option, a proof-reader ought to spell ambiguous words and arrange compounds in a methodical and uniform way" (p. 181).

With Theodore Low De Vinne and the several books (in 1900, 1901, 1902, 1904) which made up his *Practice of Typography*, a new era in printing was at hand. Even so, it is worth calling attention to the continuing tradition of responsibility for accidentals. De Vinne's second volume, *Correct Composition* (1901 and later editions) is a book of instruction for printers about style, form, spelling, capitalization, punctuation, and the like. The printer needed such instruction, thought de Vinne, because "there is a general belief that the correction of these oversights [spelling, capitalization, punctuation] is the duty of the printer, and the writer too often throws this duty largely on the compositor and the proof-reader."[65] And so the printer

[65] I quote from the New York, 1916 ed., p. viii. One of the most forthright complaints by a writer on the failure of his printer to fulfill this duty is contained in an errata notice (called to my attention by Carey S. Bliss) placed under the frontispiece of Kelly Roth's *Experiences and Travels of an Immigrant Boy* (Los Angeles, 1944): "DONT LAUGH—I WEPT. The rascal publisher who promised all corrections in my SPELLING, WAS A LIAR."

was still continuing, in a more modest way, to assume the responsibility which was more exclusively his in earlier times.

IV

Writers and printers have sometimes looked on one another with the kind of hostility which is appropriate to natural enemies. In the writer's view, printers "can neither print Sense nor English, nor indeede any other language, thô it lie never so plainely before them." In the printer's view, "it is rare, indeed, to meet with a work sent properly prepared to the press; either the writing is illegible, the spelling incorrect, or the punctuation defective"; moreover, the printer is confronted by the need to make "radical changes in the type which an author's whim or taste may demand."[66]

From my little survey, it appears that the great majority of writers in the period under review have not concerned themselves very seriously with the accidentals used in printing their writings. Every possible position on this subject has doubtless been taken by one or more writers: some have left the care for accidentals entirely to the printer, some have welcomed changes made in the printing office, some have tolerated changes, and some have resisted (with varying degrees of resolution) changes which were offered or imposed. The center of gravity among the attitudes of writers seems generally to have been in the area of indifference.

The great majority of printers were (in principle, at least) willing to follow the author's copy even to the details of accidentals provided that copy was legible, perfected, and "correct" in usage as it was understood in the printing house. In practice, however, the accidentals of the author's copy were—generally and regularly—considerably changed in the course of printing. From the printers' manuals we know that the printer felt these

[66]Evelyn, p. 392; Hansard, p. 434; Mackellar, p. 184.

matters to be his responsibility and that it was his duty to set such details right; from a comparison of printer's copy with the finished book we know that the printer did, in fact, ordinarily make very numerous changes in such details.

In general it can be said that spelling, punctuation, and capitalization were thought of as conventions that had to be treated with at least modest respect. Otherwise, they might form a barrier, small but real, between the reader and what he had before him to read. These details were troublesome to writer and printer alike, and most of the time each was content if the other would relieve him of these worrisome nuisances.

From this entire discussion of the treatment of accidentals, what are the consequences which affect the work of editors of literary texts? Our task is, I believe, to fulfill the intentions of the writer in these small details as well as in greater matters. The most apparent conclusion seems to me to be that no simple rule of thumb can be made to cover all situations. We cannot say that, in principle, it is "right" to use old-spelling for scholars and modernize for general readers, nor that one should modernize before a certain date—1800, say—and not modernize after that time.

The sound principle is, of course, to try to determine the intentions of the writer. Unfortunately, most of the time it is not clear that we know how to determine what the intentions of the writer were with respect to accidentals. In many cases, probably in most cases, he expected the printer to perfect his accidentals; and thus the changes introduced by the printer can be properly thought of as fulfilling the writer's intentions. To return to the accidentals of the author's manuscript would, in these cases, be a puristic recovery of a text which the author himself thought of as incomplete or unperfected: thus, following his own manuscript would result in subverting his intentions. (An argument could be made along these lines against the practice of the Centenary Edition of *The House of the Seven Gables*, which follows the accidentals of the extant manu-

165

script rather than of the print, with three or four thousand differences between the two.) In a good many cases, we do know the authors' intentions: as I have indicated, mostly writers have been indifferent about accidentals, but a few—such as Housman and Beerbohm—have regarded their own accidentals as an important part of their intentions. An editor will, of course, inform himself of any views on this matter that were expressed by the writer whose work he is editing. Where no direct evidence is available, the editor can often infer the writer's attitude by comparing the printed version with the final manuscript which the author turned over to the printer, by examining his corrections to proof sheets, by weighing the testimony of those involved in the process of publication, or by considering any other such evidence that is available. When the editor finds evidence that the writer took a position about the accidentals of his own work—any position at all—then the editor is, in my judgment, bound to respect that position and to give it effect in any applicable example of the writer's work. If the writer wished his own accidentals to be used, the editor should carry out that wish; if the writer was satisfied with printer's accidentals, then the editor should be also.

Marginal cases always offer opportunities for refined reasoning, and there are many margins. Under what circumstances, for example, should the editor supply punctuation for the writer? It has been argued that it is the duty of the editor of Shelley to re-punctuate his poetry so that a reader can understand it. Shelley couldn't punctuate; thus, to communicate the intention of the author you must go behind what he wrote and reveal what he meant to write, or should have written. "Shelley's poetry depends on syntax, the syntax on punctuation, and the punctuation on the editor's personal understanding and technical skill."[67] In reviewing Donald Reiman's edition of *The Triumph of Life*, the same writer says that "the result is a

[67]Neville Rogers, "The Punctuation of Shelley's Syntax," *The Keats-Shelley Memorial Bulletin*, No. 17 (1966), 22.

tragic one." "By preserving Shelley's punctuation, which corrupts it, he has restored, not only the words of the MS but the nonsense of the MS."[68] When the author does not bother about punctuation, he leaves a larger area of ambiguity than usual, with words shifting their roles and meanings as punctuation is added or subtracted or changed. The absence or inadequacy of authorial punctuation often tempts everybody else to come in as joint authors of the work. While it is a pious task to be so altruistically eager to perfect the work of art, helping hands are not always welcome. In principle, the editor is free to alter punctuation only when it is clear that he is fulfilling the author's intentions, only if he is doing precisely what the author wanted done or would himself have done under favorable circumstances. Otherwise, the editor is not free to alter punctuation simply because he thinks that the change improves the work of art beyond the achievement of the writer, nor because he thinks the author could not punctuate—he might think the writer inept with rhyme, metre, or diction and (on this reasoning) set those right also. It is not that the editor should be against cakes and ale but that he should not squeak out unsolicited additions to the author's work. The situation in which an author's manuscript is extant (with one form of accidentals) and also a reliable, "approved," printed text (with a different form of accidentals) poses a special problem for the editor; I discuss this matter toward the end of Section III of Chapter VI.

There will remain many examples for which no inkling of the writer's position on accidentals can be discovered. How should the editor then act? When there is no other principle to use as a guide, then probability must serve as an expedient. As we have seen, the probability is all on the side of the writer being indifferent about accidentals and of the printer changing, with considerable freedom, the accidentals in his copy-text: it seems reasonable for the editor to assume that such are the

[68]Pp. 25, 26.

source and authority of the accidentals when other evidence is lacking.[69]

It is evident that it is rarely possible to know whether a specific accidental—a given comma, or a certain spelling, or a particular capitalization—is or is not authorial. It is not even possible to feel much confidence as to whether the majority of the accidentals ordinarily subject to variation are or are not authorial. The attempt to penetrate the opaque curtain of the accidentals by reasoning, in order to find their source, is so fraught with uncertainties that it can rarely be expected to yield any reliable results.[70]

Part of the difficulties in making these determinations is due, finally, to one simple fact. Namely, that authors and printers did not, for the most part, feel that these matters were of very much importance. While we, as editors, are under no obligation to share that view—and, indeed, much scholarship depends on devoting a disproportionate amount of attention to relatively small details—we expose ourselves to the commission of various kinds of folly if we do not. In my opinion, the editor will do best to spend only a modest amount of his time on accidentals— mainly a losing cause—and devote himself to matters of substance. There is some good sense, as well as amusement, in Addison's essay making fun of editors:

> Indeed, when a different Reading gives us a different Sense, or a new Elegance in an Author, the Editor does very well in taking Notice of it; but when he only entertains us with the several ways of Spelling the same Word, and gathers together

[69]One sometimes meets with exactly the opposite assumption. Paul Baender writes that "obviously, if accidental changes are to house style or compositor's style, if they are indifferent choices, and if we do not know the author's wishes or his instructions to the printer, our judgment should tip in favor of the manuscript readings" ("The Meaning of Copy-Text," *SB*, 22, 1969, 316).

[70]Fredson Bowers has been at great pains to resolve the question as to which accidentals are authoritative in his edition of Stephen Crane. Donald Pizer has taken exception to some of the results because of "the tortured road of 'possibles' and 'probables' by which assurance is gained," that an "exercise in tentativeness" ends in "firm adoptions" (*MP*, 68, 1970, 214).

168

the various Blunders and Mistakes of twenty or thirty different Transcribers, they only take up the Time of the learned Reader, and puzzle the Minds of the Ignorant. *(Spectator* 470.)

The question of modernization remains. It remains, in my opinion, not so much a question of principle as it is a question of convenience. As such, it can now be dealt with briefly. Herbert Davis maintained, in 1961, that English writers of the eighteenth century would now prefer their works to appear in modernized texts. "It is amusing to reflect," he wrote, "that the writers whose works are being so carefully edited would certainly have been much more concerned that they should be read today in modernized texts than preserved in those particular forms which they feared might make their books unreadable in later times. They would some of them have disliked modern scholarly editing as much as they disliked what they called the pedantry of scholarship in their own day."[71] Most writers are glad to have an audience, and they would doubtless think that modernization—since it eliminates a possible barrier in the form of unfamiliar conventions—would increase that audience. We may sympathize with that wish without installing it as a textual principle. The writer usually has more interest in the fate of his own work than others do, but his authority does not extend into its after life. Once he has communicated it to his usual public, his control over it—at least in that version —is at an end.

The question of modernization has an analogous relationship to the question of translation. It is easier to read a text in a language or form with which one is familiar through current use, and yet there is much to be said in favor of the extra return from reading it in its original form. Is the return worth the effort? It depends on many things: the value of what is to be read, the quality of the extra return, the willingness and skill of the reader, and the further use of the skill. Or, to put it the

[71]Review of *SB*, 13 (1960) in *RES*, 12 (1961), 324–325.

other way, does the gain from translation—reading what might not otherwise be available, saving time, understanding more clearly, perhaps—overbalance the inevitable loss involved in translation? Again, it depends. Most of all, these answers depend on the nature of the audience. As there are not just one or two but many audiences, so there must be many answers. There is no rule of thumb that will relieve the editor from considering all of the relevant factors and arriving at a decision which he is willing to defend. There is at least a theoretical need—and, mostly, a practical need of some consequence or other—for both a modernized and non-modernized text of every work which is separated far enough in time from the present for changes to have taken place in the conventions governing accidentals; and it follows, of course, that a modernized text would need to be re-modernized after the lapse of such time. (It seems to me that a good deal of "modernizing" is only partial, as if it were done by someone not quite in touch with contemporary writing.) From my personal experience, I can say that the losses from modernization seem to me to be less than most textual scholars assume, and that the gains from modernization tend to be greater.

Accidentals usually involve the textual scholar in a quantity of effort which may seem disproportionate to the results. Frequently the decisions are close ones, and it is the marginal cases, like the sour grape, that set the teeth on edge. But they are decisions that have to be made even if the results are usually of negligible importance. Of all phases of textual criticism, I believe that the treatment of accidentals is the one, most of all, in which much is to be endured and little to be enjoyed.

170

CHAPTER VI

The Establishment of the Text

"DEFINITIVE" is the word that every right-thinking editor would rejoice to find applied to his work. Reviewers have caused many editorial hearts to leap up by the judicious application of words from the definitive family. When Thomas H. Johnson's edition of Emily Dickinson's poems appeared in 1955, it collected a remarkable number of these special commendations. "A definitive edition," wrote one reviewer; another styled it "this definitive 3-volume edition"; another, in a more leisurely vein, said that "serious students of Emily Dickinson have long awaited a text of her poems that could be relied on as definitive. This accolade, rarely bestowed by the reviewer, is clearly merited by the new Harvard edition." The *Bibliography of American Literature* returned to the succinct style, however, and described it simply as "the definitive edition."[1] I do not mean to suggest that "definitive" was the only term employed; "monument" was resorted to a good deal, for example, along with "majestic," "epoch-making," "magnificent," and (with suitable extolling adjectives) the old standbys "achievement" and "contribution." R. P. Blackmur said that "Mr. Johnson has done everything an editor can do," and Robert Hillyer asserted that the edition

[1]Louise Bogan in the *New Yorker*, Oct. 8, 1955, p. 190; G. D. McDonald in *Library Journal*, Dec. 1, 1955, p. 2788; Charles Anderson in *MLN*, 71 (1956), 386; Vol. II (1957), item 4701. While publishers' estimates may be classed with lapidary inscriptions, a rather unusual "Publisher's Preface" to the first volume particularly extols "Mr. Johnson's definitive edition of *The Poems of Emily Dickinson*" as "an epoch-making event" (I, xi).

171

"is not only a major work of scholarship; it is a monument in American literature."[2]

When James B. Wharey's edition of *Pilgrim's Progress* was published, in 1928, it was hailed in somewhat similar terms. The review in the *Times Literary Supplement* appeared under the heading "A Definitive Text" and described the book as a "remarkable feat of scholarship." G. B. Harrison prophesied that it "will rank with the classical editions of English texts" and that it "might with advantage be placed in the hands of a beginner as a standard of achievement." Allardyce Nicoll thought it "in every way an admirable piece of work; in many ways it may be regarded as the finest achievement in critical bibliography produced within recent years." "We take it that this book," wrote the reviewer in *Notes and Queries*, "will establish itself as the authoritative text of the 'Pilgrim's Progress'."[3] And so it was regarded.

To go back to 1912, H. J. C. Grierson's edition of Donne's poetry was for a long time thought of as a model. In an early review in *The Nation,* it was said that its textual discussions "are well done, once for all." Pierre Legouis, author of one of the most influential studies of Donne published in the 1920's, doubtless spoke for many students of Donne when he said that "Grierson's edition of Donne's poetry was hailed by my generation as *définitive.*"[4]

To recall such noble sentiments about these three editions may remind us of the statue of Ozymandias, a decapitated ruin

[2]Blackmur in *Kenyon Review,* 18 (1956), 224; Hillyer in *New York Times,* Sept. 11, 1955, p. 7.

[3]*TLS,* Feb. 28, 1929, p. 159; Harrison in *MLR,* 24 (1929), 473, 472; Nicoll in *YWES,* 9 for 1928 (pub. 1930), 218; *N&Q,* 156 (1929), 254.

[4]*The Nation,* Jan. 15, 1914, p. 61; Legouis, *RES,* NS 17 (1966), 317. Examples of such praise of scholarly editions abound, like Sir Herbert J. C. Grierson's comment on Hutchinson's edition of Herbert that "this is the final, all-inclusive edition of the writings of George Herbert, English and Latin" (*MLR,* 37, 1942, 207). Or the reviewer of Hyder Rollins' edition of Keats's letters, who asserted that "it is safe to say that these two volumes will never be supplanted" (*New York Times,* Sept. 7, 1958, section 7, p. 4).

172

in the desert sand, with the proud boast of his might still visible on the pedestal. The passage of time has revealed these editions as works which one need not look on and despair to emulate. In fact, the Grierson edition of Donne's poetry has, so far as the text goes, been supplanted; so has Wharey's edition of *Pilgrim's Progress;* and already there is reason to know that Johnson's text of Emily Dickinson is not truly definitive.

The principal lesson to be learned from these changes in evaluation may well be the cautionary tale that has recurred throughout this book: the likelihood of error in textual work, even in major matters. This is a true saying, and worthy of all scholars to be received; but there are more particular conclusions to be drawn when the editions were in many ways very remarkable achievements. As an introduction to the principles that seem to control the establishment of texts, it is worth outlining what, in the judgment of specialists today, appear to have been the flaws which prevent these editions from embodying the "definitive" texts that had earlier been ascribed to them. In thus necessarily dwelling on shortcomings, I hope it will not be assumed that I do not recognize merits; some of the merits are aside from textual matters; and while some of their textual merits have diminished with time, others have maintained their value. It is my task, however, to speak of those which have diminished.

Among Grierson's many merits as an editor of Donne, there were, of course, some flaws. The two features of his work which seem to have been most influential in causing these flaws were the fact that he did not see all of the necessary textual materials for study, and the fact that his study of what he saw turned out to be somewhat inadequate. He made a careful search for early printed editions and early manuscripts (including advertising in *Notes and Queries)* and he had remarkable success and cooperation, including the long loan of important manuscripts to him personally (the Dowden and Westmoreland manuscripts, for example). Although he located most of the important mate-

173

rial, a number of texts have—not surprisingly—since appeared: among them, several are of very great importance in establishing Donne's text—Cambridge University Library Add. MS 5778, Sir Geoffrey Keynes's Luttrell MS, the Harvard College Library Dobell MS, and the Huntington Library Haslewood-Kingsborough MS.

The inadequacy of Grierson's study is certainly understandable in view of the conditions and time in which he worked. He had only a brief look at the first edition of the First Anniversary, and he had to rely on collation notes made by someone else for the first edition of the Second Anniversary (and, of course, the second edition of the First Anniversary). He did not think it necessary to study all of the available manuscript collections, but he said that he had "examined between twenty and thirty, and with the feeling recently of moving in a circle—that new manuscripts were in part or whole duplicates of those which had been already examined, and confirmed readings already noted but did not suggest anything fresh."[5] This limit was applauded by E. K. Chambers, who did not feel that Grierson should have gone further; "the labour of such a task would have been wholly incommensurate with its critical outcome."[6]

These features of Grierson's work resulted, unhappily, in some serious flaws in the text. For the Love Poems, for example, Grierson relied mainly on the 1633 edition. Helen Gardner, after analysis of the manuscripts and printed texts, concluded that the 1633 edition "is highly sophisticated and that it needs more thorough and consistent correction from the manuscripts than Grierson undertook." Likewise, the textual value of some particular manuscripts now seems different; according to Gardner again, the second part of the Huntington Library Haslewood-Kingsborough MS "enables us to dismiss as degenerate some of the manuscripts that Grierson thought contained early read-

[5] *The Poems of John Donne*, ed. Herbert J. C. Grierson (Oxford, 1912), II, lxxix.
[6] *MLR*, 9 (1914), 269.

ings."[7] For a more particular example from the Divine Poems, Grierson printed "A Hymn to God the Father" from the 1633 edition; but he also printed what he called a variant version, from manuscripts, under the title of "To Christ." Gardner concluded, however, that Donne had written only one version and that the variants in 1633 must be regarded as corruptions. So she thought fit to print only one version, based on 1633 but incorporating the manuscript readings which preserve the uncorrupted version of the text.[8] For another kind of example, the two Anniversaries make plain the serious consequences of the inadequacy of Grierson's textual study. Grierson printed both of the Anniversaries from the 1633 edition. As Frank Manley has shown, however, 1633 offers a late, derivative, and corrupt version of the poems. The First Anniversary appeared in 1611 in a careful print; in the next year there was a second edition, less carefully done, deriving from 1611, along with the first edition of the Second Anniversary and an errata slip. There were further editions in 1621 and 1625, successively derived from 1612 and without further authority. The 1633 collected edition from which Grierson chose to print was actually based on 1625, with editorial correction of readings that seemed to be errors. To print the text from 1633 is thus to choose the fourth or fifth edition, with each edition after the first having introduced corruptions and unauthorized changes in the text. Manley used the first editions of 1611 and 1612 as his copy-text, corrected them from the errata slip, and produced texts that differ from Grierson in many ways.[9] The revisions which editors since Grierson have made to the text have had various other consequences with respect to our understanding of Donne's poems. From a textual study of the nineteen Holy Sonnets, for example, Gardner concluded that they con-

---

[7] John Donne, *The Elegies and the Songs and Sonnets*, ed. Gardner (Oxford, 1965), pp. vii–viii.

[8] John Donne, *The Divine Poems*, ed. Gardner (Oxford, 1952), pp. 109–111.

[9] John Donne, *The Anniversaries*, ed. Manley (Baltimore, 1963), pp. 50–61.

175

sist of a sequence of twelve sonnets, a sequence of four, and an added group of three sonnets. In order for the meaning of the sequences—each with its internal order—to be clear, it is evident that the sonnets must be in their intended order. Grierson, however, had printed them in the following order of the new numbering: 2, 4, 6, 7, 9, 10, 11, 12, 13, 14, 15, 16, 1, 5, 3, 8, 17, 18, 19. These various flaws in Grierson's text have caused recent scholars to think it desirable to replace his edition of Donne's poems, and new texts have been issued, based on much additional information and prepared on somewhat different principles.

The main flaw in Wharey's edition of *Pilgrim's Progress* can be more briefly described. It was that Wharey chose corrupt versions for his copy-texts. For the First Part, he selected the third edition, on the grounds that this "represented the first complete text" and is free from errors introduced into later editions. For the Second Part, he chose the second edition because it adds "numerous marginal notes."[10] This reasoning has not stood the test of scrutiny, and Wharey's publisher agreed that a new edition—with a different copy-text—was necessary; such a work was duly produced, under the editorship of Roger Sharrock.[11] This time the first editions of both the First Part and the Second Part were chosen as copy-texts, on the ground that all later editions became progressively corrupt in a number of ways, such as unauthorized "correction" of Bunyan's colloquial forms, of his grammar, his archaisms, and his provincial expressions, as well as the usual assortment of inadvertent errors. The printers of later editions trimmed and polished and smoothed over the native roughness of Bunyan's style. As Sharrock put it, "it is only in the first edition that a less officious printer allows us to see the English of Bunyan as it was in his copy" (p. cx). To be sure, there were additions thought to have

[10]*The Pilgrim's Progress*, ed. James Blanton Wharey (Oxford, 1928), pp. cxi, cxiii.

[11]Second edition, revised by Roger Sharrock (Oxford, 1960).

176

some authority in editions after the first. For the First Part, additional passages in the second and third editions and several further marginal notes in the fourth; for the Second Part, additional marginalia in the second edition. These additions were incorporated by Sharrock into the copy-text of his second edition of Wharey's work, thus presenting a text which is considerably different from Wharey's. "Second edition of what?" exclaimed one reviewer of Sharrock's "second edition." "The late Professor Wharey took as his copy-text in 1928 the third edition of Part I and the second of Part II. Mr. Sharrock takes the first edition of each, so that the text is different throughout and the critical apparatus necessarily different also."[12] The resulting edition is one (it is hoped) which is nearer to Bunyan's intentions than has heretofore been available. Is this edition now "definitive"? Alas, perhaps not. While the theory under which Sharrock worked seems correct, one reviewer has noted "a distressing divergence between theory and practice," with (for example) the new edition following its predecessor rather than the announced copy-text in a great many cases.[13]

Finally, a word about Johnson's edition of Emily Dickinson.[14] The first disquieting account of this edition that I have met with came a decade after its publication. The subtitle of Johnson's edition is: *Including variant readings critically compared with all known manuscripts.* It was therefore somewhat surprising when an article appeared in 1966 under the title of "Twenty-

[12]C. L. Morrison, *RES*, NS 12 (1961), 296.

[13]G. Blakemore Evans, *JEGP*, 60 (1961), 171–174. For example: "In the first 120 lines of 'The Authors Apology for his Book' I note some 29 unacknowledged variations from the first edition in spelling, punctuation, and capitalization, and one substantive variation.... The majority of these variations... appear in Wharey's text.... Turning to the text proper, in the first 12 pages I count 46 further unacknowledged variations from the first edition(s) in spelling, punctuation, and capitalization. Again, the majority of these variations agree with the readings of Wharey's text" (p. 172). One might guess that printer's copy for Sharrock's edition consisted of a corrected copy of Wharey's edition—in which the corrections had been by no means complete.

[14]*The Poems of Emily Dickinson*, ed. Thomas H. Johnson, 3 vols. (Cambridge, Mass., 1955).

five Poems by Emily Dickinson: Unpublished Variant Versions."[15] The author had indeed discovered, for twenty-five Dickinson poems, twenty-six versions that do not appear in Johnson's edition. Moreover, all of them came from the Dickinson papers of Millicent Todd Bingham, who (wrote Johnson) had made "available for study and photostating all of the large number of manuscripts of Dickinson poetry in her possession" (I, xiii). To the article, Johnson supplied the following footnote: "Although all Dickinson material in the possession of Mrs. Bingham had presumably been made available to me before its transference chiefly to the Amherst College Library, the existence of these twenty-five variants was not brought to my attention" (p. 1). While this new evidence hardly overturns an edition consisting of some 1,775 poems, it does make it seem to tilt a little. Moreover, the extensive study by R. W. Franklin (*The Editing of Emily Dickinson: A Reconsideration,* 1967) at least makes it clear that there is still work to be done and that Johnson's edition was not truly definitive.[16]

The definitive edition is the target which scholars are expected to aim at. Fredson Bowers recognizes two kinds of editions: practical texts and definitive editions. The former is a "commercially inspired product" which presents "to a broad audience as sound a text (usually modernized and at a minimum price) as is consistent with information that may be procurable through normal scholarly channels and thus without more special research than is economically feasible." The maker of this product he dubs "a non-definitive editor." On the other hand, "a definitive edition attempts (quite simply) to present an established text that, with luck, will never need to be done

[15]By David J. M. Higgins in *AL*, 38 (1966–67), 1–21.

[16]Here is one summation, by John S. Van E. Kohn: "It [Johnson's edition] was generally assumed to be the definitive edition of the poet's work. Twelve years later R. W. Franklin, in *The Editing of Emily Dickinson*, showed that the variorum, while immensely valuable, was far from definitive. The editorial process of giving Emily Dickinson to the world will continue" ("Giving Emily Dickinson to the World," *PULC*, 31, 1969, 50).

again in its particular manner, and in all its detail, in the foreseeable future."[17] Among its many accomplishments, "the definitive edition establishes with absolute accuracy the exact documentary forms of all authoritative early texts of the work being edited" (p. 52). As a result, prophesies Bowers, examples of such work will in fact be "definitive editions like the Centenary Hawthorne" (p. 70); "the scholarly judgment of posterity" is "likely to see in the Centenary *Scarlet Letter* the first truly bibliographical and definitive critical editing of a printed American-literature text" (p. 49). And perhaps it may be so. If the past is a measure, however, we can expect that posterity will discover that "definitive" editions have flaws or that they will not last forever. This outlook is not an argument against accuracy or against trying to follow all the steps which now seem necessary in establishing a sound text.

All editions carry the taint of time. They are for the here and now, whether that is a decade, a generation, or a century. Ultimately they must all be replaced for most purposes. There will probably be new discoveries or new standards or new methods which will cause them to be supplanted. As language changes, they will at last require a new form for most readers and new explanations. I hope that this certain prospect for their efforts will cause scholars to feel, not gloom, but relief in not having to carry all the future on their shoulders.

II

Most of the important principles for the establishment of texts could probably be adduced, either positively or negatively, from these examples of editions that have been thought of as definitive. I would like now to discuss those principles in connection with outlining the major steps that are normally involved in establishing a text. I proceed in this way, as a matter

[17]"Practical Texts and Definitive Editions," in *Two Lectures on Editing*, by Charlton Hinman and Fredson Bowers (Columbus, Ohio, 1969), pp. 26, 62.

of convenience, in order to use the editor's procedures as a framework for the discussion. Let me say again, however, that describing the procedures as such is not my object. My purpose is to identify the chief principles that govern the establishment of a text and to discuss the considerations that should be weighed when trying to decide how the principle is to be generally understood.

In my view, the two most important principles governing textual work are so homely and so plain that they are usually passed over in favor of their younger and more exciting sisters. Their importance for all textual work is, however, so fundamental and pervasive that they can hardly be admired sufficiently. One is the necessity for the editor to have a thorough knowledge of the work he is to edit, along with a thorough knowledge of other works by the same author and of other related works. The second principle is that the editor must have a thorough knowledge of the external evidence which has a bearing on the composition, transmission, and publication of the work being edited. To be sure, familiarity with the craft of editing is also essential, but it will not take the place of the forms of knowledge indicated in these principles. We have recently seen an increase in the tendency to believe that a person who is well versed in the technical details of printing (plate corrections, press numbers, casting off copy, compositor analysis, and the like) is therefore ready to edit any literary work that comes to hand. Perhaps he is; but not unless he also has the knowledge that I have indicated, of and about the work that he intends to edit.

Some of the necessary knowledge of the text—the first principle—can come from collating different versions or multiple copies of one version. Fredson Bowers says that he finds that kind of "drudgery useful as a means of closely acquainting myself with the minutiae of a text before attacking it as an editor."[18]

[18]"Practical Texts and Definitive Editions," p. 31.

180

The *"minutiae* of a text," however. I once had occasion to collate a couple of dozen texts of Rochester's "Satire against Mankind," with the result that I could complete most phrases or lines in the poem; but I came to realize that I had never really read the poem as a whole, nor fully observed its structure or dramatic method, nor understood various of its larger effects. So, the kind of knowledge of a text that its editor ought to possess is one which comes from thorough, even exhaustive, study. That study should include all the rewarding scholarship and criticism which aid an understanding of the text, and it ought to encompass (as I have already said) related works by (and not by) the same author. I believe that a person who undertakes the job of editing *Mansfield Park* should also have a thorough knowledge of—among many things—all of Jane Austen's other writings, and the editor of *The Castle of Otranto* should, of course, have the other Gothic novels within his intellectual control.

The necessary knowledge of relevant external evidence, the second principle, is sometimes difficult to seek, sometimes scarce and sometimes extensive, but always of primary importance to the editor. The main types of information include observations by the author, accounts by other persons who knew relevant facts or views of the author, and information from the publishing house or its staff. The sources of such information are so various that it is hardly worth mentioning any, except as examples. Some are obvious sources, like letters by the author, accounts by his editor, and printing-house records. Some may be less obvious, such as letters by friends and associates of the author, or relevant comments in prominent or obscure printed books. The story of the composition and publication of *The Waste Land*, which I discussed at the beginning and at the end of Chapter II above, can serve as one general example of the many and various sources from which necessary information was obtained: some of it came easily, and some only with great effort; some was soon known, and some required half a century to appear; some that is not now known will probably appear hereafter, and some perhaps never.

The editor does well to remember that his task is to learn the intentions of the writer and, so far as they lie within his province, to put them into effect. Intentions are often obscure and sometimes unknowable, but they are most nearly understandable when they are recorded in such sources as I have been describing. It is thus of the first importance to canvass all of the likely sources of these kinds of information and to exploit everything that one can discover and that others have found. The material, being (potentially, anyway) of such crucial value, deserves at least the expenditure of the amount of energy that editors are so often enjoined to devote to proofreading or to other mechanical details. Of course, the seeker may come back empty-handed, but that is no worse than the risk in many other forms of research; and in reports on this form of research, other people are less easily deluded into believing that empty hands hold valuable new material.

Although these first two principles are of first importance, they cannot always be first fulfilled before other steps in editing begin. In this sense they are not true preliminaries to the editorial process but constant aspects of it. While one might wish to take one thing at a time and be done with it, the kinds of knowledge possible within these principles are rarely exhaustible on schedule. One hopes to exhaust the apparent opportunities for understanding the text and its history through such sources as I have mentioned. But then leads for further sources will sometimes appear as work proceeds, and of course following those leads may provide additional material of prime importance. In fact, it is unusual to feel that there is nothing left to be learned from these important sources of information.

It has become usual to staff the large cooperative editions with a Textual Editor and another person (or persons) as the Editor responsible for the introduction, explanatory material, and other matters of literary history. This division may be advisable if the labor is extensive, provided the two editors consult one another regularly on all matters that look both ways; but any split by which textual editing becomes a technical craft separated from the sources of prime knowledge about the text can only lead to a weakening of textual criticism.

III

As a matter of convenience, let me divide the editor's procedures into the five major steps that are ordinarily involved in establishing a text. Sometimes one and sometimes another is more important or more time-consuming, and sometimes one or more require very little attention. Nevertheless, all of them have to be reckoned with in general practice as well as in principle. I wish to use them as convenient stages in considering principles, but I am not trying to set forth (as a handbook or manual might do) the procedures or methods of technical details that they involve. The five major steps are: 1) *Collecting the texts*; 2) *Analyzing the texts*; 3) *Selecting the copy-text*; 4) *Perfecting the copy-text*; and 5) *Explaining the perfected text*.

1. *Collecting the texts.* I am using the word "text" to mean a form of the literary work being edited, a form which is or may be different in readings from other forms of the same literary work. Each manuscript or typescript of the literary work (whether written or typed by the author or copied by someone else) is a text; each printed edition and each issue of an edition presents a text; and each example of publication in periodicals (whether all in one issue or in serial) and of publication in parts offers a text.

All of these texts must be assiduously collected, except those where it is plain that the text has no authority independent of whatever source or sources from which it derives, provided that source (or those sources) are available.

It used to be thought that the date of the death of the author was the continental divide for collecting texts; on the one side, all texts were to be collected and on the other side none, on the grounds that the author could have provided copy, or revised or supervised any on the one side but none on the other. If children did editing, that might be a useful rule to lay down; otherwise it has no merit. Often—perhaps usually—texts dating before the death of the author have no independent authority, and sometimes texts from far after the author's death are a prime source of his intentions.[19]

The most reliable testimony as to what texts have independent authority, and therefore should be collected, generally comes from such external evidence as I have spoken of in the preceding section. Otherwise, recourse must be had to the analysis of texts—the subject of the next section—in the hope of identifying readings with independent authority.

2. *Analyzing the texts.* The collection and the analysis of texts must, in part, be simultaneous processes, since analysis often has to be relied on to determine which texts are to be collected, rather than being simply examined and rejected. The use of analysis to identify texts with independent authority is much more uncertain than is usually assumed. Once variations have been discovered between two texts it is by no means easy to determine with assurance—beyond the level of typographical error—which one embodies the intentions of the author, or whether both do or neither one does. In the absence of external evidence, the textual scholar is left to the mercy of his own critical faculty, which is (for many of us) a slender support, and risky because we often submerge our reasoning in language and in places that few are hardy enough to explore.

The textual scholar tries to reason whether the changed read-

[19]"We have recently discovered that Richardson's last and most elaborate revision of *Pamela,* long believed to have been lost, was actually published in 1801 [forty years after his death] and reprinted in 1810." (T. C. Duncan Eaves and Ben D. Kimpel, "Richardson's Revisions of *Pamela,*" *SB,* 20, 1967, 61).

ing is likely to be the work of the author, and his reasoning has to take into account every likely consideration such as the style, the apparent motive, and the anticipated effect of the new reading. It is not surprising, therefore, that analysis cannot always be relied on to determine whether a given text does or does not embody the intentions of the author. Analysis is often the only method we have at our disposal—if guesswork is not counted a method—in trying to form a considered opinion on this matter, however, and it is then an essential tool for the textual scholar in deciding which texts to collect.

Collation of variant readings is first necessary in order to make two kinds of preliminary distinctions. ("The duty of a collator is, indeed, dull, yet, like other tedious tasks, is very necessary."[20]) First, it is by collation that one identifies which texts can be interpreted as different from all others that have been collected of a given version of a literary work. For this purpose, a text would be considered "different" if it varied from the others in some way that could not be readily accounted for by changes in the process of transmission, such as typographical errors, but that did not constitute it as a different version of the work. Second, it is by collation that one identifies the different versions which are represented among all the forms that have been collected. It is necessary to make a practical distinction between the differences which characterize changes within one version of the literary work and those which characterize changes which create multiple versions of a literary work. For this purpose, a version would be considered "different" if it is a major revision of the work of art. When an author revises a work so radically that he can be said to have produced a work which creates a changed aesthetic effect, the result should be thought of as a different version. The two forms of *Great Expectations* and of "In Time of War" which I discussed in Chapter I, section IV, are examples of different versions, as are the two ver-

[20]Samuel Johnson, "Preface to Shakespeare," *Works* (Oxford, 1825), V, 137.

185

sions of *Every Man in His Humour, The Rape of the Lock,* "La Belle Dame Sans Merci," and the like. On the other hand, a revision which does not constitute a different version is one which corrects, modifies, or extends a text without substantially changing its essential character. For example, all the printed texts of *The Waste Land*—which I discussed in Chapter II, section I—represent a single version of the poem.

I offer this distinction between "versions" of a literary work and "texts" of a version of a literary work as a useful way of proceeding to think about the principles involved and to carry on the editorial process. To make these distinctions useful, a knowledge of the extant information about the author's intentions is essential, as well as the exercise of critical judgment. It will sometimes happen that two textual scholars disagree as to which texts represent different versions of a work. These disagreements do not invalidate the existence of the distinctions, however, nor prove them arbitrary, any more than differing judgments about the excellence of a poem prove excellence arbitrary; disagreements of this nature spring from such causes as knowledge and interpretation.

When several texts or several versions have been identified, analysis is then used to try to determine the relationships that exist among them. I have considered textual analysis in detail in Chapter IV above. The general purpose of analysis, as there discussed, is to try to determine which text among the various possibilities most nearly fulfills the author's intention. As there are major limitations to all of the three main methods of analysis, many risks are involved in complex analysis. Although not all problems can be solved by analysis—and many can be solved only tentatively—the application of analysis is often necessary and useful.

3. *Selecting the copy-text.* The selection of the copy-text is the editor's decision as to which text will be the basic one for his edition. I use the term "copy-text," throughout, to mean the

"basic text" that an editor chooses for his edition.[21] If there is more than one version of the work, the first part of the decision is to settle on which version should be the basic one for the edition. I have discussed in Chapter I, section III above, the considerations involved in making this decision where the author has provided us with more than one version of a literary work. There I have argued that no simple rule of thumb should be used to make the choice, and that the common prescription —take the author's last version or his final intentions—is not sound in principle.

The editor should first distinguish between "potential" and "actual" versions. Any versions which are not communicated to the public—like drafts or working versions—may be "potential" works of art. I believe that a "potential" work should be the basic text for an edition only if there is no "actual" version that the author communicated to what he conceived his public to be.

Even so, an edition of a "potential" work of art is a special undertaking. It should usually be presented for study purposes or for tentative consideration rather than as if it were a literary work comparable in status to the "actual" works of the author, and the nature of the collaborative role of the editor should be plainly indicated. This is true of any work which the author leaves unfinished, or incomplete, or with alternative choices of readings, or in draft form.

The category of "potential" is descriptive rather than evaluative, and it includes some very fine works, such as poems by Emily Dickinson. It should provide a warning both to editor and to reader, however, as to the status of the work that is set before him, when it looks like an "actual" work of art. I believe that a good deal of confusion about Melville's *Billy Budd* would have been avoided if these considerations had been clearly

---

[21]I am aware of the objections raised by Paul Baender to the use of the term "copy-text," and his conclusion that the only viable meaning for it is "printer's copy" ("The Meaning of Copy-Text," *SB*, 22, 1969, 311–318). I believe that the response by G. Thomas Tanselle is, however, convincing ("The Meaning of Copy-Text: A Further Note," *SB*, 1970, 191–196).

stated by editors and understood by readers. Melville left it unfinished, of course, and editors have tried to present what they thought Melville would have published if he had himself prepared the manuscript for the press. Since some problems of the text have alternative solutions which can be reasonably supported, any reading edition of it must necessarily be a collaboration between Melville and the editor, and it ought to be so labelled.[22] The natural inclination of editors to rejoice when they reveal an unfinished work to an unsuspecting world should be tempered by the realization that what they are dealing with is not quite in the status of an "actual" work of art.

The editor chooses an "actual" version, whenever there is one, for his copy-text. When there is more than one such version, complex problems of decision arise. Under the definition I have given for "version," every version is really a different work of art. Consequently, any version may be chosen for the copy-text provided the editor makes plain which version he has chosen and why.

Sometimes it may be possible to make a choice which is logically preferable as the best reading text because it better fulfills the author's artistic intentions, and an effort should always be made to see whether a choice is possible on those grounds. If there are two versions, one might ask such questions as these. Was the first version a hasty job released under some form of pressure and later put into what the author thought of as proper order? Was it full of printer's errors or editorial "improvements" that the author tried to set right and, in the process, made other revisions? Was it inconsistent from one part to another—as in serial publication, when the writing was separated

[22]The 1962 edition by Harrison Hayford and M. M. Sealts, Jr., presents a reading text, being what these experienced and skilful editors guess that Melville would have published, and it also reproduces the manuscript itself as accurately as possible, including the revisions and additions and deletions. Reviewers have not, however, generally recognized the status of the literary work presented. Since Melville cannot be brought back from the dead to do what he did not do while he was alive, it is not possible to prepare a "definitive" reading text. See Paul Brodtkorb, Jr., "The Definitive *Billy Budd*: 'But Aren't It All Sham?'," *PMLA*, 82 (1967), 602–612.

in time—and the author revised it to correct the inconsistencies? In such cases, the editor might be led to choose the revised version. On the other hand, sometimes the revised version may be rejected in favor of the original version. Was the revised version shortened to meet the demands of a magazine editor? Was it altered because of the insistence of the publisher?

A clear choice on such grounds is usually not possible, however. When it is not, the decision must ordinarily be made on aesthetic or historical grounds. An editor might decide on historical grounds to select, for example, the version which is considered most representative of the work of the writer at a given time; that method of choice is legitimate provided he makes plain his basis and grounds of choice. Most commonly, however, his choice will be on aesthetic grounds.

From my earlier discussion of this topic (in sections I and III of Chapter I), I hope it is clear that one should not shrink from the realization that the basic decision of the choice of version is an aesthetic judgment as to which is the best work of art. Accordingly, it is not surprising that there are arguments about which version of a novel by Henry James should be chosen as the best text for an edition of the novel; those arguments are similar in basis to arguments as to which of several different works by James is the best work of art. In some sense, the question is unanswerable in either case; the heat of debate is often not enlightening, and the rightness of a critical preference for one version (or work) over another can rarely be demonstrated.[23] While one is not usually obliged to choose the

---

[23] I have discussed James's revisions in section III of Chapter I above. To cite one other example of argumentation about versions, not many people can feel such certainty as this: "A mistaken preference persists for the intermediate version of Poe's 'Lenore,' a preference expressed by critics as widely spread chronologically and as various in their approaches as Thomas Wentworth Higginson, Marie Bonaparte, and Edward Davidson. . . . My own belief is that Poe strengthened his poem in successive revisions. . . . I believe also that the poetic superiority of the final version can be demonstrated through analysis" (John C. Broderick, "Poe's Revisions of 'Lenore'," *AL*, 35, 1964, 504). It will be a day of general revelation, accompanied by the sound of trumpets, when poetic superiority can be demonstrated through analysis.

best among several different novels, yet practical considerations of editing often require the choice of one version over another. The duties of an editor include informing himself of all the relevant facts and studying all the arguments and opinions that bear on the choice, and then (after mature consideration) of making the decision that seems best to him, knowing that he must clearly state that decision in his edition, along with his reasons for making it.

There is a natural temptation to try to evade the decision by mingling what he thinks of as the best features of all the versions. The result is an eclectic text which has been assembled from the different versions, which are really to be thought of in this context as different works of art. The result may very well be the confusion of several different sets of authorial intentions. While this procedure is not always impossible as a sound editorial procedure, it is always dangerous.[24] It should be undertaken only after careful study and a conclusion that no disservice will be done to the intentions of the writer. Otherwise, the result may be like an automobile which was constructed by the use of parts from a 1925 Ford Model T, a 1930 Ford Model A, and a 1935 Ford V8. You still have a Ford, all right, but that may be the best that can be said of it. The chances are slight that it will run; were it to do so, it would perhaps be a machine strange enough to cause the foundation of the earth to shake like a coward. Moreover, it seems to me improper for an editor to try to construct a single "definitive" reading text out of various versions which represent different authorial intentions at different times. An editor cannot do for readers in this way

[24]Whitman's *Leaves of Grass* is a difficult example. Fredson Bowers feels that although "some of the alterations of the final authorized edition of *Leaves of Grass* may seem to a literary critic to be inferior in merit to the readings of earlier editions, . . . when only a single definitive reading text is being constructed (and not independent definitive editions of the two or more forms of the text), an editor must choose Whitman's final intentions" ("Established Texts and Definitive Editions," *PQ*, 41, 1962, 11). This view seems to me to be an effort to find a handy rule to solve an impossible problem.

what the author did not choose to do.[25] There will, of course, be differences of opinion as to whether two texts represent different authorial intentions. Donald Pizer has criticized volume I of the Virginia edition of *The Works of Stephen Crane* for mingling the two significant texts of *Maggie*, which he considers two different kinds of books, and the mingling of the two becomes (in Pizer's view) a third kind of book; the editor, on the other hand, presumably considers the two versions as reflections of the same authorial intention.[26] If the edition being prepared is intended to satisfy the need for studying versions of the work other than the one chosen for reproduction, consideration should be given to the possibility of supplying the variant passages from other versions either in footnotes or in appendixes. Sometimes this procedure is practicable and useful, but sometimes it is so confusing that a complete reproduction of more than one version is necessary to provide an adequate basis for scholarly study.

If we now assume that the editor has chosen the version to be reproduced, we can proceed to the question as to which text of that version he will select as the copy-text for the edition. The only proper answer is, of course, that he will select the one which most fully satisfies the intentions of the writer. Again,

[25]The rare cases when the intentions of the writer can be ignored are ordinarily works being disseminated for a special historic reason. Here, for example, are the criteria for choice used by George deF. Lord in the first volume of the edition of *Poems on Affairs of State: Augustan Satirical Verse, 1660–1714* (New Haven, 1963): "The version having the fewest errors of historical fact, the fewest inconsistencies in meaning, and the fewest faults of style (especially in matters of meter and rhyme) has been adopted as the copy text" (p. 442). These standards of selection for works which are to be modernized in the edition should identify the best reading text without regard for what the author wrote; if a poem was improved by a copyist or a wit, so much the better. This plan is perhaps defensible in dealing with lampoons or subliterary works, or in trying to determine the best contemporary version; but it is a dangerous principle to follow with works of art. It found favor with such an experienced editor as H. T. Swedenberg, Jr., who said that Lord had "very sensibly adopted" his procedure, and Swedenberg admired the "reason and practicality" used "in dealing with the materials of which this book is made" (*PBSA*, 58, 1964, 314–315).

[26]Pizer's review is in *MP*, 68 (1970), 212–214.

there is no rule of thumb to guide editors, though we often try to create one. Greg's essay on "The Rationale of Copy-Text" is sometimes taken as the source of a pat answer for the editor in time of adversity. Greg suggested that the text which was originally printed from manuscript—usually the first in a series of editions—should be selected as the copy-text, and this view has come to be taken as a general preference in the choice of copy-text for the first edition over any revised edition. It is not always kept in mind, however, that Greg's suggestion governed accidentals only, on the grounds that the compositor would be more likely to preserve the author's accidentals when setting from manuscript than when resetting from print, and on the assumption that an old-spelling text was being prepared; as far as substantives are concerned, Greg urged the preparation of an eclectic text, with authoritative readings chosen from wherever they were to be found; he repudiated the idea of treating the copy-text as "sacrosanct" even for accidentals, and made room for a "frankly subjective procedure"; he limited his discussion to the editing of printed books (rather than manuscripts), and his scope was material of the sixteenth and seventeenth centuries; and he concluded by asserting that "my desire is rather to provoke discussion than to lay down the law." When these special assumptions and restrictions are remembered, Greg's essay provides very limited assistance for the editor in search of a rule of thumb. And we are thus back to the basic principle of selecting the one which—to the best of our knowledge—most fully satisfies the intentions of the writer.[27]

The choice of copy-text may be complicated in cases where an authorial manuscript is extant. I believe it is usually felt that such a manuscript is always without rival as a statement of the author's intention and therefore is automatically seized on as the copy-text. It is indeed paramount so far as substantive readings are concerned, unless the author corrected or revised in proofs or in later editions. But a question should always be

[27]*SB*, 3 (1950–51), 19–36.

raised about the accidentals of the manuscript. In many cases the author expected that his intentions would be completed by the agency of editor or printer in the matter of accidentals; I have discussed this topic at length in Chapter V, especially section II. It is clear that a reversion to the authorial manuscript would, in such cases, actually thwart the author's intentions. We might then end with a poem punctuated entirely with dashes which the author had confidently assumed would be translated into a current formal style. In practice, it is necessary to determine—from external evidence, from observing the habits of the writer in dealing with proofs, from the form he adopted or accepted for his other works—whether it is more reasonable to think that his intentions with respect to accidentals were fulfilled by the manuscript or by a print.

In any event, the editor should include in his edition all substantive readings which he judges to be authoritative from all texts within the version which he has selected. It follows that the choice of one or another of these texts as the copy-text is significant only if he is preparing an edition in old-spelling, and Greg's suggestion may in that case be followed; even so, whether it is important to try to preserve the author's accidentals is itself a complicated question which I have treated in section IV of Chapter V above. Wherever an edition is not in old-spelling, the proper eclectic procedure will amalgamate all of the texts with authoritative readings and thus it is of no importance in principle as to which text within the version is chosen as copy-text. In practice, it would always be prudent to choose the text which needed to be amended the least, on the grounds that our proneness to err by failing to incorporate other authoritative readings may thus be potentially less damaging.

4. *Perfecting the copy-text.* Once the copy-text has been selected, there are three kinds of changes that may have to be made in order to bring it into conformity with the writer's intentions and to present it effectively to the reader.

One of these—and by far the most important—is the inclusion of authoritative readings from sources other than the copy-text. I have spoken of this important matter in the preceding section, in view of the bearing that it has on the selection of copy-text. The sources other than the copy-text might include revised editions, corrected printings, changes in proof, press corrections in printed copies, plate corrections, lists of errata or revisions, directions in letters to the editor or publisher or friends, and the like. Such readings have to be sought at their source, wherever it may be, and identified by collation. Some people shiver at the thought of any changes being made in the copy-text, on the grounds that an eclectic text is an impure text. Such hesitation is very proper under two circumstances. One, the old-fashioned editing by which the editor assembled all the variant readings (from any version, and never mind whether they are authoritative) and chose those which made, according to his taste, the best text. Such editing has been likened to the description of Bishop Lancelot Andrewes' manner of preaching, that "he did play with his text, as a Jack-an-apes does, who takes up a thing and tosses and plays with it, and then he takes up another, and plays a little with it. Here's a pretty thing, and there's a pretty thing!"[28] The other circumstance for hesitation is when there is doubt as to whether the variant readings are by the author, or when they come from another version of the work. Otherwise, readings which can be reasonably attributed to the author and which were intended by the author for the version of which the copy-text is one form should be included; under these conditions, an eclectic text is not only permissible but essential in order to fulfill the author's intention.

Although the determination as to which readings are authorial is of the utmost importance, those decisions are—let me say again—exceedingly difficult. One problem about *David Copperfield* can serve as an example. Dickens sent a heavily

[28]Quoted by F. P. Wilson, "Shakespeare and the 'New Bibliography'," *Studies in Retrospect* (London, 1945), p. 77.

amended first draft to the printer as copy for the monthly parts, and Dickens revised the proofs which are extant. Since each part was to consist of thirty-two pages, he made last-minute changes to cause the part to come out right; he cut some passages and wrote some others for this purpose alone. It is not easy to decide which of these variant readings should be regarded as the fulfillment of Dickens' intentions.[29] Moreover, it is sometimes easy to confuse or distort the author's intentions, as Mary Shelley so frequently did when she edited the poems in Shelley's notebooks.[30] And it is a great temptation to "improve" the author's intentions, as I have discussed in section II of Chapter I above.

Nevertheless, it is encouraging to notice that the intentions of the author are more attended to in modern editing than used to be the case. Even texts designed mainly for undergraduates are now more often based on a fresh examination of the evidence, with particular attention to the intentions of the author; some of the Riverside Editions, published by Houghton Mifflin Company, can serve as good examples of concern for what the author wrote.[31]

A second method of perfecting the copy-text is emendation. (I ask the reader to recall my discussion of this topic in section II of Chapter I.) In textual studies of the writers of classical antiquity, emendation has stood second in importance only to

[29]See John Butt, "*David Copperfield*: From Manuscript to Print," *RES*, NS 1 (1950), 247–251.

[30]See Joseph Raben, "Shelley's 'Invocation to Misery': An Expanded Text," *JEGP*, 65 (1966), 65–74.

[31]For example, the edition of Thackeray's *Vanity Fair* (B 66, edited by Geoffrey and Kathleen Tillotson) was the first to use the Pierpont Morgan autograph MS to emend previously undetected errors; Gordon S. Haight supplied, for George Eliot's *Mill on the Floss* (B 54), cancelled passages and other alterations in textual footnotes; Hyatt H. Waggoner prepared, for Hawthorne's *House of the Seven Gables* (A 89), a new critical text incorporating material from the Houghton Library autograph manuscript; George H. Ford printed, in an appendix to Dickens' *David Copperfield* (B 24), some passages omitted from the proof sheets; Andrew Wright, in editing Jane Austen's *Persuasion* (B 95), included the so-called cancelled chapter (an original draft of the climactic scene) in an appendix; and so on.

analysis as a method of criticism. In textual criticism of English literature, it has been counted of considerable importance, in some measure (I imagine) because textual studies of the early part of this century revolved so fixedly about Shakespeare and other sixteenth and early seventeenth-century dramatists, whose texts have been studied closely and reverently. For those writers, the texts are often corrupt and sometimes extant in only a single version, with occasional need to resort to emendation. Samuel Johnson observed that "where all the books are evidently vitiated, and collation can give no assistance, then begins the task of critical sagacity"—by which he meant emendation.[32]

The most celebrated of all emendations in English is, I suppose, Theobald's alteration of the passage about Falstaff's death from "a table of greene fields" to "a' babbled of green fields"— though even this model has been under attack. Critical sagacity has been exercised in many other fields, sometimes to good effect; it has also been highly praised, particularly by its practitioners. W. W. Greg, for example, called it "an inspiration," a "stirring of the spirit," "an art"—all terms of the highest honor in a romantic vocabulary of criticism.[33]

One view of emendation which has long been considered a basic "principle" has to do with whether it is better to attack a sound text or let a corruption pass. Paul Maas, as a representative of classical scholars, held that "of course it is far more dangerous for a corruption to pass unrecognized than for a sound text to be unjustifiably attacked." Samuel Johnson, however, adopted for his edition of Shakespeare "the Roman sentiment, that it is more honourable to save a citizen than to kill an enemy," and he said that he had "been more careful to protect than to attack." "Diffidence in emendation" has been the usual attitude in the last generation or two among the leading textual scholars of English literature. "The risk of too little

---

[32]"Proposals for Printing the Dramatick Works of William Shakespeare," *Works*, V, 99.

[33]*Principles of Emendation in Shakespeare* (London, 1928), p. 3.

emendation," writes Madeleine Doran, "is far less serious than its opposite—too much." In fact, to H. W. Jones this is the main textual principle: "Apart, however, from diffidence in emendation as a prime requisite, one can hardly postulate definite criteria of the textual critic."[34] I must confess that this "principle" of emendation seems to me about as sound as asserting that it is better to get wet than to wear a raincoat unnecessarily. I should imagine that some thought as to the likelihood of rain (or of error) would first run through the mind of a sensible man, who would also realize that his guess (or "probability conclusion") might well be wrong.

The density of corruptions that can be dealt with only by emendation tends to be greater in the earlier periods, of course, when the techniques involved in communication were more dependent on human agency and more liable to human error. At the same time, it should be remembered that some corruptions cannot be cured by emendation. Many notable corruptions in Shakespearian texts that stood in obvious need of emendation have been corrected only because of our good fortune in having other texts extant with the readings apparently uncorrupted. Let me mention several examples from a single scene in *King Lear*. Who would have been able to make sense of "a nellthu night more" (uncorrected Q1), "anelthu night Moore" (Q2), "anelthunight Moor" (Q3), without access to the corrected Q1 and F1 reading of "He met the night-mare" (III. iv.124)? Or who would have dared to emend "this crulentious storme" (uncorrected Q1) or "this tempestious storme" (corrected Q1) to "this contentious storm" (F1) (III.iv.6)? Or "come on bee true" (uncorrected Q1) or "come on" (corrected Q1) to "Come, vnbutton heere" (F1) (III.iv.111-112)?

Emendation has indeed served useful purposes, but it is salutary to remember its limitations. Principally, that it is essentially guesswork of a high order, by its nature unverifiable.

---

[34]Maas, *Textual Criticism* (Oxford, 1958), p. 17; Johnson, "Preface to Shakespeare," *Works*, V, 148; Doran, *JEGP*, 59 (1960), 288; Jones, *SB*, 14 (1961), 70.

No sequence of "tests"—such as Greg proposed—can "prove" the rightness of an emendation; likelihood can only approach certainty, without ever embracing it. The discovery of a confirmatory reading is presumably the only way to verify an emendation, and I do not recall any significant instance of such a verification. (I am afraid we cannot have the satisfaction that a nuclear physicist may enjoy in predicting the existence and characteristics of a new subatomic particle and later having his predictions confirmed by experiments.) It is well to remember that Samuel Johnson came to use the term "conjecture" for emendation, and that in classical textual criticism it is aptly called "divinatio."

A third method of perfecting the copy-text is modification of the accidentals. (Chapter V above is devoted entirely to this topic.) Except in the case of facsimile or diplomatic reprints, it is almost inevitably necessary to make some changes in the accidentals. With almost equal inevitability, someone will be prepared to argue that the editor has tampered with the accidentals excessively or to ill purpose, and someone else to maintain that he has followed an overcautious course and not done enough for the benefit of the gentle reader. One or the other is probably right, but the beleaguered editor may hope that their arguments are mutually destructive. In short, whenever good sense is the judge, it is idle to hope for agreement among advocates.

The basic principle is that the author's intentions with respect to accidentals should be carried out. The complication of this principle is that one needs to learn what the author's intentions were. This involves the method in which he expected or wanted his manuscript to be treated, the way in which he treated the proofs, and the response he made to the prints of his work. Whenever these intentions cannot be learned, they must be inferred as accurately as possible. Whether the text should be presented in old-spelling or in modernized accidentals is mainly a matter of convenience for the intended audience, and the editor will have to take many factors into account before making this decision.

5. *Explaining the perfected text.* The major task of the editor is putting the text into the shape that, in his opinion, best fulfills the intentions of the author. When that work has been completed, it remains for the editor to give an accounting of his text. The principle which ought to govern is that this accounting should be as brief as the purpose of the text requires and the users of the edition need. A text for general reading by undergraduates generally requires the explanation of only a brief note. On the other end of the scale, a critical edition which has been prepared to resolve complex textual problems should present all the essential information that might be needed by specialists of the text or of the author. Those needs would include a textual introduction giving all of the external evidence that happens, in the case at hand, to bear on the text or on the decisions involved in the collection and analysis of the text, and in selecting and perfecting the copy-text. The evidence may be drawn from such sources as letters or other testimony by the author, proof sheets, editorial testimony, publishers' records, and the like. Those needs may also include textual notes or appendixes which present variant readings, historical collations, departures from the copy-text, the reasons for making editorial decisions, and so forth.[35]

It seems to be an occupational disease of editors to tell all that they have learned, rather than what readers need to know. Often a vast amount of labor lies behind a single negative statement—"there were no substantive changes in . . ."—and it is tempting to expand unnecessarily, to put oneself forward, or to indulge in rhetoric. In the "Preface to Shakespeare," Samuel Johnson made splendid fun of these our frailties: "The art of

[35]These matters are treated in detail in various manuals or "rules and procedures" handbooks. The *Statement of Editorial Principles: A Working Manual for Editing Nineteenth Century American Text* (Center for Editions of American Authors, Modern Language Association, 1967) gives a compendious statement.

writing notes is not of difficult attainment. The work is performed, first by railing at the stupidity, negligence, ignorance, and asinine tastelessness of the former editors, and showing, from all that goes before and all that follows, the inelegance and absurdity of the old reading; then by proposing something, which to superficial readers would seem specious, but which the editor rejects with indignation; then by producing the true reading, with a long paraphrase, and concluding with loud acclamations on the discovery, and a sober wish for the advancement and prosperity of genuine criticism."[36] Wordsworth had a blunter way of objecting to Todd's *Spenser:* "three parts of four of the Notes are absolute trash. That style of compiling notes ought to be put an end to."[37]

In short, the textual explanations should at least be as brief as possible.

"A correct text is the first object of an editor," wrote Wordsworth; "then such notes as explain difficult or unintelligible passages, or throw light upon them; and lastly, which is of much less importance, notes pointing out passages or authors to which the Poet has been indebted, not in the piddling way of a phrase here and phrase there (which is detestable as a general practice), but where the Poet has really had essential obligations either as to matter or manner" (p. 542). The part of an edition which offers commentary on the perfected text—"Such notes as explain difficult or unintelligible passages," say—is, of course, not (strictly speaking) textual criticism at all. Although this knowledge is sometimes necessary for the textual critic as a background for his work, it is within the province of literary history. For the convenience of the user of an edition, however, it is often advisable to include explanatory material of this nature. It normally consists of an introduction, explanatory notes, and (in the case of major problems which require longer space to

[36]*Works,* V, 149–150.

[37]*The Early Letters of William and Dorothy Wordsworth,* ed. Ernest de Selincourt (Oxford, 1935), p. 540.

elucidate) explanatory appendixes. Since the editor has had to inform himself of the facts of and about the work being edited, he ought to be in an admirable position to write all of this explanatory material.

The amount of space and attention that should be given to these matters depends, of course, on the difficulties that the work poses and on the level of knowledge of the readers for whom the edition is intended. It is a matter for the editor to determine, at his discretion, how long and how detailed and how elementary or advanced his explanatory material should be; it is a matter for critics and users of the edition to judge the discretion of the editor in making these decisions.

There have been very wide variations in the proportions of space that editors have chosen to give to this explanatory material. The Yale edition of Milton's Prose Works is an example of what I consider very full explanations. The shortest historical Introduction in any of the volumes published so far is 183 pages, while one approaches 300 pages; in addition there are prefaces to the individual works, appendixes (including some textual notes), and indexes. The intention is to trace "in minute detail the hundred complex strands of Milton's age, background, ideas, and art" (I, ix), and one would judge that the influence of Masson's biography of Milton ("Narrated in Connexion with the Political, Ecclesiastical, and Literary History of His Time") is still strong. On the other hand, Herbert Davis' edition of Swift's Prose Works is relatively spare in explanatory material. The introductions are only about 35 pages per volume; explanatory footnotes are not given for the text; each volume concludes with textual notes of about 15 pages and an index.

There is also a wide range in the amount of annotation in the editions of the historical papers of the American Founding Fathers, despite the similarity of the problems and despite the fact that the work is going on more or less simultaneously. In the trade, the Hamilton papers have the name for giving the least amount of explanatory material, and the Madison papers for giving the most; the Adams and Jefferson papers come in between, with Jefferson (at least in the earlier volumes) nearer to the Madison level. The majority of the specialists in the field seem to be scornful of the practice of what they consider "excessive" annotation, and one hears talk of certain editions pulverizing the subject.

It is true that each of the two styles represented by the Milton and the Swift Prose Works may suit the problems that are posed by some authors, and each may satisfy the needs of some readers. At the same time, some general reservations can be made. I believe that introductions should introduce the work being edited. When they attain to the length of monographs or separate books, they should be offered for publication as monographs or separate books; such volumes are more effective and more appropriate when published separately than when yoked with an edition. Furthermore, S. Schoenbaum has objected to introductions that give controversial interpretations; it is his view that the editor who goes beyond explaining words and phrases is "having a free ride at the expense of a captive audience that has paid its money for the plays."[38] It is always the text that should be the center of interest in an edition, and all else in the edition should be auxiliary and subordinate to the text.

The establishment of the text is, normally, the comprehensive act of textual criticism. It is to this act that the textual critic brings all of the accumulation of all of his knowledge and all of his skill and all of his experience. He has one final purpose, and that is to fulfill the intentions of the writer.

---

[38]"Editing English Dramatic Texts," in *Editing Sixteenth Century Texts,* ed. R. J. Schoeck (Toronto, 1966), p. 20.

INDEX

This index refers to general topics discussed and to authors and scholars whose works are commented on. It does not include references to casual allusions, to minor topics, or to titles of works.

208